When An ECHO RETURNS

Linda Kay Silva

Bella BOOKS
2011

Spinsters Ink
P.O. Box 242
Midway, Florida 32343

Printed in the United States of America on acid-free paper
First Edition

Editor: Katherine V. Forrest
Cover designer: Linda Callaghan

ISBN: 13 978-1-59493-225-0

Dedication

This one is for Lori…who believed in Echo right from the start…who believed in me before she knew me. People ask how I can write so many books a year. The answer is easy…I have a partner who is supportive of my work, who feeds not only my belly, but my mind and heart as well. This writing gig is a solo endeavor…it's not romantic to be with a writer. ..it's downright difficult. You have to be self-reliant, independent, and understanding of all the other women who share your writing partner's life inside her head (and quite often, her heart). You have long stretches of alone time while she finishes a chapter, a scene, a thought. You see her staring wistfully out the window, wanting her thoughts to be of you, but knowing she's probably in some other land, far, far away, inside another character, saving the world or dancing on the moon. Writers are an eccentric breed. We think differently. We see the world differently. We have strange habits and odd hours. And not one of us could do this without the kind of love and support we get from our partners. Thank you , my love, for all you do for me, for us.

This one is just for you

About The Author

Linda Kay lives in California with her partner of 14 years, and a menagerie that includes Lucy, a black cockapoo, Buddy, a Green Cheek conure, Big George, a desert tortoise, Baxter a Russian tortoise, Butler, a box turtle, Cleopatra, a red ear slider, King Henry, an Asian water lizard, and an assortment of tree frogs. When not writing, she teaches World Lit, Sci-Fi Lit, Epic Fantasy, American Lit, British Lit, Asian-American Lit, and Women's Lit. She loves what she does and is one of the happiest people she knows. Life has never been better for this writer of three series, as evidenced by the number of works she is churning out each year, the places she has traveled to, and the amount of time she gets to spend on Lucky, her Harley. You can find Linda Kay on Facebook, or email her directly at iamstorm@yahoo.com. She responds to all emails personally.

She is currently finishing the sixth in the Echo series and the sixth in the Across Time series, as well as the second in a new series about a CIA operative. Busy, busy!

"Oh...my...God," Danica whispered, edging closer to me as we stared at the wreckage of what was once known as the Big Easy.

Not in a million lifetimes could I have ever envisioned my beloved New Orleans looking like this—a waterlogged maze of death and destruction out of a Stephen King novel. Nothing I had seen on television could have prepared me for the complete obliteration before me. Buildings lay collapsed on top of each other, debris floated lazily past, destination unknown, all in an eerie silence chilling the marrow in my bones.

"You okay, Clark?" Danica reached for my hand; we were two soldiers staring at a battlefield with no idea how to win this war. The stench of rotted death assaulted my nostrils, burning my nose and watering my eyes. "Clark? Talk to me."

My foster name was Jane. As in Jane Doe, baby nobody wanted. Jane as in, we don't know your real name Doe. When I was drop-kicked to the curb of the foster facility at the age of five, I wasn't speaking and no one knew my real name, including me. I changed it to Echo shortly after I ran away from a mental hospital. Dani calls me Clark for several reasons; first off, I am a reporter for the *San Francisco Chronicle*, and secondly, because, like Superman, I have paranormal powers, albeit not to his extent. I cannot leap tall buildings in a single bound.

My name is Echo Branson, and I am an empath. I can feel people's emotions, sense their intentions and desires. I can tell when someone is lying and when they are telling the truth. It is a power, a gift I was born with. It is both who and what I am, but that power could never prepare me for what I was feeling at this moment. "I…can't believe this."

The damage from Katrina was complete—the destruction total—and my heart cowered in a dry corner for fear of what lay around the watery bend. Whole streets were submerged under water lapping at broken windowsills like the flicking tongue of a snake. Television could not convey how wickedly evil the water was. Like a giant serpent slithering through the streets of my adopted home, the water had cruelly snatched both the living and the dead in big, gaping jaws. Winding its way through every nook and cranny, the murky water polluted everything it touched, leaving an alien-like slime and mold spores clinging to everything in its path. Things you never expected to see floating in that disgusting water bobbed up and down like miniature buoys. In the five minutes we stood there, we saw a toilet seat, a golf shoe, dentures, a dead cat and several wooden picture frames float by. I was staring down at a photo of five small children when a young black man pushing a refrigerator made his way through the water. Nothing made sense. It was as if we had fallen down the rabbit hole.

"Hey." He nodded as he waded by us. Inside the hulled out refrigerator were two little girls, maybe five or six. I had to blink several times, trying to fit the pieces together into some sort of sense. It was like standing on the movie set of an old Seventies disaster film; but this was no fantasy, and there were no breaks for commercials. This was as real and as ugly as it gets, and Dani and I had arrived none too soon.

"You okay?" Dani asked, squeezing my hand.

Not even the few reporters I'd listened to had adequately described the horror of what was happening on the bayou. Try as they may, there was no way for them to convey the horrid stench creeping into your nose like sulfur after a match was lit, burning your nasal passages and triggering the gag reflex. No one could bring to life the horrific odor of death and decay permeating everything around us, including, now, our clothes and hair. The water, a shade of brown close to melted milk chocolate, carried with it oil, gasoline, feces, sludge, slime, blood and God knew what else, creating a toxic mixture I was afraid to touch. No one had mentioned the number of corpses floating in the water. No one had the right colors on their palette to accurately paint the grotesque portrait before us.

But we were here to help people like this young family and paint the correct picture for the rest of the country.

"I got my lil' one, but ain't nobuddy seen they mama." Two tears rolled down his cheeks to add to the grimy water. "Ya'll know Chantal Petterson?" He was not talking to me. He aimed his question at Danica. I was just some skinny white woman standing with her mouth agape, but Danica was one of *them;* a woman of mixed race, but clearly of African descent. I turned slowly toward Danica, as if seeing her for the first time.

When you've known your best friend for over a decade, you naturally take some things for granted; things like her ethnicity. We'd both gone to an all-girls Catholic school in Oakland, California and then to Mills College. Surrounded by black people and having one for a best friend is the surest way to become color-blind. It wasn't until times like these when I remembered Danica was half black. Her caramel coloring might have passed for another race, but her full lips and wiry hair indicated a noble African heritage that turned heads of all races.

It was the people who shared that heritage who had taken Katrina's beating the hardest. Suddenly, I wondered what this must have looked like through the eyes of someone sharing the same skin color...how it must feel to Danica to see the injustices of our still very segregated country—our nation's poorest had what little they had torn away from them, and Danica felt this loss to the very core of her being.

Being the best friend of an empath has its drawbacks. When we were fourteen, I had my first empathic episode that nearly drove me insane and caused me to beat a kid's head in with a math book. One nuthouse and a thousand miles later, I ended up in the bayou of Louisiana where I was tutored by one of the most powerful supernaturals in the world. And though I spent the next four years learning how to control my powers, Danica never abandoned me nor did she ever tell a living soul what I was. Instead, she embraced my new life, coming often to visit in my four-year stint on the bayou, and in doing so, she learned how to protect herself against mental and emotional invasions from empaths and others like me.

"Did you see his eyes?" she asked softly.

I nodded. I didn't need to lower my shields to know how this was affecting her; poor, black America stood helpless in the water as our government turned its back. Danica may not have been poor, but she was still black America.

And that was when I knew what my story would be.

Danica looked over at me. "Thinking about your story?"

I grinned. "Are you sure some of me isn't rubbing off on you? I was just thinking that."

Danica grinned back slightly. "What's your angle?"

My "angle" was the article I was here to write. I am an investigative reporter for the *San Francisco Chronicle*, and I was sent here, like thousands of other reporters, to report on what was really happening to New Orleans after Hurricane Katrina blew in and decimated the entire Gulf Coast, but I was different. Unlike most of the other reporters trying to get access to the emergency zone, I wasn't an outsider. I had spent my formative years on the river, in a stretch of land few had ever experienced outside of Pirates of the Caribbean in Disneyland. I had ins and connections my colleagues could only dream about. I knew these people, this city, that river. I owed who I was to all three.

And that was why my story would be different. These people, *my* people, needed help, and if the government wasn't going to do it, the American people would. The American people always had; we just needed to know the truth about what was going on. Since I was an empath, getting to the truth was somewhat easier for me than it was for "naturals." A natural being someone without supernatural powers. Mine allowed me to sniff out the lies and see the truths, and I had come to New

Orleans to write a piece that would accomplish both things.

"Personal stories. My guess is most reporters will come at us with the whole enchilada. Well, the whole enchilada isn't what makes Americans get off their asses to do something. It's personal stories that create empathy."

"Create empathy? Now that's right up your alley." Danica sighed. "Stories like a father pushing his two daughters in an old refrigerator?" Looking away, Dani made a sound like a bird chirp. "I'm sorry, Clark. I know I should have snapped a photo, but—"

Putting my arm around her shoulders, I pulled her to me. "But nothing. You did the right thing."

She pulled away and wiped her face. "How can we get pictures of this…this…mess without exploiting these people's misery?"

I shrugged. "Maybe we don't. Maybe we wait until someone says, *Hey, get a picture of this.* We'll know when the time is right. In the meantime, go ahead and put the camera away for now."

Nodding, Danica slipped the small camera back into her waterproof fanny pack. As my best friend, she had volunteered to come, but she did not work for the *Chron.* In college, Dani majored in computer science and developed a security software program that eventually made her millions. With that money, she opened a computer software firm, called Savvy Software where she continued making big bucks. When I told her I was coming, she put her business on autopilot, grabbed her camera, and met me at the airport. That was the kind of friend she was.

"We should have brought some masks or something. That stench is awful." Dani looked down at me. At six feet tall, she towered over my five-foot four-inch frame. "You feeling any of this?" She turned and I followed her gaze. Two men were struggling to keep an old woman in a wheelchair above the waterline. The wheelchair teetered this way and that as they fought to keep it balanced. It would have made a great photo to accompany the first part of my story, but I couldn't do it. "No. It's too much. I…I can't."

She nodded. "Who's picking us up?"

"Melika just said to watch for Bones' boat."

Bones reminded me of the legendary boatman on the river Styx. His dilapidated boat carried everyone from the outskirts of the city to the deepest, most inaccessible parts of the bayou. It was rickety and somewhat scary, but it was Bones who looked a hundred and two years old. He knew the fingers of the delta better than any man alive, and I trusted him with my life.

"He never comes this far up."

I nodded. "All rules are being bent, don't you think? Things are different now." I sighed. "Guess they'll never be the same. Come on." Danica and I tentatively waded into the soupy water up to our waists to help the two men with the wheelchair.

It wasn't until we were able to set it down that we realized the old woman was dead.

Looking over the old woman's head at Dani, I knew. I needed to get her out of here. Something happens to people once the feeling of hopelessness subsides. It's called rage. Danica was beginning to feel the kind of anger that sears your heart forever, like a brand, and I wasn't about to let her go to that dark place. "Dani?"

When her eyes met mine, there was a fire burning beneath them. "We've got to *do something*, Clark."

"That's what we're here for."

She shook her head. "We have to do more than report a story. These people need our help *now*."

She was right, of course. I had used the same logic when trying to convince Wes Bentley, my boss, that he needed to send me down here. It didn't take much convincing. Three months earlier, I had broken an international story that pretty much made me the Golden Girl of the *Chron* (a pseudonym given me by the *Los Angeles Times*). In the three months since that story broke, I had had two other stories of national merit. Wes knew I had been courted by every major newspaper and television station in the country, so keeping me happy was in his best interest at the moment. What none of them knew was that I was coming with or without the newspaper's backing.

I had been summoned by a different boss.

For the first time since I left the bayou, Melika had sent a summons; and when Melika calls, you don't keep her waiting. We all knew when we left the bayou, we would forever be obligated to it and those still living here, like one feels toward family.

And we *were* family with Melika as our matriarch. Well, our queen bee had buzzed, and the call to arms was never to be ignored. Most of us wanted to get down before Katrina landed but Mel would have none of that. She wanted to make sure we were all out of harm's way and were adequately packed and ready for what was to come. Given her supernatural connections, it wouldn't have surprised me if a seer or clairvoyeur hadn't warned her. Something of this magnitude had surely been seen by a precog or someone who receives premonitions. Whatever the case, Melika forbade any of us from rushing into the eye of the storm, thereby giving us a chance to get our affairs in order before heeding her summons.

For me that meant getting my assignment, making sure someone would feed Tripod, my three-legged cat, and explaining to the woman I had been dating for three months that I needed to go home and wasn't at all sure when I'd be back.

"Home?" Finn had said over dinner.

Sergeant Marist Finn did not know what I was nor did she know anything about the years I'd spent on the bayou. It wasn't that I was ashamed or embarrassed. My silence was necessary. My power and the people who helped me tame it needed protection. I was twenty-four years old, and the only natural I had ever brought to the bayou or shared my story with was Danica.

"Isn't that them?" Danica asked softly.

Shielding my eyes, I watched the familiar canoe-shaped boat as it made its way down what used to be a street. Danica and I were standing on a strange little incline that rose about two feet above the water. I had seen Bones maneuver the boat in about a foot of water, so I had complete confidence he could get to us without any problem.

"Zack is with him," I said.

"I thought Jacob Marley was going to be here."

I frowned. "Maybe he had a harder time getting here."

Danica's eyebrows rose. "Harder than we did? I don't know, Clark. That wasn't the best fourteen hours of travel I've ever experienced."

If we hadn't run into a Canadian Mountain Police Officer, who took a fancy to Danica, we'd still be waiting at the airport. I may not have known where our own government was (I had a pretty good idea it was somewhere sunny and sandy), but I *did* know there were other countries coming to our rescue.

"Damn, that kid's grown," Danica murmured.

It had been over two years since she had seen him, and Zack had, indeed, grown up. Zack was a TK, the acronym for telekinetic. A telekinetic has the ability to move objects without touching them. As with most paranormal powers, it's all about energy. TKs were able to use the energy surrounding an object in order to lift it or push it. A strong TK had the ability to knock windows out, but those were few and far between. The famous spoon bender Uri Geller was thought to have been a TK, and maybe he was, but spoon bending was an amateur sport compared to what some of the TKs I knew could do. Bend a spoon? Hell, Zack could bend rebar if he really put his mind to it.

Ten years ago, when I first met Zack, he was only twelve and, like me, had just come into his powers. Now, at twenty-two, he was an incredibly handsome young man, standing well over six feet tall and all grown out of his awkward teenage ways. Even from where I stood, I could see his carrot red hair sticking out from under the baseball cap he always wore.

"That red hair never settled down, did it?" Danica mused.

"Not really." Though his hair had not, *he* had. Zack had grown up thinking he was a freak and weirdo, but once Melika taught him how to control his abilities, he eased back into normal life and was now a scout for the Atlanta Braves with a fiancée and two-year-old baby girl.

"I'm a little surprised he came," Danica said, fanning herself. The fumes were beginning to take actual form as the heat made the stench unbearable.

"Melika must have her reasons for tearing him away from his family."

"He's a mover. What good can that do down here? It's not like he can risk being caught using his powers."

Risk being caught. Danica well knew the dangers in using our powers in public. If anyone suspected what we were, if there was ever a time when someone could actually *prove* our existence, we would all be in mortal danger. What the American government, or any government, for that matter, would do if they had a telepath in their ranks was a scary notion. What if a telepath didn't *want* to spy on people or listen in to important thoughts? Would they be forced into it?

You betcha.

And even if we weren't forced, we'd be poked and prodded like some new bug under a microscope. Even normals would eventually be affected, as scientists would find some way to test people to see who was and wasn't normal.

As if on cue, Zack moved his arm, as if waving, and a small bookshelf floated swiftly by and out of the way of Bones' boat.

"What in the hell is he doing?" Danica asked.

"Keeping it from colliding with the boat." I nodded to Dani, who pulled her camera out and snapped a few photos of Zack and Bones in the rickety boat.

Lowering the camera, Danica looked over it. "How old is Bones now, anyway?"

"Three hundred and twelve?" We both chuckled, knowing that Bones lived in a cinder block house at the mouth of the river that made ghetto living look palatial. "He's the best boatman there is. He could have found us blindfolded."

"Thank God for that. I don't know how much longer I can take it out here."

"The heat or the smell?"

"Neither. My heart. I've never seen anything like this. All the money I have and it can't do a damn thing to help these folks. I feel so helpless."

"Just wait, Dani. When it comes time to rebuild…"

"Fuck that, Clark. They need help *now*."

Before I could say anything else, Zack saw us and leapt from the boat. Wading over, he threw his arms around my waist and lifted me up. "Here's my favorite feeler!"

I chuckled and squeezed him tightly. His shirt was soaked and mine stunk of this sewer water, but neither of us cared. "It's great to see you," I said when he put me down. "Though I wish it were under better circumstances."

"No doubt." He turned to Danica and gave her a less enthusiastic hug, but a big one nonetheless. "You get more beautiful every time I see you."

Danica smiled softly. "The Braves pay you well for your bullshit?"

Zack tossed his head back and laughed; an unfamiliar sound among this carnage. "Very well."

"How's Melika?" I asked. After Katrina, we were all worried about Mel's house and the aftermath. Most of the homes along the river were made of wood. Not Mel's. Like Bones' house, hers was built from cinder block cemented together. As we had seen, nothing was impervious to the power of the water. That much was obvious.

"She's been better."

"Her house?"

"Still standing. If the hurricane didn't get the bayou folks, they're pretty safe. The levees don't affect people that far out."

"Good." Inhaling deeply, I asked the question I wished I had bitten back. "Is *she* here?"

Zack nodded. "Are you kidding? Of course. Tip came down days before Katrina ran aground. Typical of her, you know, going against the grain. When everyone was leaving, she was coming. Pissed Melika off something awful. You know how she is, but Tip insisted she come and batten down the hatches. She appeared out of nowhere and secured everything Mel had."

I grinned. "That's so Tip."

"Absolutely. Bones was telling me she pulled Mr. Wyatt out of his house just before it blew over. Damn Indian always has to play the hero."

I was certain Zack was referring to the time he got us in trouble in town by showing off his powers to me. When some thugs started harassing us, Tip came to our rescue and kicked some thug ass. That was the way of Tip.

Tiponi Redhawk was one of the most powerful telepaths on

the planet. When I first came to the bayou, she scared the crap out of me. Tall, dark, mysterious, she spent most of her time glaring at me or brooding in the shadows. It wasn't until I left for college I realized she had always had it bad for me. Coming to Oakland, Tip and I tried to make a go if it, but it was just too hard. She couldn't stop herself from reading my mind, and I wasn't strong enough to keep her out. In the end, we went our own ways, still managing to maintain a tenuous grasp on our friendship. Now, she spent her days collecting new supers, studying with gurus all over the world and keeping track of all of us in times like these. She was loyal to Melika, dedicated to training supers and a trustworthy friend.

"What about Jacob?"

Shaking his head, Bones pulled the boat closer. He looked more like a blackened skeleton than a man. "De boy kint get true. Too many dead knockeen at his door."

Zack and I stared at each other. "I hadn't thought of that. He must have gotten bowled over by the spirits."

Bowled over was super-speak for having your shields busted down. All telepathy, whether it's empathy, TK, clairsentience or straight up telepathy require us to erect psionic shields to keep all the feelings and thoughts of others out of our consciousness. Without shields, we would all go insane from the sheer magnitude of mental noise bombarding us. Each of us learned how to construct these shields from Melika. It was the first lesson we learned; not how to control our powers, not how to strengthen or use them, but how to protect ourselves from naturals and supers alike. The amount of mental noise from a crowd of people could be devastating. In times of sickness, stress or exhaustion, our shields could fail us, and all that noise would come crashing in.

I had seen what happened to someone when that noise couldn't be stopped, and it wasn't pretty. In the mental hospital I had been sent to when I bashed a kid's head in with my math book I saw a girl my age who hadn't been able to keep the noise out. She was rocking back and forth in a padded cell with spittle on her lips and a foot long piece of drool hanging from her chin.

"I'll see if Tip can find him."

"Maybe he's just not in the city yet."

We both looked to Bones. I was pretty sure Bones wasn't a super, but just what he was, I wasn't sure. "Bones?"

"De water always talks to Bones. He here." Spoken in his broken Cajun, Bones preferred Patois as his first language.

"Let's get you out of the sun, Echo, so you can concentrate better." Zack handed our backpacks to Bones who was leaning on a long pole called a gator getter.

"De folk need me help. I be back. Go higher. I meet you der."

The three of us made it to higher ground and that was when I realized what was happening: People could not get *out* of New Orleans. Out. Off of. Away from. Suddenly, I understood. Were my shields crumbling, or was I just now seeing what Danica had been seeing all along?

We were trapped.

"Over here, Clark." Danica said, reaching for my hand. The three of us climbed onto a porch that had no house. It was a porch lodged between a telephone pole and a cyclone fence. The house was submerged to the roofline, as so many were.

"Bones hasn't stopped patrolling the bayou and backstreets since Katrina left," Zack said, adjusting his Atlanta Braves ball cap. The brim was already stained with sweat. "Okay, Echo, let's see if you can contact Ms. Wonderful."

A bead of sweat rolled into my eye, stinging it. "If she doesn't want to hear from me, Zack—"

"Who are you kidding? Just let down your shields. She'll come a runnin'."

Danica nodded. "Get a hold of that hunky Indian so we can blow this pop stand."

Tip and I had been lovers for a nanosecond the year after I left the bayou, but having a girlfriend who could read my mind and communicate with me across the distances was too weird even for me. Danica knew as well as I did that Tip still loved me and wanted to be a bigger part of my life, but I had moved on in California. I had a job I loved, friends who were fun to hang with and a new woman in my life who thought I hung the moon. As much as I cared about Tip, I couldn't see myself going back down that road again.

Sighing, I let down my shield and sent my energy outward. *"Tip, we can't seem to get a bead on Jacob. Any idea where he might be?"*

"Hey, kiddo. Sorry I couldn't come do the meet and greet, but as you can plainly see, we're in a helluva mess here."

She sounded tired. As an empath, I not only heard her words inside my mind, I could feel the energy with which they were spoken, and hers was tapped out. "*You okay?*"

"Tired, but fine, which is more than I can say for Jacob Marley. Let me see where he is now. I had to put a block on him. His fear was sucking the life out of me."

Tip was the telepathic equivalent of a giant cell phone tower; she could tune in to any supernatural anywhere as long as their shields were down. That was why she was a collector. This skill enabled her to collect young supers so Melika could get to them before they killed themselves. Having special powers might seem like fun to the outside world, but there was a steep price to pay for those who couldn't handle them.

"Jacob's in a bad way. You gotta get him out of there."

"Where is he?"

"He ducked into Henderson Elementary and is trying to regroup, but there's just too much…go grab him and I'll have Bones meet you on the backside."

"Gotcha."

"Be careful. A lot of weird shit is getting ready to go down. Stay low. Get in, get out. Watch out for gangs, groups or guns. Get Jacob Marley and then DD outta there and meet me at Mel's, you hear me? No extra stops and don't let your emotions run away with you. We can't save them all."

"Right."

I opened my eyes to find Danica and Zack watching a family of five pile out of Bones' boat. "Things are going to get uglier," Zack whispered, reaching for my hand. "You feel it too, dontcha?"

Nodding, I asked Bones to take us to Henderson.

We found Jacob in a semi-flooded classroom crouched on a desk, holding his hands to his ears and shaking his head.

"I'll go get him," Zack said. "If he gets violent, at least I can handle him."

I nodded and motioned for him to make a go of it.

Zack approached him cautiously. The water rose to his waist as he waded over to Jacob. Every movement of the water was like bursting a boil; you could smell the pus seeping out. "Jacob Marley, we're here."

The sound of Zack's voice made Jacob unclench his eyes and look up. He was drenched in sweat, his eyes flashing wildly about. "Zack? Oh my God—" Jacob flung his arms around Zack's neck like a little boy and clung to his childhood friend. Jacob wasn't a little boy. Two years younger than Zack, Jacob was a grown man fighting off demons of another sort.

"It's okay, buddy. We're going to get you out of here." Zack helped Jacob to his feet and into the murky water.

"My fault. My fault. I didn't realize—" Jacob shook his head, and sweat and water flew from his dreadlocks.

Jacob Marley was one of the blackest boys I had ever seen, and I had seen a lot. He had been training with Melika when I first arrived, and had taken me all over the bayou. He was twelve then, and instead of acting like some possessive alpha male, he showed me everything he knew, and then some. Now, he was a young man of twenty-two getting his doctorate in theology from NYU. It was an appropriate degree for a necromancer—someone capable of speaking to the dead; a power I was so thankful I didn't possess. The amount of dead energy surrounding us had overloaded his circuits.

What most people don't realize is the importance of energy to everything on earth. When someone dies, their corpse no longer retains energy, but their spirit does. It was these newly departed spirits who were driving Jacob Marley over the edge. There were simply too many of them and his shield had cracked. What they were saying to him was anybody's guess, but too many voices at once makes it hard to fend off and maintain a shield, so we needed to get him out of the neighborhood and quickly.

"There are so many—"

Danica and Zack got him to the boat. "We need to clear out," Zack said to me. "Does Bones still have an engine in that thing?"

He did, and though Bones seldom used it, it managed to fire right up and carry us rapidly away from the dead and their lingering spirits.

Reaching out, I took Jacob's hand in mine. He was slightly calmer than when we first reached him. "How you feeling now?" I asked Jacob once we reached the outskirts of town. It had taken longer than I thought even with so much debris in the water.

"Better."

I nodded, sensing his relief. "Get your shields back up. There's bound to be more death along the way." Jacob took a deep breath and closed his eyes. He looked peaceful, not at all like his namesake, Jacob Marley, the main ghost in Dickens's *A Christmas Carol.* Seven years prior to the main events of the novel, Marley had died on Christmas Eve. After his death, Marley's spirit was condemned to walk the Earth for all eternity as punishment for his shutting out of his fellow man. Marley's ghost could observe, but not interact with, living beings. Marley saw that Scrooge, his only friend in the world, was following a path to Hell, so he helped Scrooge avoid this fate by arranging the visitations of the Ghosts of Christmas Past, Present and Future. Like me, Jacob chose a new name befitting his powers to talk to the newly departed. It was the "ghosts" of the many dead who had forced Jacob into hiding.

We had always called him by both names together: Jacob Marley, and though he once told me what his real name was, I had long since forgotten it.

Opening his eyes, he looked at me with a twisted grin. "Justice," he murmured.

"What?"

"Justice. They were all crying out for justice. That's all I could hear when I got stampeded."

A stampede was necro talk for being bombarded by groups of dead people, especially when those souls suffered violent deaths. Often, there was an anger or rage accompanying a visit by a soul who was torn from its body in an untimely manner, and given the way many of Katrina's victims died, there was bound to be a great deal of hostility. If there is a necro nearby, they will often complain, demanding answers.

He looked over at me and forced a smile. I didn't need to read his energy to know this had exhausted him. Taking his hand again, I held it tightly. There had been many nights when we were kids that Jacob Marley sat on the edge of my bed and held my hand after I'd had a bad night terror. Quiet, thoughtful, soft-spoken, he was one of the neatest people I had ever met. "We'll catch up later," I whispered. "Right now, close your eyes and get some strength back. I've a feeling there won't be much time for rest."

He nodded and squeezed my hand. "Good to see you, Echo. I've missed you."

Smiling softly, I patted his hand. "And I, you."

We were quiet the rest of the way to Melika's.

If you've never been to the bayou, you're really missing out. It is a world unto itself with its mazelike waterways snaking in and out of the delta. There are no signs, no maps, no real landmarks to speak of out here, and many a drug runner has died after failing to find his way out. Of course, those who live here see plenty of landmarks and signs. All of us can. Once you understand the distinctiveness of nature, you realize that no two trees are alike, no patch of grass like the previous patch. Sure, they may look alike to the untrained or unappreciative eye, but they are as different as two people. To come here without a Cajun or native guide was risky business indeed.

Like so many Cajuns, Bones could navigate these waters in the dead of night with only a penlight, and maybe not even that. These waterways were both mysterious and dangerous. What New Orleans was to Louisiana, the bayou was to New Orleans.

"I'm sorry about your house, Bones," Zack said softly.

As we passed by where his house had stood, no one said a thing. Bones didn't even give it a cursory glance. "All dem wymmin hurricanes like de Bones' house." He shrugged. "I build a new one later."

And so went the true spirit of Louisianans in the days after Katrina. No jumping up and down and hair pulling, just a silent resignation about what needed to be done; and there was *a lot* needing to be done.

As we reached Melika's dock, we all exchanged glances and smiled at each other. No matter where we lived or went in the world, this would always be our home and Melika, our mother.

There she stood, as always, wearing a black dress, a wide brimmed straw hat, and her black galoshes. She was waving, as usual, and though she was too powerful a blocker for me to read, I knew her well enough to notice the exhaustion on her face.

"She looks tired," Danica said softly, shifting in her seat.

"De storm it come and it go…but de people hurricane…it comin'," Bones said.

Danica and I exchanged glances and shrugged.

"You all made it, I see." Melika waited for Bones to pull alongside the dock before offering her hand to Danica to help her from the boat.

"Danica! It's been so long." Melika hugged Danica, who towered over the diminutive Haitian woman with the waist-length black hair and flawless skin. "I am so glad you accompanied Echo."

"She wouldn't let me come alone," I said, getting out of the boat, my eyes scanning the dock for any sign of Tip.

"Because she is a good friend." Melika released Danica and hugged me tightly. "I have missed you, child," she said, then whispered, "She is waiting on the porch for you, and is jumping out of her skin to see you."

At first, I thought she was talking about Tip, but then I felt the childlike energy of someone else and immediately smiled.

Looking over at the small porch wrapped around the cinder block house perched on the riverbank, I saw two pairs of eyes staring out at me. One pair was Tip's, who always got my last hug. The other was a ten-year-old girl I had brought to the bayou myself.

"Cinder!"

Her eyes lit up when I called her name and she leapt from the porch and into my arms without hardly touching the ground. She had grown so much in the three months since I brought her that I was barely able to hold her up.

"I think you've grown two feet since I last saw you!" Setting her down, I stood back and looked at her. "Maybe a foot and a half." Her long, blond hair hung loosely past her shoulders and her blue eyes danced as she smiled up at me. It wouldn't be much longer before she was taller than me.

Three months ago, Melika had me retrieve Cinder from the same mental ward I had spent time in as a teenager. Melika's son, Big George, works at the hospital and is what we supers commonly refer to as a spotter. A spotter's job is to find or spot supernaturals before they are either driven insane or bring notice to themselves. It is important we not only help each other through that moment when our powers come to a head, but it is vital we keep those powers under wraps in order to protect us all. It is Big George's job to spot any of us who come through the mental ward.

Big George was my savior when he spotted me just days after another empath arrived at the facility. When the drooling mess of a girl lost all touch with reality, her life as she knew it was over. Big George got to me in the nick of time, and I returned the favor to this little girl I'd grown to love.

Kneeling down, I smiled into her face. Her blue eyes were positively aglow, and I realized just how much I had missed her. "I hear you're a very good student. Melika speaks very highly of how quickly you catch on."

Cinder grinned and nodded. Still, after all this time, she had spoken but one word, and that was her name. I mistakenly kept calling her Cindy, but when I saw her power, when she used that power to save my life, she looked at me with solemn eyes and simply said, "Cinder."

When she saw Danica, she practically bowled me over to get to her. Cinder and Danica had formed a special bond while Cinder stayed with me, and they Instant Messaged constantly. Danica was crazy about our little mute girl and was just as excited to see Cinder in person instead of via webcam. Danica's think tank, three techno geeks who made it all happen for Savvy Software, had developed a checkbook size computer called a vidbook, and Cinder used this to "chat" with Danica on a daily basis. Well, Danica chatted. Cinder typed because she had stopped speaking long ago.

"Hey there, Firefly!" Danica said, scooping Cinder up. "You're all grown up now."

Cinder giggled and looked hard into Danica's face. Unspoken words passed between them.

"Tired from traveling is all, Danica answered the unasked question. "We'll be fine once we get some food and a little catnap."

Melika turned from us and helped Jacob from the boat. "You go upstairs and rest, Jacob Marley. I'll be up to see you shortly."

He grinned weakly at me. "We'll catch up?"

"As always."

Melika hugged Zack before turning her attention back to me. "Tip will fill you in on why I sent the summons. I expect the both of you to comport yourselves as if you were on the same side. I must see to Jacob Marley first. I had no idea he was under such stress. I should have better prepared him." We walked arm-in-arm down the dock. "Here, on the bayou, it is as if the very land were grieving. Have you ever seen it so quiet and still?"

Actually, I hadn't. Not only that, I hadn't even seen one gator on a boat ride that usually had two dozen of them sliding into the water. There were also no bugs, no bug sounds, nothing. It was eerily quiet…deathly still.

"I'll bet it's quiet like this after a California earthquake, huh?"

I felt her before I heard her, and trudged up the stairs and into her hug.

"Hi," I said, tossing my arms around her neck and pulling her closer. There was a solidness about Tip I needed right then; a grounding of sorts after all we had seen. When your home is ravaged and your people left homeless, it tears a gaping wound in your heart. Mine was no exception.

"It's good to see you again. Thank you for getting here so quickly. We have a lot of work to do." Pulling away, Tip smiled softly. With big brown eyes beneath long lashes, long black hair, deep red skin and piercing eyes, Tip was a gorgeous specimen of a woman. Her broad shoulders met a tapered waist attached to legs like tree trunks. To say she was intimidating was an understatement, but what people didn't realize was it wasn't her body that could hurt them. As a pure telepath trained by some of the greatest minds in the world, she could bring a natural to their knees without breaking a sweat or moving a muscle.

"You're tired," I said, running my fingertips over her brow before I could stop myself. Some things from past relationships are hard to excise from our lives.

She shook it off with a shrug. "Who isn't? Come on. Mel's been anxious to get started."

As Tip turned to leave, I felt another, unfamiliar energy, and stopped where I stood. "Tip?"

"You'll see. Come on."

I followed her into the living room, and when we were all situated, Melika came downstairs with another super in tow—the energy I'd just felt.

"Everyone, I'd like you to meet Bailey." As Melika handled all the introductions, I struggled to remember where I had heard of her before. Bailey…Bailey…that's right! She was a twenty something hybrid super who was both telepath and empath. I had never met her; she was before my time. If I recalled correctly, she was a blackjack dealer in Atlantic City or something like that. Her blond hair and blue eyes made her look younger than she was, and I could tell she took great care of her skin.

I cut my eyes over to Danica in a "What do you think?" question, and her single left eyebrow raise told me she wasn't sure. Danica could size up any woman in two point two seconds. She could tell you if they were single, divorced or after the same type of man you were. It was her…gift, as it were.

Bailey took a seat next to Tip. If I was the jealous type, which I wasn't, I might have had some petty feelings going on toward her. Tip was a free agent, after all. I had no claims on her. Still…there was something proprietary about the way Bailey sat there, and I averted my eyes before she could look at me. She might have been older, but she was nowhere near as strong an empath as I.

"Thank you all for coming so quickly," Melika said, sitting down.

I looked around the small room. "Is this all?"

She nodded. "Not everyone was called. As you can see, our home and the surrounding area is in ruins and help is slow in coming. While I have never advocated that you use your abilities for personal gain, this is one of those times when the rules must be bent and we must use our powers for the greater good." Melika took a shuddering breath and it was the first time I realized how much this had choked her up. "We are all connected to this wonderful place in one way or another. To many of you, this *is* home, and I have called you back to it because it is dying. Literally."

Zack reached over and held my hand. It was unnerving to see Melika so emotional…like we were all little kids seeing our mother cry for the first time.

"A scryer from the backwoods came to me with a vision she had had the day before Katrina hit. She told me you all would be needed or many more people would die needless, tragic deaths. She could not be more specific than that, other than to say there was a great evil afoot that may or may not be the source of the deaths." Sighing, Melika shook her head sadly. "There are people trapped all throughout the lower Ninth. Children, the elderly, pregnant women, all the folks who could not get out in time. The only real help we're getting is from the Coast Guard, but that is not nearly enough to help the unfortunate. The Coast Guard, bless their souls, can't help what they can't see or hear, but you all can. That's one of the reasons you were called. You are needed."

"What's the other?" Danica asked.

Melika shook her head again. "I do not yet know that. The scryer only said it was evil and that you might be the only ones capable of handling it."

"Broken levees are bad, Mel, but evil?" Bailey put her palms up. "That's a little melodramatic, dontcha think?"

"Like I said; what that is, is unknown to me at the moment. Until it comes into play, our main job is to help these poor people any way we can."

"You want us to be human bloodhounds." This came from Zack.

"Precisely. Bones will take two of you out at a time. Echo and Bailey, you will lower your primary shields for any sign of life: fear, exhaustion, despair, any emotion will do. If you can get to them without risking your own lives, do so. If not, you will spray an orange triangle on something nearby and we will send some of the bayou boys down to lend a hand."

The bayou boys were guys you might have seen if you watched the movie *Deliverance.* These were guys who grew up wrestling gators, catching snakes bare handed, and daring each other to see who could lift a dead tree out of the mud and muck. They may not have been the brightest guys on the river, but they were the muscle we needed.

"Zack, your job is to help Bones cut through the waterways faster by getting the debris out of the way."

Zack nodded. "Gotcha."

"And Jacob Marley…when he is rested, he will see if the newly departed can't help lead us to the living who might be trapped."

I know getting used to being an empath was tough and nearly drove me crazy, but communicating with the dead? Yuck. I would have been fitted for a straitjacket for sure.

"I know you are all exhausted from the ordeal of getting here, but time is of the essence. Zack, Jacob Marley and Echo will all go out this afternoon. Bones knows where to go." Turning to Danica, Melika ordered, "You and Cinder will stay here. Her powers are, as of yet, uncontrollable, so I can't risk taking her out yet."

I had seen Cinder's powers once and with devastating results. She'd used them saving my life, and I have to say, I was more than impressed. Unlike the rest of us, if Cinder miscalculated or made a mistake in using her powers, she could wind up a ball of flame.

Cinder was the rarest of all supernaturals. She was known as a firestarter; a pyrokinetic, or PK. A PK had the ability to manipulate energy in such a way as to create fire. Sometimes she created flames, other times, balls of fire. I had seen her make both, and to tell the truth, it was a little scary seeing two balls of flame emanate in the palms of her hands; balls she could hurl like flaming softballs. She was a very powerful firestarter who somehow hadn't burned herself up, which was what happened to 99 percent of the PKs in the world. Scientists called the phenomenon *spontaneous combustion*—when a human being seemingly bursts into flames for no reason. There were about a dozen or so on record throughout the world. Spontaneous combustion was the incorrect term for what had happened to those poor firestarters. What usually happened was that a PK caught themselves on fire before they even knew what they were or how to control their powers. Sometimes it was a temper tantrum, sometimes, stress of another sort, but most PKs never made it through puberty.

Cinder was different. With Melika's guidance, she would learn how to contain and control that energy and send it outward instead of letting it control her. Cinder was a good kid with an enormous power she seemed quite comfortable using. Whatever had happened in her life before us had caused her to stop talking altogether, and now, three months into her training, she still did not speak. No one knew why.

"Where will *you* be?" I asked Melika.

"Tip and I are going to try to find some of our people."

I sat up, my blood running cold. *Our people* could only mean one thing. "Bishop?"

Bishop was Melika's mother, a fortuneteller of some renown who worked in Jackson Square in New Orleans. Bishop was like a second mother to us, and though she seldom came to the bayou, whenever any of us were in town, we took Bishop out to lunch and listened to her tell us what was coming down the pipeline. Bishop was a precog—a clairvoyant of the greatest kind. She could see, with incredible precision, events of the future unfolding. It was another power I was happy not to have.

Looking at Melika, I felt chills run up my neck. "Oh God..."

Melika's eyes met mine. She had never lied to me. It was impossible to lie to an empath. "I…the truth is…" She looked away. "We don't know."

Zack leaned forward. "What do you mean you *don't know*?"

Melika held her hand up. "I have yet to hear from her. Tip cannot seem to make contact, but that doesn't mean I want you all jumping to conclusions. Katrina brought with her the kind of energy that can disrupt our powers, so I am not going to put the cart before the horse, as they say and think the worst. There are reasons why she hasn't contacted us. Let's not think the worst."

We were all on our feet now. "Then we should all be out looking for her," Zack said.

I nodded. "I agree. As much as I want to help others, this is our *family* we're talking about, our—"

Melika held up her hand for silence. "My mother's whereabouts will be known shortly. It isn't as if she is off the grid. None of you have the strength Tip has of finding other supers so your powers are better left to helping others. Is that clear?"

We all nodded. "You'll let us know, though, the moment you hear anything?"

"Absolutely. For now, focus on those you can help. If Bishop ends up being one of those, we shall cross that bridge when we get there." Melika rose, signaling the end of the meeting.

Turning to Tip, I whispered, "Why can't you find her? You're the most powerful telepath we know. There's only one reason why you can't find her—" I stopped short. I could not say the words, but Bailey could.

"And that's if she's dead."

We waited for Melika and Tip to leave before starting in on both the food and the questions. There's nothing in the world like Melika's jambalaya and corn bread, and she had a big pot of it on the stove.

"I was so hoping she'd make us some of this." Zack leaned over the pot and inhaled with his eyes closed. "This is heaven."

"How can she not know?" Bailey demanded. "It's her *mother*, for Christ's sake." She paced around the large picnic table Melika used for a dining room table. Danica was elbowing Zack out of the way so she could pour the jambalaya into bowls.

"Everyone sit and eat something," Danica ordered, placing the first bowl in front of Zack. At home, she was the matriarch over the geek squad, her three geniuses for whom she had an enormous office built where they could play and create to their heart's content. The boys, as we called them, had come to her as a package deal and made her millions right out of the gate.

Unmarried and unencumbered, the boys were her main responsibility in a world where business was her first love. By taking care of the boys, they, in turn, took good care of her. In their absence, she naturally gravitated toward the guys in our family.

"I don't get it," Jacob Marley said. He was standing at the bottom of the stairs looking tired. "Tip may be able to find any super as long as they're conscious, but if Bishop crossed over, *I* would know."

"Jacob Marley is right," I said to the others.

Bishop was perhaps the most incredible woman I had ever met. She maintained near celebrity status in the French Quarter with her fortunetelling business. Bishop, unlike her daughter, believed in hiding in plain sight. It was Bishop who foresaw the levee breaking, which was why Melika had plenty of stored food and first-aid supplies. For reasons none of us knew yet, Bishop did not leave New Orleans before Katrina hit. Like many who stayed, she'd refused to flee. This was her home and no storm or flood was going to drive her out. It was a mentality many Louisianans held.

It hadn't always been like that for her. Bishop had been brought to New Orleans from Haiti by the master of the plantation when she was just a little girl. She had saved him and his family from an impending boat crash when she suggested he not get on the boat. He then brought her to America, and on his death bed gave her her freedom, and she went to the city to capitalize on her abilities.

Abilities didn't seem to be a substantial enough word for what Bishop could do. She was an amazing seer with a high success rate in the accuracy of the things she saw.

"Right now, there are a lot of folks who need our help," I said, sitting next to Zack and pulling my own bowl toward me. The jambalaya did smell like heaven. "Cells aren't working, so if you need anything..."

Danica held up her vidbook. "This gets reception everywhere. It's via satellite, so let me program the number into your cells in case you're able to get coverage at some point."

Everyone piled their cell phones into the middle of the table and Danica started fiddling with them in between bites.

"Thanks for coming," I whispered to her while everyone was chatting and eating.

"I'll always have your back, Clark. You know that." She took a big bite. "Besides, you may have grown up here, but these are my people, too. Still..." Danica reached into her fanny pack and pulled out a small handgun.

"How in the hell?"

"My boys know all about metal detectors. They sprayed something on it. I have no idea what, but they assured me—"

I whirled around. "Are you insane? What if airport security—"

"Oh, pish posh. My guys can get around anything, you know that."

"But airport secur...never mind." I waved it away. "Now put that thing away."

She continued to hold it out to me, so I took it before any of the others could see it. "Will it work underwater?"

"How the hell should I know?" Danica reached over and laid a hand on Cinder's shoulder. "I have all the protection I need right here, don't I, Firefly?"

Cinder beamed. Danica had been calling her that ever since the night the lights went out and Cinder gave us light by the flick of her finger.

Ten minutes later, Zack, Jacob Marley and I were back out on the river and headed toward the city's lower Ninth Ward. As we skimmed along the top of the water, we caught up on each other's lives since we last saw one another. Zack loved his scouting job for the Atlanta Braves and was looking forward to his upcoming nuptials. He had decided against telling his fiancé what he was, and doubted he ever would. He did what we all did whenever we met someone special to us; he felt her out. She didn't believe in heaven or ghosts, witches or reincarnation. He even prodded her further about her feelings on ESP (a term none of us use because it is not *extra* to us. It just *is*.). When she practically laughed in his face, he knew he could never tell her; not because she wouldn't believe him, but because he was afraid she would think him a freak.

As for Jacob Marley, be had been working at coffee shops and working toward his doctoral degree, but he hadn't managed to find love. Not for lack of trying, but when the dead are constantly knocking on your mental door, it's difficult to stay focused on reality. After several failed relationships, he was keeping his focus on his studies and not much else.

"And you're still seeing the woman in uniform? How's that going?" As a very black black man, Jacob Marley had no love for a law enforcement system that continually pulled him over for no other reason than the color of his skin.

"It's going pretty well, actually."

"Is it getting serious?"

"If you mean am I getting a U-Haul, no. We're avoiding that lesbian cliché like the plague." I grinned at my own cliché. "She's a really sweet woman and a lot of fun to be with, but you won't be seeing a ring on my finger any time soon."

The boys looked at each other.

"What?"

Zack shook his head. "Nothing."

I pulled out Danica's gun. "Don't make me shoot you."

Zack laughed. "You carry a gun now? It *must* be serious."

"Yeah, maybe that's the ring," Jacob Marley chuckled. "They have matching guns."

"It's Danica's, you nitwits. Now tell me what's going on."

Zack blushed and looked away. "The Big Injun threatened to scalp us if we let anything happen to you."

"Yeah, we tried to tell her to get over it, but she started to do that mind meld bullshit of hers until we cried uncle."

I laughed. "She's still doing that to you guys?"

"We're still afraid of the big lug. You might not notice, but her eyes never leave you. Ever."

"Yeah, it's creepy," Jacob muttered. "She needs to move on. I tried telling her there are more fish in the sea and I thought she was going to turn my brains to mush. She may have told you she's moved on, but her eyes say she's locked onto you like a heat-seeking missile."

"She knows I'm seeing Finn."

"Doesn't really matter to her. She's got it for you bad, Echo; always has. I'm thinking it was love at first sight all those years ago and she's never really gotten over it. Put that gun away and don't do anything stupid. I'd hate to have Tip melt my brains out."

"I won't." Looking around at the devastation, I tried to shake off the feeling of Tip's eyes following me as I made my way across the room. The boys thought I didn't notice, but I did. Tip's feelings were so strong for me, even her own shield couldn't contain them. I knew. I felt it the moment she touched me.

"So, are you in love with her?" Zack asked.

"Who, Tip?"

Zack and Jacob Marley exchanged glances once more. "No, the cop."

I sighed. "It's complicated. I like her a lot. I might even love her, but it's not that gooey, sweet sort of love that makes people yell at you to get a room. We're not like that."

"What did she think about you coming here?"

Leaning back, I recalled our last conversation with my hunky little police officer.

"I'm going to New Orleans," I had said over a quick counter lunch.

"Now?"

I nodded. "People need help. I'm going to cover the story."

Finn nodded. "Want company?"

"What?" I nearly spewed my coffee all over the counter.

"Sure. I've got a bunch of comp time due me. It's not quite an idyllic vacation spot, but I'd feel better knowing you had some…some…"

"Protection?" I put my hand over hers. "I don't need protection, Finn. I just need to go cover the story and check on my…people."

"Do you realize you never talked about *your people* and suddenly, you have to run off to a federal disaster zone? When are you going to fill me in about your *people*?"

I looked at her, feeling guilty for not divulging anything about Louisiana or my time there. "Nothing to tell, really."

She stared at me. "I can tell you'd rather not talk about it, but if you're flying to the worst disaster in the last decade, whoever is there must be really important to you."

They were. "Finn. It's not like that. I appreciate the offer, but—"

"Okay, okay, I get it. You're not the business and pleasure kind of gal. I hear you."

Oh, I was pretty sure she didn't. I felt a little bit like Marilyn of the Munsters; how did you explain to your new girlfriend your family held the kind of powers we possess? How do you tell her the guys you hang with all the time are really only your brothers, oh, except for the large Indian woman who used to be your lover? How do you explain that connection?

You don't.

At least, not yet. Unlike Zack, I couldn't really marry someone who didn't know the truth about what I was. It would feel like I was constantly looking over my shoulder, waiting for the moment when she would suspect and want to know the truth…and why I hadn't been honest. Or, or, or.

"She wanted to come," I said softly. "But…you know the gig." As I watched a heron land on a dead branch, I shook my head. The *gig* was that we weren't allowed to bring naturals to Melika's. Danica was one of the few exceptions.

"Dis is where you wan' begin," Bones said, as we neared a porch of a sunken house.

Jacob Marley reached for my hand. Having already felt the emotional pull of the recently deceased, he knew the risk of me lowering my shields, but I wasn't afraid. This was what we came here to do: find the living.

It was the best use of our powers I could think of. Most

of us spent about 98 percent of our time trying to stay on the downlow. We were teachers, garbage men, even nuns. A very small percentage of us were out there posing as psychics, palm readers, tarot readers, and even TV stars talking to people's past loved ones. Americans would not pay a lot of money and attention to something it didn't really believe in unless they had nowhere else to turn. Those of us raised in the bayou learned how to fly under the radar.

But Bishop was different.

She used her platform to find more of us…to keep her very skilled hand in the game. She had the perfect vantage point to scout for others. Of course, it didn't hurt that she made good money at it, but that had never really been her purpose. She was all about saving as many of us as she could, and from her palm reading chair, she could scan hundreds of people daily for any sign of psionic presence. She was the best of any of us at hiding in plain sight.

"Echo?"

I looked up from my thoughts. "I'm ready." Lowering shields was easier than constructing them, and I could do so with very little effort. But it's a little like taking off a piece of clothing in front of a stranger; you feel vulnerable. Squeezing Jacob's hand, I nodded to him.

It was eerily quiet on that water. The lapping sound I'd come to love sounded ugly as it beat against the flooded porches and sides of sunken buildings. The stench wafted in and out with the warm breeze that blew west to east across the bow of the boat. Like most odors, it seemed to fade the more you inhaled it. It's amazing how the human body copes.

We cruised in silence for maybe five more minutes before I felt the distress from someone in a battered yellow shotgun house listing to the left. An odd creaking sound emanated from it, as if the house itself were crying for help.

"Over there," I said, pointing to the house. Bones pushed the gator getter deeper into the water, and we floated up to the gutter. Zack flicked his hand at the debris in front of the porch, effectively moving it aside.

"Hello?" Zack yelled, cupping his hands around his mouth. "We know you're in there! We want to help!"

We all leaned forward, listening. Then, ever so softly came a tiny voice.

"Daddy said…" It was a child's voice. "Daddy said never to talk to strangers."

Jacob and Zack looked at me. Why do most men think handling a child is a woman's job?

"Honey," I said, raising my voice as Bones pulled us right up to the porch. "Do you know where your daddy is?"

"Up in the attic with mommy. She sick."

I looked over at Jacob, who was shaking his head. He held up two fingers.

Dead. Both her parents were dead.

"Where are you?"

"At the top of the stairs. I got tired of being in my bedroom… and…and…" The little girl started crying.

Zack started to take off his shirt, but Jacob stopped him. "You can't go in that water, man. Look at that shit. It's toxic. Just spray the house and let's keep going. We can tell the authorities later."

Zack glanced at me. I knew he was going in. "Echo?"

"You have to get her, Zack, but Jacob Marley is right about the water." I shuddered. "It's not safe."

He nodded. "I'll try to stay out of it as much as I can."

Jacob Marley grabbed Zack's arm. "Saving people is one thing, Z, but don't do something foolish at the cost of our own lives."

I nodded. "Be careful, Zack."

When Zack went into the water, I felt his whole being shudder. He was filled with disgust, dread and something like fear but not as strong. When he disappeared through the doorway, I held my breath along with him. Time did not move as we waited to hear his voice, and though I could feel him, I wouldn't feel any better until I *saw* him come out of there.

When at last he emerged, he held a little black girl clinging tightly to his neck. It looked like she would never let go.

Handing the girl over to me, Zack peeled off his shirt and

did something I had never seen him do before: he used his power to dry himself and get the muck off of him. It was the weirdest thing I'd ever seen him do.

"Holy crap, Z. That was awesome."

Zack managed a slight grin. "A few years ago I discovered I could use my hands like blow-dryers." Reaching out, he stroked the little girl's back. She was crying softly into my neck and asking where her parents were. I whispered we could talk about it after we ate.

"Where to now?" Jacob asked.

"De Red Cross tint. Down de way." Bones pointed north.

For the remainder of the afternoon, we rescued as many as we could find. By the fourteenth victim, we were hungry, exhausted and filthier than any of us could ever remember being. Zack was so drained, he wouldn't have been able to move a feather. Having my shields going up and down made my head hurt, and I was terribly tired from the onslaught of emotions I'd felt all afternoon. An empath like myself cannot filter out the noise from all the emotions. This means I feel everyone's emotions within a certain radius. That radius grew smaller the more exhausted I became. Melika had taught me how to focus on just one person's emotional state so I could pick that person out in a crowd, but I had to be operating at full capacity, and this wasn't the sort of mission where that particular skill was needed.

It was time to head back to the bayou, where the water didn't cling to you like dog shit on your shoes, and the air was breathable. We all nodded off on the way back, with none of us needing to say anything to the others. We had done a good thing, but there was still so much more to do. We had seen so much devastation…so much death, but every time Zack or Jacob had pulled someone from the muck, it was all worth it. Never had I seen so many Americans need so much and get so little.

It was somewhat comforting to see others besides ourselves pitching in, people helping others out of their flooded homes, helping get pets off roofs. The water took no prisoners. Those who could get higher than it survived, and there were plenty of people stranded on rooftops, in trees, anywhere where the water wasn't—which wasn't much. There would be more work to do in the morning, but for now, we were all spent.

When Bones finally pulled up to our pier, Danica and Cinder met us on the dock. "We've got dinner on, bath water ready and a first-aid kit. You guys look like shit. How did it go?" Danica helped me out of the boat first.

"Fourteen in all," Jacob replied. "Not bad, but it only scratches the surface. There are a lot of people who need help."

"Any word from Mel or Tip?" Zack asked.

Danica shook her head. "Oh God, you reek. We'll have to burn your clothes. Come on, let's get you guys into some clean, dry clothes, and some food in your bellies."

I stood on tiptoe and whispered in Danica's ear, "You can't cook."

"Says you." Danica giggled. "Don't think Melika doesn't know that. All we had to do was reheat it, which is easy with Firefly around. She's my own little Bunsen burner."

Cinder beamed. They had become quite a duo.

I turned to Bones. If he was weary, I couldn't tell. He had the kind of face that always looked like death on a cracker. "Would you like to stay for a bite?"

He shook his head. "Tank you, no. I got de Lane family to bring in. Ah'll see you in de mornin'."

When Bones pushed away, a feeling of isolation, and perhaps, desolation seeped in through the dusk. I remembered feeling this way when I was a kid, as if he were our link to the outside, but this was different. This felt so real.

"Come on, Clark." Danica put her arm around me and led me to the stairs of the porch. "You don't look so hot."

"I need…I need my shields back up. I'm exhausted."

"Why don't you go upstairs to rest and I'll see to the boys."

Nodding, I went to my usual room, the blue room, and stripped off my disgusting clothes. In my bathroom, there was a tub filled with lukewarm water. I sighed, wishing it was warmer to help wipe away the grunge. Three seconds after my wish, Cinder appeared and held her hands over the water.

"How sweet. Were you reading my mind?" I asked, touching the water. It was perfect. "Nice job."

She grinned from ear-to-ear, then pointed to her temple and shook her head. She hadn't read my mind. Danica must have sent her up.

"Thank you, sweetie. Did you have a good time today with Dani?"

Cinder nodded rapidly, then, she moved her hands like she was dealing cards, playing checkers and rolling dice.

"Cards, checkers *and* Yahtzee?"

She shook her head. Reaching into her pocket, she pulled out change. "She didn't…did she…did she teach you how to gamble?"

Cinder's eyes grew wide and she shook her head. I waited for her to retract the lie she was about to tell, and slowly, the shake turned into the slightest nod. I couldn't keep from smiling.

"It's okay. You're not going to get her in trouble. It was fun, huh?"

Vigorous nodding. Danica was an adept poker player and loved the craps table. It didn't surprise me that she taught Cinder how to play. Danica always knew how to keep herself busy.

Sliding into the large, claw-footed tub, I closed my eyes, regrouped and built my primary shields back up as the water washed away some of the aches and pains accumulated during our journey. I was tired to the bone and still had my story to write. There was just so much to say, so much I wanted to convey to the world. I was in the unique position of writing my article from the bayou, from *within* the target area of Katrina's wrath. I just didn't have the energy to begin it tonight.

As I soaked, I mentally searched for Tip. She and I shared a special connection enabling me to let her know I was looking for her, and after a few minutes, she answered.

"Sorry to take so long. You okay?"

"I'm fine. I was worried about you and Melika. I can tell something's wrong. What's going on?"

"We can't find Bishop. Mel's managing to keep it together, but who knows for how long? She's pretty rocked. She's never not *been able to feel her mother. She's scared..."*

I could only imagine. *"And you?"*

"Exhausted. Jacob said he didn't find her anywhere, so that's promising…but—"

"He's been wrong before, I know."

"I've been trying to get Mel to take a break, but you know how she is."

"Relentless?"

"Something like that."

"Tip, what's happening? All day long, we pulled people out of the muck with no sign of FEMA or any other organization other than the Red Cross, and they had their hands full with the injured. People are missing loved ones, and I heard something about the Superdome. What in the hell is going on?"

"The city was unprepared. The poorest blacks couldn't get out, and now martial law is needed to keep people in line. This is going to get worse before it gets better, so make sure you all rest up…and be careful. Desperate times call for desperate measure and desperate people do desperate things."

"Operative word: desperate?"

"You know it. This thing is gonna blow up in a big way, so please be careful out there. Saving naturals at the cost of any of us is not going to happen."

"I hear you. Be careful your own self."

She faded from my mind, but some of her energy remained, and I could see how close *she* was to freaking out. After all, Bishop was in her 80s, and if she was okay or conscious, she would move heaven and earth to let Melika know.

My big question was, how long were we going to pluck strangers from the wreckage when our matriarch was missing?

"Until Mel tells us to stop."

"I hate when you do that."

"I know. It's why you broke up with me."

"Or something. What do you want, besides to eavesdrop on my thoughts?"

"I want you to keep your eyes on the boys. They don't have the restraint or discipline you do. Mel doesn't want them to take things into their own hands and go looking for Bishop on their own It's not safe out there."

"I'm all over it."

"Good…oh…and one more thing…"

"Don't. I know what you're going to say, so don't. Finn is a damn good woman, she's fun, she's good to me, she—"

"I was going to tell you that you look really happy…really good."

"Oh. Thanks."

"Sleep well. Good night."

"Good night, Tip."

Sliding deeper into the tub, I let the water come up to my chin. Helping these people really mended my spirit.

It wasn't that my spirit was broken. It was just that my job seemed to always bring me in direct contact with people who were less than good, far less than dishonest. I spent time with CEOs who cheated their companies, companies which dumped raw sewage and toxic chemicals into the rivers, and people who, for the most part, abused both authority and power to line their pockets. As an investigative reporter, my job was to find the dirt and then dig even deeper.

I hadn't realized how dirty I had become, but I realized it now.

I was so into being the prize reporter, the Golden Girl of the Golden State, I hadn't taken any time to feed my soul. I had become one of those icky ladder-climbing bitches I wrote about, and my spirit was sick because of it.

Even the woman I was dating spent the majority of her time within the dark underbelly of San Francisco. Sometimes, usually over dinner in a diner on her beat, we would swap stories about the lowlifes we'd dealt with during our day; it was these lowlifes who were slowly draining the light from my spirit, and I hadn't even known it.

Until now.

Here I was, in a small cinder block cottage with no electricity, surrounded by white candles, and the people I call family, and I could actually feel the change in my spiritual energy. Nature has a way of showing us back to our path, and I had seen this firsthand during my time on the bayou. Again, my soul was mending.

Maybe that was what the bayou was about for all of us. It was more than home; it was a hospital for our souls. Like all of nature, there was a rejuvenating essence to it even as we suffered at the hands of Katrina. When I was fourteen, it had healed me. At twenty, it had shown me the way. Now, it reminded me of the fragility of human life, making me more appreciative of those around me.

I came here whenever I was tired or broken. Now, the bayou needed me. There was no dirt to dig in or mud to sling. This was as real as it gets and what these people needed was for me to help them by telling the truth of what was happening down here. It was time for me to pay back to the bayou what it had always freely given me.

The bath water started getting cool, so I climbed out of the tub. A little shadow appeared in the doorway handing me a towel.

"You and Dani are having a good time together, huh?" I said to Cinder.

Big nod followed by her pointing toward the river.

"I know you want to be out there with us, but it's not really safe. It's dirty and creepy and…" I could have gone on, but she made a flaming B with her index finger. "I know you want to help. So do the rest of us, but we can't do anything until we hear back from Tip and Melika."

Toweling off, I slipped into my robe and took her hand as we headed downstairs where the boys sat eating what looked like lasagna.

"So, what's the plan?" Zack asked, pushing a plate full of food toward me. "We're not just gonna sit around waiting, are we?"

"We're going to do what we came here to do, and that's to help. Until Tip tells us what Mel wants done, we are staying on that path."

"Well, you're not leaving me here with that fireball," Bailey announced loudly. "I've got mad skills and—"

Danica came to her feet. "What *the hell* did you just say?" She rose to her full six feet and took one long stride toward Bailey. She was in her face in a heartbeat. "I'll rip your fool tongue right oughtta—"

I stepped in between them, putting my hands on Danica's

shoulders. "Whoa. Down, girl." Turning to Bailey, I glared at her. "A little tact might be wise under the circumstances."

She narrowed her eyes at me, unafraid. I had to give it to her, not many women were unafraid when Danica got in their faces. "I didn't come here to babysit, Echo. Danica is the only one of us who is a natural and has nothing…has no power. Why is she even here? It makes sense to me—"

"It makes sense I ought to *let* her kick your ass, Bailey, but I'm not going to. We're going to do what Melika tells us to do, and not one damn thing else." As our eyes locked, Bailey made the one greatest mistake one supernatural can make with another: she tried to read me. "Are you out of your mind?" I stepped forward. "Are you fucking crazy?"

She may not have been afraid of Danica, but she was afraid of me. "What?" She looked away, but it was too late. She had tried to sneak around my shields and I knew it.

"Oh puhlease, Bailey. Trying to read an empath as strong as I am with your very meager skills is pathetic at best. If you're going to take *me* on, you better be a helluva lot stronger than you are." I stepped closer. "If you *ever* try that again, not only will I let Dani make mincemeat out of you, I'll blow your brains out the back of your head with one thought... So why don't you do the smart thing and make your apologies."

Bailey crossed her arms. "I don't apologize when I'm not sorry."

Danica started for her, but Zack managed to keep her back with a field of some sort.

"Oh, *hell* no, Zack!" Danica growled. "Get this fucking thing outta my way."

"Calm down, Dani."

"Let me handle this," I said quietly to Danica. She moved her eyes from Bailey and then back to me before taking a half a step back.

"Take the goddamned wall away, Zack, or I'm comin' after *you*. Nobody calls Cinder names without spittin' out a few teeth."

I looked at Zack and shook my head. Danica meant it. It was best to have her corralled for the time being.

Turning back to Bailey I said, "Look, I know you were before our time, but—"

"You don't know jack about me, *Princess*."

"That's it!" Danica looked to Cinder, who flicked her fingers, sending enough flame toward Zack to break his concentration. Then, Danica pushed me aside, and before anyone could stop her, had Bailey pinned up against the wall with her forearm to Bailey's neck. You don't grow up a mixed race kid in the ghettos of Oakland without knowing how to defend yourself.

"Dani!"

"Zip it, Clark." To Bailey she growled, "Apologize," and pressed her forearm deeper into Bailey's neck. I don't know what would have happened if a titmouse hadn't run across the mantel right next to where Danica was standing. Danica hated mice.

"Shit!" She spat, backing away, her face still holding its anger.

Bailey rubbed her throat and stepped toward Danica. "Instant karma, Danica. If you ever touch me—"

Before she could finish, there was a bright light like a super nova. When we could all see again, we looked at Cinder, who stood in the middle of the room shaking her head at us. We were acting like fools.

Stepping back between them, I said, "Cinder's right. Now is not the time for bickering. Bailey, the rest of us don't go against Mel's wishes or plans. We don't take things into our own hands simply because we don't like the direction things are heading."

"That's just it. They aren't heading anywhere! We could be doing so much more to help find Bishop!" Bailey looked around, realizing she was outnumbered. I wondered where *her* people were. Surely, her time here had been spent with others. Why hadn't they been summoned?

"When Mel wants our help finding Bishop, she'll ask. Until then, we do as we're told."

"Fine. Until then, call off your dog."

Danica lunged for Bailey and would have gotten her hands around her neck, had Zack not pushed Bailey out of the way.

"That's enough!" I said, grabbing Danica's arm. "Let her be."

"If she thinks I'm a dog, let's see how she likes my bite."

"Not now. Please."

Danica glared over at Bailey, weighing her options, but relaxed and sat back down. "We're not through here."

I nodded. "I understand." Turning to Bailey, I locked eyes with her. "Danica may be a natural, but she can take you out like that." I snapped my fingers. "She's not a guest here, Bailey. She's family, like the rest of us."

Bailey cleared her throat. "Family. Look, when I was here, none of us got along, all right? It was five years of cat fights, of arguing, of vying for Mel's attention."

Ah, so that explained why Melika had not summoned the rest.

"So all of this touchy, feely bullshit going on here is getting to me. I keep waiting for your real feelings about each other to show."

"These are our real feelings," Zack said from the table. "I don't know why your experience here was so bad, but ours was awesome. We really like each other. If you'd warm up just a tad, maybe we could like you as well."

"I don't do warm."

Bailey sat back down and finished her meal in silence. The boys were smart enough to stand clear, but the tension remained until we were all too tired to keep our eyes open.

After cleaning up the kitchen and sending everyone off to bed, I sat next to the fire with Danica and told her about our day. She said she had taught Cinder how to cheat at cards and then Cinder showed her all of the things she could do with her powers.

"The kid's pretty amazing, Clark. She can throw fireballs as well as shoot a straight line of fire from her fingertips. She's still not very accurate, but it's impressive nonetheless. And that bright light thing she did? It can knock you on your ass if it's strong enough. Mel's done amazing things with her in three months."

I smiled softly watching Danica talk about Cinder. I realized at that moment that I had underestimated their bond. "What happened with Bailey?"

Danica looked away. "That bitch was treating Cinder more like Cinderella earlier today; bossing her around and having the kid schlepp wood in for the fire and shit like that. When I came downstairs and realized what was happening, I called her out on it. All she did was shrug her shoulders and walk away, which was a damn good thing to do, because I'd have eaten her fucking lunch."

I nodded. "Well thank you for not doing that. You don't have to like her, but obviously she brings something to the party or Mel wouldn't have summoned her."

"I realize that, but if she says anything like that about Cinder again—"

"Then you have my permission to kick her ass."

Danica smiled. "Deal." Gazing into the fire she sighed. "You're going to have to talk to Tip, you know?"

"About?"

"Oh come on! You can't tell me you don't see how she looks at you! Most women would kill to have someone look at them like that."

"In case you haven't noticed, I am not like most women."

"Neither is she. You have to talk to her, Clark. You have to find a way to help her let go."

Turning my own gaze to the fire, I shrugged. "What's left to say? I'm *seeing* someone else."

"That doesn't seem to matter. Whatever you two have left unsaid needs to be said."

I went to bed with those words banging inside my head, and when sleep visited me at last, it was more welcome than even the best lover.

The next morning, we were up and at it again, only the atmosphere around the lower Ninth had changed dramatically in the short time we were gone. The air wasn't just hotter and muggier, it was thicker, somehow, harder to breathe in, like there was a steel band around my chest.

“We need masks,” Zack said after pulling our third person from a rooftop.

Jacob nodded. “Echo, I don’t like what I’m feeling at all. Are you feelin’ it?”

How could I not? There was a wild desperation in the air; a feeling like chaos lurked around every corner rubbing its hands together as the city’s residents fell apart. There was rage and hostility. As the water slowly receded, temperatures quickly rose. It had been five days so far, and the President of the United States was nowhere to be found. Rumor had it that he was on vacation, and Condi Rice was out buying Manolo’s while the rest of the world watched and waited for some sign of intelligent response.

I felt all of this and I hadn’t even lowered my shields yet.

“There’s a mini-mart over on that corner,” Zack said, pointing about a hundred yards away. “Maybe we can get bandanas or something.”

“Good idea.”

Turns out, it was a bad idea. Getting out of the boat so we could walk the rest of the way, we turned a corner and the whole world turned upside down. I felt like I was trapped in a snow globe and some child was vigorously shaking it up and down. People were looting, smashing the glass of all the stores, and fighting like rabid dogs. People were running and carrying handfuls of CDs, electronics and even televisions.

Zack and Jacob both took protective steps toward me, hemming me in.

“We have to get out of here,” Zack growled, grabbing my arm. I turned to Jacob and saw the same trapped animal expression he wore when threatened. Jacob’s fight-or-flight response was forever stuck on flight, and I knew he would bolt any minute so I reached out and held his wrist. “Stay with us, Jacob Marley.”

We had been cornered by a gator once when we were out picking mushrooms for Melika. One second, Jacob and I were face-to-face with a ten footer, and the next second, I was alone, staring into the eyes of a prehistoric creature who wanted less to do with me than I wanted with it. He’d apologized forever for that day, and Melika explained that necromancers have a very different view of life and death. While many are not afraid of dying, there's a small fraction who are incredibly frightened of the afterlife. Jacob is the latter.

"Bones won't be coming back for us, Jacob Marley. We're going to have to make a run for it to get to the boat."

"Then let's get g—"

Shots rang out. We hit the wet ground. Then more. I covered my head with one hand and Jacob Marley's with the other. Then more glass broke. I looked up and saw a cop running from a store with his arms full of merchandise.

A cop?

In my snow globe moment, I was completely upside down. Did I just see a cop *stealing* from an electronics store? Suddenly, above the noise, came an odd chirping sound.

"What in the hell is that?" Jacob Marley asked.

We all looked down at my fanny pack. "Oh. It's me. I mean—" Pulling my vidbook out, I flipped it open. Mine was the prototype of a GPS satellite computer Danica's geek squad had developed. When you opened it, the caller's face filled the screen with as much clarity as high definition television. The whole thing was revolutionary, and bound to make Danica even more money than she already had. It was a great little device, and had saved my life once. Well…it and Cinder.

"Yo, Princess." It was Roger. Number one geek. Of the three, he had the biggest crush on me. "You all right?"

I started to say yes, out of habit, when a brick sailed just a little too close to my head. "Umm…not really."

"We figured. We've got all three big boys on and it's looking pretty scary down there." Big boys is what the guys called their three 80-inch jumbotron television sets mounted on one wall. "We've got you located on the system and you're laying smack in the middle of an LA-type riot."

"We know. We just—" Another gunshot rang through the air.

"We can get you outta there. We have a map of the city up and can help you dodge and weave until you're out of that crap. You gotta get a move on, Princess, 'cause the mob is moving toward you."

"How—"

"Not important, Princess. Who's with you?"

The boys did not know about my status as a supernatural, and I was pretty sure they would think it was "boss" that I was. The real question they were asking was whether or not their *boss* was with me. All three of those men would have eaten hot coals for Danica.

"She's not with us."

"Okay. You guys need to get off that street by taking Second Avenue. Do you see it?" The three of us looked around.

"There," Zack said, pointing. "That way."

We both grabbed Jacob Marley's hand and pulled him to his feet before scooting around a fight that had just broken out.

We reached Second quickly and Roger had us take a left at Pierre. We may have waded through water yesterday, but today, we were wading through human carnage that reminded me of one of those horrible zombie flicks. People who weren't looting and pillaging were actually attacking the looters and pillagers. You couldn't make this stuff up. It was insane.

"Get a move on, Princess. The third right is Staton. Take it."

We did, and I pressed the mute button. "I've tried contacting Tip, but she's not answering," I said to Zack.

"That's never good. That bugger always answers."

"Probably working too hard to find Bishop," I answered.

"We have to get outta here," Jacob Marley muttered. "I can feel it coming. It's *coming*!"

As if on cue, we trudged past an old woman slumped in a wheelchair with flies buzzing around her, reminding me of just how fragile life was, especially for the city's oldest citizens. It hurt my heart—the dead hurt Jacob's soul.

"Please, Echo," Jacob Marley whispered. "We have to go now!"

"We're going." I unmuted.

"Take a left on Harrison. Get a move on, Princess."

Zack glanced over his shoulder. "What's he got on that thing? A heat sensor?"

"Close enough, boy-o," Roger retorted. "Satellites make the world go 'round, and Danica's boys are seldom wrong. Now pick it up!"

We did, but it wasn't fast enough for Jacob, who was jumping out of his skin. "What are we going to do once we get there? We're heading back toward the water. What then?"

In the distance, a woman screamed for help. If there was a hell on earth, surely, we were in the middle of the glowing embers.

"I have no idea," I answered, leaping over what looked like a pile of human feces. Fortunately for me, I didn't need an idea. When we reached the end of Harrison, where the water was beginning to rise, Bones was making his way toward us in the boat.

"I'll be damned," Zack murmured. "He knew."

I glanced down at the vidbook. No, he didn't know, but Danica did. She must have been watching the news on the vidbook and contacted the boys to get us out of there. Leave it to Danica. "My guess is it's Danica who knew."

"Then how did she send for Bones?"

"She didn't. Bailey must have. She's the only quasi-telepath on the river."

Jacob Marley shot me a glance I knew instantly. "I know. I know as much about her as you do, but we have to trust her."

"Oh no…" Jacob uttered. "Look." He pointed to our left and I lost part of my shield when I saw a gang of five teenage boys wading toward Bones' boat yelling and hollering like dervishes. It was frightening and creepy in its similarities and it took all my strength to keep Jacob Marley from running.

"Princess—"

"Gotta go, Roger. I'll keep you posted." Closing the vidbook, I tossed it in my waterproof fanny pack. Already, Zack was wading toward the group, who were going to make it to Bones before we did.

"We gotta run, Echo," Jacob Marley muttered trying to pull away. "We can't stay."

"Zack?"

He shook his head. "Too far." His powers were no use from this range.

"Echo, stay back there. There's nothing you can do." Zack pushed his way through the mucky water trying to get to Bones before the gang did.

I was right behind him. When I came to the bayou, the only power I had was the ability to feel what others were feeling. Four years and one Tip later, I had learned how to take all the emotional energy around me and create a wall I could project outward. Like an invisible force field, it could be used both defensively as well as an attack. It was a power I practiced the following four years until I could erect a shield forceful enough to knock over someone Tip's size.

"Yeah, like that's gonna happen, Z." Jacob pushed ahead of me and suddenly, he and Zack were hip to hip and about forty feet from the boat when the gang reached it. The first thug's head met the end of Bones gator getter pole and slumped into the water. I had to give it to the old guy; he wasn't going down without a fight.

As long as we were there, he wasn't going down at all.

The second kid grabbed the large pole and tried vainly to shake it out of Bones' grasp. I daresay, if a half-ton alligator couldn't do it, no city hoodlum was going to.

It was the third kid who posed a problem. He had grabbed the old dinghy and was trying to rock it from side-to-side, and as we made our way closer, it was clear Bones would not be able to wrestle for control of the stick *and* the boat at the same time.

Just as Bones was starting to list in one direction, Zack made his move. Though we were still too far away for his powers to be fully effective, there *was* one thing near enough for him to use against them: water.

Putting his hands to his chest, palms facing outward, Zack thrust them forward as if he were making a chest pass in basketball. A wall of water about three feet high raced toward the boat and slammed into the kid wrestling with the pole. He went under the water, and in one swift motion that belied his age, Bones recovered his balance and smashed the third kid on the side of the head. It made a sickening thump and the kid sank like a stone, leaving the fourth and fifth boys fleeing for the safety of land, their buddies lingering somewhere in the muck below.

"You okay, Bones?" Jacob asked when we reached the boat.

He nodded once. “Zack done good. He know ol’ Bones kip his balance no madder what de water do.”

Quickly climbing in, two of us looked over the sides for any signs of life. Jacob shook his head at us. “Only one is still alive,” he said, feeling no remorse.

“Gator food, den,” Bones said shrugging, and that was that. Without another word, we all silently agreed this was one of those moments when you have to turn your back on what’s right and do what’s best. Which meant getting us the hell out of here.

After Bones made sure we were far enough away, he pulled his pole in and leaned against it. “Tank de girl. She come to Bones and say *Bones, you get back der now.*” Bones motioned with his chin to the outboard motor. “Bones use de motor.”

“That’s probably why they came after you…for the boat.”

Bones nodded, but said nothing more. None of us did.

As we made our way to the outskirts of the city to rest and eat the lunch Danica had made for us, I plucked the vidbook from my fanny pack and let the boys know that we were out of harm’s way. They were relieved and reminded me to check in every chance I could.

I stared wearily out at the water. Our beloved New Orleans had gone from Katrina to a flood to a war zone overnight, and it didn’t appear as if the cavalry was anywhere in sight.

If the looting and rioting disquieted my spirit, the sight of regular people doing extraordinary things to help their fellow New Orleanians rejuvenated it. People pulled family and strangers alike from the rubble. I was pretty sure I’d even seen a couple of Hollywood’s finest helping out in the fray, but Zack claimed they were only lookalikes. I wasn’t so sure.

It was with this momentum that we managed to pull twenty-six living and five dead from the ruins of the Ninth Ward, a feat exhausting us to the point that our chins were on our chests when Bones pulled up to the dock well after sundown.

“Thank the Gods,” Tip said, swooping down and scooping me up in her arms. “I’ve been trying to locate you for hours.”

With my shields down and all that extraneous noise, hearing Tip had been near impossible. “I’m sorry…it’s just—”

“Shh,” she whispered, holding me tighter. “You’re not hurt anywhere, though, right?” Stepping back, she surveyed me from top to bottom. “You’re okay?”

“Put her down, Tip,” Melika ordered. She appeared more haggard than I had ever seen her look.

Tip obeyed and stepped aside so Melika could take my chin in hand and gaze into my eyes. Melika preferred the truth filtered through her own eyes rather than through someone else’s mouth. “*You are very brave*,” she whispered inside my head. “I am proud of all of you for staying the course.”

“What about Bi—”

“Go inside, clean up and eat. We’ll discuss everything once you’ve all had a chance to settle down for the evening.”

When I walked into the cinder block house, Cinder practically threw herself at me. “Hey, you!” Picking her up, I hugged her tightly.

“Firefly was worried sick about you,” Danica announced, cutting up what looked like tuna sandwiches. She glanced casually over at me with a gaze far deeper than her actions portrayed. She’d been worried and rightly so. “Glad to see my boys’ gadgets come in handy every now and then.”

Letting go of Cinder, I walked over to Danica and pulled her to me with one arm. “Thank you,” I whispered. I wanted to cry—wanted to just let go of all the sadness I felt from those poor people who had lost everything. Everything. Nothing I was going through in slogging through that toxic waste could even remotely compare to families who had lost all they had, including each other.

“Clark?” Pulling slowly away, Danica looked down at me. “You’re not all right, are you?”

“I’m okay. Just…a little overwhelmed from it all. You have no idea…” Sighing, I shook my head. “Thank you. The boys got to us in the nick of time.”

The door opened and we were quickly joined by everyone else.

"Don't thank me," she said, handing one plate to Jacob Marley and one to Zack. "I'm not the one who called for backup."

I turned to Bailey and nodded. "I know. Thanks."

Zack and Jacob Marley both added their thank yous as they sat at the table.

Bailey sighed with a pained expression. "I'd love to take the credit, but—" She glanced over at Cinder. "Apparently, the flame thrower has some telepathic abilities or something. *She's* the one who made the call. Not me."

"Is that true?"

It wasn't Cinder who answered.

"I'm sorry I didn't mention it, Echo," Melika explained, "but with Bishop missing and all…anyway…Cinder is not telepathic in the strict sense of the word, like Bailey or Tip. Theirs is universal. Cinder has what's called selective telepathy."

"Selective?" This was new to me.

"Yes. Cinder has an emotional and telepathic link to you and Danica. I do not yet know if this is a latent ability or just something that happens during certain episodes in her life, but it's there. We just don't know what to do with it yet."

I knelt and took her hands in mine. "Pretty cool, eh, you and me?"

She smiled and touched her temple with her index finger before doing the same with mine. Her eyes filled with tears and I hugged her to me.

"When the boys initially called on the vidphone to make sure they had a bead on us, Cinder went outside," Danica explained. "I thought she was just going for some fresh air. By the time the boys got you out of the danger zone, she had already sent a message to Bones."

I rose unsteadily, and Tip reached out to keep me from going down. "She's selective with Bones as well?"

Melika nodded. "They have spent a great deal of time together since you brought her here. He has shown her all over the bayou. He gets her, I suppose." Turning to Cinder, Melika ruffled her hair. "You've done Echo proud, Cinder."

When Melika stood at the head of the table, we all stopped eating and listened.

"We hit every hospital. Most of them are completely inoperable and nonfunctioning. There are elderly strewn about like last week's garbage. No one knows where anyone else is; the doctors have done what they can with limited supplies and no electricity, but it is not enough. We did not find Bishop nor did we sense her presence anywhere in the area." Melika blew out a breath and pinched the bridge of her nose. Inhaling deeply, she continued. "If Jacob Marley has yet to detect her in the spirit world, then it's safe to say something has happened to her that took her off our present plane."

No one said a word.

"Which is better than her being dead. We did find out that the authorities are opening the Superdome and Convention Center for people who have lost their families and such. We'll go there tomorrow and see if she is being taken care of there. It is possible she suffered injury, which would explain why we cannot locate her, so we will go there first."

"We're going with you," I said softly.

"Like hell," Tip barked.

I leveled my gaze at Tip. "We are no longer children who are threatened or intimidated by you, Tiponi. It is up to *all* of us to help find her. We're either all going with you to find Bishop, or we're going out on our own, but either way, we're done rescuing strangers until we get Bishop back. This is our *family* we are talking about, and we're going after her with or without your permission."

Tip's pupils were pinpricks, and just as she was getting ready to fire back, Melika held her hand up. "Echo is right, Tip. I would have thought by now we would have located her. It is time we pooled our considerable resources. I appreciate your acute observation of the situation, Echo, but until Jacob Marley can confirm her demise, we must assume she is too injured to help herself or to contact one of us." Melika stepped away from the table. "I am exhausted, as I'm sure you all are. Do not stay up long and please do not argue." She looked hard at Tip. "Now is the time for coming together. Keep that in mind. Good night."

Melika passed Bailey on the stairs, and when Bailey sat down, the table remained quiet for a long time, save for the sounds of us eating. I was surprised when the first person to speak was Danica. "When you said *all* can I assume that to mean me, Bailey and Cinder as well? Because it would seem to me that three more pairs of eyes would be far more helpful than having us stay here."

Everyone naturally turned to Tip for a response, but her only reply was to level her gaze at me. Maybe she was miffed that I had challenged her in front of everyone. Maybe she felt it was just too dangerous out there for any of us. I couldn't tell what her deal was; I just knew the gauntlet had been tossed down and she was waiting to see what I was going to do about it.

I would do nothing. It wasn't my place to lead this group and she knew it.

"Tip?"

She looked away from me to Cinder. "I don't see why not. My only issue is to keep Cinder under wraps. She is nowhere near ready to go out in public with her powers. Her control is questionable at best, and with all the hysteria out there, we don't need to bring any of that attention on ourselves. I'd have to agree with Danica, though. Three more pairs of eyes are better than leaving you here."

I nodded. "Cinder? That means no powers. You understand?"

She nodded, her eyes bright with excitement. Who could blame her? She had been cooped up in this house for far too long.

"We'll leave at sunup," Tip said, setting her napkin on the table as she rose. "Can I talk to you outside?" This was directed at me.

I joined her at the door. "Sure."

When we stepped outside on the deck, Tip took her usual seat at the top of the stairs. I remained standing. "If you're going to bust my chops, can't it wait until tomorrow? I'm beat."

Patting the space next to her as she had done a hundred times before when I was a teenager, she shook her head. She was too gorgeous to be legal: jet black hair that shimmered like velvet, dark brown eyes that inhaled everything she studied, and a build of an Olympian. She was stunning personified. "I'm not busting anything. You said what you needed to say. I just… well…we haven't had any time to visit."

"We haven't had any time, period." I sat next to her. "How's Mel?"

"As stoic as ever, but the more time goes by the less sure she is that we'll find Bishop in time."

The last two words were like a slap across the face. "In time? What does *that* mean?"

Tip stared out over the river and shrugged. "She didn't say it in so many words, but there's a sense of urgency…like I can hear a clock ticking, but it's hidden from me. It's the strangest damn thing."

"Wait. You mean—"

"There's something she's not telling me. That much I know. What that is, I have no clue. But it's got to be pretty bad for her not to say anything to me."

"Hey, as long as Jacob Marley hasn't seen or heard from her, we have hope, right?"

She didn't say anything for the longest time. When she finally did, it was about something altogether different. "Does your new girlfriend know?"

"No, and she's not my girlfriend. That's so…"

"True?"

I pushed her, but she didn't budge. "Hush."

"You seeing anyone else?"

"No."

"Girlfriend."

"You are such an ass sometimes."

Tip grinned. "Sometimes? Look, I'm just calling it like I see it."

"Finn is a really good person."

"A *good person* would have come with you, or at least tried."

"She offered, but under the circumstances—"

"Those being that you have yet to tell her what you really are?"

I hesitated. "Well…yeah. I suppose." We both chuckled, probably more from exhaustion than anything else. Then we faded into that protracted silence very good friends experience without discomfort. As the crickets slowly began their night chirp, I realized there was an absence of other dusk-related sounds. I suppose a hurricane will do that.

When Tip put her arm around me, I leaned into the crook and let out a loud sigh. "The whole world has gone mad."

"I know. Pretty scary, huh?"

"Is *any* help coming?"

"I have no idea. Once we secure Bishop, we'll resume helping the folks along the river, but not if it's going to be as dangerous as it was for you guys this afternoon. I'm…I'm really sorry I couldn't be there. If anything happened to you—"

I reached over and held her hand. "You can't spend your entire life looking out for me. You've always been here for me. Always. Now, it's time for you to be there for Bishop." I heard the familiar sound of a gator sliding from the bank and into the river. "We *are* going to find her, aren't we?"

The length of time between my question and her response chilled me to the bone. "Tip?"

She let out a deep, defeated breath. "We should have found her by now. I've looked everywhere…thrown my mind as far as it can go, and still…nothing. If Bishop is in Louisiana, she's either in a coma, or somewhere else where I can't reach her."

This made me turn out of her grasp. "Somewhere else? I thought Jacob Marley—"

"Is a mediocre necromancer at best. We need a much stronger necro, a more experienced one than Mr. Marley."

"What about Rupert?" Rupert had helped me on my very first reporting assignment.

"Too far away. We need help *now*, and Mel's at her wit's end. So many of her gifted friends escaped Katrina and the flooding only to have been moved to Houston, Miami and even Oklahoma. Our strength is scattered among the ruins…and Bishop along with them."

I had never seen her so hopeless, so needing someone to prop her up. "Tomorrow then. We'll get a fresh start, new eyes, and we won't stop until we find her."

Tip blinked back tears. "Right. Won't stop."

I took her hands and held them. "We're all in this together, Tip. Maybe that's why we were the ones summoned. Maybe Bishop knew something like this was going to happen. You can't beat yourself up for not finding her yet. You still have us. *She* still has us."

We sat in silence for another ten minutes before I barely heard Tip say, "People's loved ones shouldn't be left out on the side of the road like trash."

I put my arms around her and pulled her to me. I didn't need to say anything…I had seen it as well. Her greatest fear was that Bishop was one of those people. "We'll find her," I said softly.

Tip nodded and found her stride again. "Keep your shields up, especially in crowds. I don't want you being overwhelmed like Jacob Marley was. There's more sickness and sadness and despair out there than I've ever witnessed. You have to take care of yourself, you hear me?"

I did, and told her so as I rose to retire for the evening. "Tip, you don't have to carry this burden alone, okay?"

She nodded and in that instant, I felt her shield collapse. She was exhausted. "Go get some rest," I said. "We'll all be fresher in the morning."

To my surprise, she did not argue, and tromped up the stairs, the weight of our world on her shoulders.

I went to sleep thinking about the word that kept dodging in and out of my mind, teasing me…baiting me to figure out what feeling it was that I had had when both Melika and Tip spoke about Bishop.

Sinister. That was the word.

I would have worked it out had I not immediately fallen to sleep, only to be awakened a few hours later when my vidbook started chirping. Glancing at my watch, I saw it would only be midnight back in San Francisco, and the boys were known to stay up way beyond three or four.

I flipped it open, and there was Roger's face again. I hoped I didn't have drool on my face.

"Sorry to wake you, Princess, but we've been watching the news reports about NOLA that are frickin' scaring the beejesus out of us and we wanted to give you and the boss a heads up in case you're headed that way tomorrow."

Sitting up, I rubbed my eyes. "What way is that?"

"The Superdome. All hell is breaking loose."

Roger showed me some of the news reports from the Superdome. Needless to say, I didn't sleep much or well after that. There were hundreds if not thousands of people standing outside the Superdome in heat you could die in. Some people were handing out water, others were begging for some, and all were miserable. It was a tragedy waiting to happen.

"We thought you and the boss ought to know so you could steer clear. Things are swirling around the toilet bowl down there, eh?"

It was an apt metaphor, and when I finished watching, I thanked Roger and closed the vidbook, knowing I would be in the middle of that toilet bowl tomorrow.

When I woke up, I made coffee and waited for Tip. She was an early riser and true to form, she was the first downstairs.

"The mob at the Superdome is getting out of hand," I told her as I handed her a cup of coffee. Her mug had a picture of wolves with a dream chaser hanging from a tree on it.

"I told you this was going to get worse before it got better."

"But we're going anyway, right?"

She looked at me. "What do *you* think? Get everyone ready to go."

I never doubted it, and in less than two hours, all of us descended on the conflagration of the Superdome.

"Oh. My. God," Jacob Marley said, reaching for my hand.

Not in my wildest nightmares could I ever have envisioned that the Superdome would turn into a prison run by the worst offenders. Never could I have dreamt of anything like that happening in the United States.

"You still packing heat?" Danica whispered as we approached a blocks-long line of miserable people fanning themselves and muttering epitaphs for the likes of George W. There were those who were trying to stay calm despite the weather and the inhumane conditions, and there were those who had slipped on their "fuck it" boots and strode up and down the street riling everyone up.

Then there was the majority of them looking out through blank eyes; eyes too exhausted, scared, and worst of all... helpless. At the onset of the flood, people were desperate. Now, they were hostile and ready to fight anyone and anything. Not only had they lost everything, now they were being treated like cattle, shoved into buses for destinations unknown.

That was the reason for Danica's question about the gun—one didn't need special powers to see what direction this event was heading.

"Heat? What do you think this is, *Miami Vice*?"

Her answer was a raised eyebrow.

"Yes, I still have it. Want the nasty thing back?"

"I have my own, thank you."

"I thought this *was* yours."

She groaned. "It was. I have two more just like it."

"I would ask if you were kidding, but I know you're not. You only have two hands. What in the hell do you need three for?"

She flashed me a grin. "One for you, two for me. I'm probably the only black woman in the nation who watched every single John Wayne movie ever made. I just got all goosepimply watching those western gunslingers."

I stopped walking and stared at her. "You always made it sound as if your dad *made* you watch those with him. But three?"

"Have you checked out the people around us, Clark? This is no party we're going to. This is worse than the ghetto. Shoot or be shot is my motto, and like the Duke said, 'Courage is being scared to death, but saddling up anyway.' I'm not as scared with my guns in my pocket."

"You know, I don't think I've ever seen you scared."

"Black chicks know how to hide fear better than white chicks. So, if you have any Jane remnants left, now would be a good time to access them."

Jane. Jane Doe. Jane-as-in-I-don't-know-who-my-parents-are-Doe. I was Plain Jane for most of my life; until I met Danica.

Meeting her changed my life. Protecting her changed my future. We were just two young girls trying to get over the hormonal hurdles of adolescence when Todd, a premier football player, came upon us. *That* Jane bashed his head in with a math book. *That* Jane was shipped off to the booby hatch because of it. *That* Jane was someone I never saw again after that day. Occasionally, Danica would still refer to me as Jane, and it was usually when she was driving home a point.

She was making a vital one now. "Just keep it handy and don't be afraid to use it. This whole stadium feels like one big ghetto, and the ghetto is a dog-eat-dog kind of place. Shoot first, ask later, but don't be afraid of pulling the damn trigger."

When we finally made it to the front door of the Superdome, Tip divided us up. Danica, Cinder and I went east, Tip and Jacob went west, Melika, Zack and Bailey went north, and we would meet at the southernmost part of the Dome. Each of us had a photo of Bishop, which we began showing to people who either stared vacantly and shook their heads or focused in and shook their heads.

"Damn it, Dani, even the ghetto doesn't smell this bad. What in the hell is that *stench*?"

"Near as I can tell, and this is a guess, mind you, is a mixture of urine, body odor, rotting food and..."

"Rotting corpses?"

"Maybe. Look over there."

I did. Pushed into one corner of the stadium were a dozen or so corpses in wheelchairs. Someone had tried to cover them up with one of those blue tarps, but it had come undone and you could see the people underneath it were dead. Each body had a name and phone number pinned to it, although one lady's name and number was scrawled on the thin gray blanket dangling off her wheelchair. It was the saddest thing I'd ever seen—unclaimed family members left like detritus.

"Shit, Clark. Can you even imagine rolling someone you love into a corner and leaving them there?"

Danica's mother had died in our sophomore year; it was a

loss that had carved its initials in the bottom of her soul and made her a stronger woman for it, but she'd never really gotten over it.

I felt Cinder inch closer to me. The noise level inside was deafening, second only to the disgusting stench hanging in the air, tangible in its thickness. It was hard to breathe; the heat inside was stifling, stagnating, without a single breeze. It felt like you had to push it aside in order to walk.

But the worst of it was the screams. Every now and then, a frightening scream pierced the air and reverberated off the walls. Bad things were happening to good people…really bad things. The emotions were so awful, they crashed effortlessly through my shields, and I had to stop more than once to regroup. It was times like these when I had to be very careful. It was too easy to get hammered by the sadness and sense of overwhelming loss.

That was why Cinder had moved closer to me. On some level she felt it also. Felt it *and* heard it. It would have been terrifying to a normal child, but Cinder threw her shoulders back as if she wasn't afraid. I didn't know who postured more, her or Danica.

"You okay?" I asked Cinder.

She nodded and then pointed to me.

"I'm okay." I felt another emotional grenade break through my barriers, but shook it off. There was work to do.

"Give a shout if you need to bolt out of here, Clark. You know me, I can clear a path faster than a hot snowplow."

I started toward a group of people who looked like family, when Danica's hand shot out and grabbed my wrist. "Uh-uh. Skip them."

Frowning, I turned back to see what it was she saw. It wasn't a family after all, but three twenty-something boys wearing red do-rags, baggie jeans and white wife-beater tank tops. "Oh. Yeah." We skirted around them, but not quickly enough. One of them made a sexual remark toward Danica before making sucking sounds. Normally, she would have whipped around and given them as good as she got, but this wasn't normal, and she knew better. Girl from the 'hood and all that. Instead, she threw her shoulders back and kept walking.

Unfortunately, so did they.

"Clark?"

I focused on one of the men behind us and quickly read him. "Trouble," I said out of the side of my mouth. My radar clanging madly, I picked up the pace. Instinctively, I knew it would do no good. They wanted what they wanted, just like Todd all those years ago; and just like Todd, these guys would get what was coming to them.

When one of the guys grabbed Cinder and one grabbed me, Danica reached inside her purse. A dirty hand clamped over my mouth as I struggled to get free. My eyes never left Cinder's face, and I was amazed at her calm—amazed and afraid. Powerful emotions were never good for a firestarter, and Cinder's calm under the circumstances was almost frightening.

The same powerful emotions weren't very good for a girl from the 'hood, either, and Danica's calm demeanor was equally as scary. Why was I the only one really afraid?

"Let. Them. Go. *Assholes.*" Danica had her gun out so fast, I never saw her pull it. She pointed it at the kid holding me, her face a stone scowl, her eyes cold and hard. She held the gun sideways—like a hoodlum—like she'd held one a thousand times before. It wasn't until I looked at the guy holding Cinder that I realized these weren't kids; these were hardened gang members sporting jailhouse tattoos, pushing twenty, maybe older.

"Whoa, hey, sista, be cool," the one holding me said, tightening his grip on me.

"I'm not your fucking *sister*, asshole, now do what I told you to do and you and your buddy might live to see tomorrow." She raised the gun and stepped closer. I read her intentions and they were deadly. She was not bluffing. The guy with his hand over my mouth put a knife to my throat; a very sharp knife. He wasn't bluffing either. I glanced down at Cinder, who had not once bothered to struggle, and barely shook my head, telling her in my mind, *No. Don't.* It was a futile gesture because she had her shields up, so it wasn't likely she heard me.

She did not acknowledge one way or the other if she understood what I wanted. I needed her to because of the unpredictable nature of her powers, she could inadvertently burn herself up in an effort to save us.

"Drop the gun, bitch," the guy behind me ordered, "or I'll cut her."

The gun didn't move, and neither did Danica. Instead, she looked over at Cinder, who was staring intently back.

Oh no.

"I'm not fuckin' kidding, bitch! Put it down or I cut her fuckin' head off."

Danica didn't blink, but turned her cold, dark eyes back to me. I would have given anything to be a telepath at that moment, because I was so unprepared for what came next.

"Here's the thing," she said conversationally. "How come you assholes didn't grab *me*? What am I? Chopped liver? You know, that really pisses me off. First, my old man leaves me for some skinny white bitch like this one, and now this? I oughtta just fuckin' blow your goddamn head off myself." Suddenly, she wheeled around and pointed it at the one guy who wasn't holding anyone. "It's a good day to die, dontcha think?" She pointed the gun right between his eyes. Her hand unwavering. "'Cause that's what's gonna happen if your *amigo* doesn't let the bitch go *pronto. Comprende, Ese?*"

For a moment, no one moved. No one blinked. Then, in a voice I had never heard her use, Danica growled, "Do it." Her voice cold as frozen steel, my gut tightened at the sound of it. Heart pounding, I understood in a nanosecond what she meant and who she was talking to, but I was too late to stop her.

The next few seconds dragged by in slow motion as Cinder's hands burst into flames. The first fireball flew from her hands hitting the guy Danica was aiming at, sending him crashing into a partition in a burst of flames. I ducked as the second fireball flew past us, narrowly missing me. The heat from it unbearable—singed hair smell filled the air. The guy holding Cinder tried to let go of her, but she grabbed his wrists and held him there. He cried out in agony as her hands melted his skin down to the bones. The smell of burnt hair replaced now by burnt flesh. I tried to call out her name to make her stop, but it was too late for him. He crumpled unconscious to the dirty floor of the Superdome, two sections of his wrists gone. It looked like he was wearing blackened bracelets on his boney wrists.

Two down, and my guy to go. I could only imagine what he was thinking as he watched his friends die. I *knew* what he was feeling. Instead of letting me go, he held me closer to him—a shield to protect him from her.

"What the fuck *are* you?" He asked. I did not struggle even as I felt the bite of the knife at my throat. We were too close together for Cinder to fire off another. Her powers were not quite there yet.

Cinder looked at Danica and shook her head.

"My turn, then," Danica said, taking three long strides toward us and raising the gun to his face. "You got two seconds to let her go, asshole. One. Two." Before I could say a word, she calmly squeezed the trigger. I felt the heat from the gun on my cheek and the sound exploded in my ears like a bomb. I didn't need to look to know the wet on my neck and shoulders were blood and brains. He fell to the floor at the same time his knife clattered to the ground.

Danica pushed past me and stood over the dead guy, his one good eye fixed up at the ceiling. "What she *is*, you son-of-a-bitch, is better than the three of your sorry asses put together, *asshole*." Danica stood over the body for a moment longer, then she turned, dropped the gun back in her fanny pack and turned away. "Let's get the fuck out of here." Grabbing my arm, she moved swiftly toward Cinder, and turned her away from the carnage we had wrought. "Good job, Firefly."

We were ten feet beyond them before I managed to find my voice. "Dani—" My throat was still burning from the knife and me knees were wobbly.

Danica shook her head at me as she pushed me in front of her. "Don't get on your high horse, Clark. This isn't about right and wrong. It's about *survival*." She moved more quickly now, pushing me forward. I turned to find people attracted to the flaming piles of what used to be men, the stench of burnt flesh and hair filling our nostrils.

"High horse? Dani, you…you…"

"Killed a man? Wrong, Clark. I took out the trash. Like wiping dog shit off my shoes."

"But Cinder—"

"Understood this is a kill or be killed environment here, Clark. Wake up! Look around you!"

I picked up my pace trying not to look over my shoulder. Cinder was practically running to keep up with Danica's long strides. "But the cops…The—"

"Are you kidding me? Do you see any five-oh?"

"But I…I—" I stammered feeling helpless in a hopeless situation.

"You told Cinder not to, didn't you?"

I was breathing quickly now, panic crumbling my shield. "It's not that."

"What did *you* want to do? Try to talk them out of it?"

"I won't make a killer out of her."

Dani stopped and grabbed me with both hands. "Damn it, Clark, what choice was there? Being gang raped or setting some dirtbag on fire?

"I protected you like you did me all those years ago." Releasing me, she turned and kept walking. "Over here," she barked, pointing to a side doorway. "We gotta get outta this shithole."

When we got near the door, I was out of breath, sweaty and trembling. Kneeling down. I grabbed Cinder's hands. As usual they were very warm to the touch. "Cinder, honey…it's not that I don't appreciate what you've done—"

"Cut the crap, Clark. You think she doesn't *know* what the hell is going on here? She *knows* how powerful she is. She understands she's killed people. She *gets* it. Maybe it's time you do, as well."

I glanced up in question, realizing, too late, what Danica already knew.

"She's an emotional telepath, just like Melika said, and she's connected to four of us: you, me, Mel and Bones. I told her to fire on that guy and she did. It was as simple as that." To Cinder she said, "Tell her."

Cinder nodded, looking in my eyes. *"I don't mind killing bad people, Echo. Melika told me I am not a killer. I'm a…a…cleaner."*

I glared up at Danica, who shrugged. She couldn't hear our conversation, but she knew we were talking. Apparently, she knew far more than I. "A cleaner?" I asked out loud.

Cinder nodded. "*Yep. I clean the world of dirty, ugly people. She said dis…dis…*"

"Disinfect?"

"*Yep. That's the word. It's a good one, right?*"

"Right, but Melika doesn't want you to kill people, Cinder. That's not what we use our powers for."

"*It's not what you use* your *powers for, Echo. I use mine to protect us. I like Danica. A lot. She makes me feel good. I wouldn't ever ever ever let anyone hurt her. Or you.*"

Heaving a loud sigh, I rose. I would have to finish this conversation another time. "Yeah, I kind of like her too," I looked over at Danica. "Even if she pisses me off."

"Call us even and stop worrying so much about Cinder's spirit. The kid understands that killing people doesn't make her a killer. Killing people *for no reason* makes one a killer."

Before I could respond to such flawed logic, someone else did it for me. "What a fascinating supposition." The tall man standing before us stood eye-to-eye with Danica's six-foot frame. His complexion was lighter than hers, but not by much, and had a reddish tint to it. He possessed incredible light green eyes that focused on all of us at once. Unlike the other survivors who were in bedraggled dirty clothes, he was wearing an Armani jacket, pressed khaki slacks, shined up patent leather shoes and a maroon collared shirt open at the neck. He had jet black hair graying at the temples with other sprinkles of gray here and there like a light dusting of snow.

Danica started for her gun.

"No need for that thing."

She paused and glanced over at me. I tried to read his intentions, but he was completely blocked.

Completely.

And that meant only one thing—the hackles on the back of my neck said it wasn't a good thing.

"You must be Melika's protégés," he said, a half grin forming on his lips. He was one of the most beautiful men I'd ever seen when he smiled. His teeth were flawless and his left cheek sported a deep dimple. I put his age somewhere near fifty.

"And you are?" I put my hand on Cinder's shoulder and told

her telepathically not to do a damn thing. And I meant it this time.

To my surprise, he bowed. "My name is Malecon. Perhaps you've heard of me."

I watched him as he tried to prod Danica's mind. "Don't do it, Malecon. It's rude and presumptuous to assume she can be read."

Turning to me, his gaze flickered from friendly to something else. "But she is not—"

"She's been trained." My hackles moved to the pit of my stomach and I squeezed Cinder's shoulder tighter to keep her where she stood. Danica would not be so controlled.

Danica stepped closer to him, something tough girls from the ghetto do to let you know they are not going to be intimidated. "What can we help you with, Mr. Malecon? We're a little busy here."

"Busy? Oh…yes…of course. I see. Blasting the naturals back into the holes from which they crawled must be exhausting. The psionic energy the two of you send forth could awaken the dead, though I have noticed that stoic Apache has yet to come running to your aid. Isn't that odd? I thought she was your personal bodyguard, Echo."

Danica started to get up in his face, but Cinder reached out and touched her leg. Whatever Cinder said to Danica made her back off.

"Come on, Echo, let's split. We wouldn't want to keep *the Apache* waiting." Danica turned.

I didn't move. How did he know my name? How did he know about Tip? Who was this guy who clearly did not belong in the Superdome? "What is it you want, Malecon? We have a lot to do."

"Like finding Bishop?"

Danica stopped and slowly turned back to him. It wasn't what he said that bothered me, but the way he said it. There was an iciness in the way he spat out her name that gave me the chills. "Maybe," I said, willing myself to move on.

"Tell Tip and her mentor they better find her before I do… because if I do—"

Cinder held a small fireball in her hand, and before I could stop her, she tossed it at his legs. To my surprise, it fizzled out halfway there. Cinder looked stunned. Malecon merely shook his head. "You don't want to make an enemy of me, little girl, so I'll chalk up that pathetic flame to youth and ignorance." To me, he warned, "Keep your charge in line next time we meet, Echo. I'd hate to see what might happen if those fireballs were turned against her." Malecon turned on a dime and disappeared into the crowd, leaving the three of us gaping.

"Who in the *hell* was that?"

"I have no idea."

"Did he actually stop Cinder's fireball?"

We both looked down at Cinder, who nodded.

"Uh-oh."

I nodded. "We better find Melika."

"And fast. I mean…who in the hell can stop a fireball?"

"My brother," Melika answered when we all gathered near the southern entrance of the Dome. The moment Danica started with, "There was this guy…" Melika ushered us all out of the Superdome as quickly as possible. When we were far enough away, Tip led us through alleys in the French Quarter I never knew existed until we came to a small, pink hotel.

"In here."

One by one we entered the side of the building before moving to a large conference room with a gorgeous maple table in the center. Melika motioned for all of us to sit while Tip went to speak with someone at the reception desk. When she returned, Melika was sitting at the head of the table with Tip on her right. It was so weird…like we were sitting at King Arthur's Round Table or something. No one knew what to say to Melika's announcement. I was pretty sure no one but Tip even knew she had a brother.

"I apologize for this," Melika said softly after Jacob closed the doors. "I never thought we would need to have this conversation."

"You don't owe us any," Bailey said.

"Please, Bailey, let me get this out before you say anything. It is vital that you hear this, for your own safety. Malecon is more than my brother. He is my twin." No one uttered a peep. "He is the yang to my yin in the universe. I have spent my entire adult life trying to help those like us live better lives with their powers, to help society if possible. Malecon has always used his to help himself. Since we were very young, he has sought to rise above his station using our innate powers. He has stopped at nothing to get the things he wants in life." She sighed, showing signs of strain. "When Bishop came to this country, she was a young girl possessing many strong abilities. She used those skills to obtain her freedom, but she didn't get very far. She ran into a roadblock called love…maybe it ran into her, I've never really been sure. All I know is there was a passionate love affair, but when she became pregnant, he disappeared. She never heard from him again. This singular act drove Malecon his entire life to want to find the man who did not want him. It made him a very bitter young man."

"He never found him?"

Melika shook her head. "Never. That only made things worse. Malecon sank deeper and deeper into despair, and his powers started changing, like all of ours do at puberty. Before we knew it, he had turned himself into what Bishop refers to as an empathic vampire, among other things."

"A what?" Jacob asked.

"It is exactly as it sounds. An EV is an empath who thrives on chaos and misery. The more there is, the more powerful they become. It was thought that Joseph Mengele, the Angel of Death in Auschwitz was one, as was Idi Amin, the African dictator. The empathic vampire is called a vampire because they actually feed off the negative energy, much like a vampire feeds on people's blood."

I turned to Cinder, whose eyes were wide. "Don't worry, Cinder, it's just an example. Vampires don't really exist." She seemed to accept this as she blinked quickly and swallowed hard.

"Not in the literal sense, no, but make no mistake about it, that is precisely what my brother is. He is happiest when those around him suffer. My mother knew this when she moved us all the way out to the bayou. Out there, there's no one but us, so there was nothing to feed from. It kept his powers, and that's plural, in check."

"What else is he?" Zack asked.

Melika sighed. "The easier question to answer is what is he *not*. When his powers are at their peak, his telepathic skills rival Tip's and his telekinesis skills…"

"He has both?"

"No. He has what we call a triad: empathy, telepathy, telekinesis all rolled into one sick person." She held up her hand. "And he *is* sick. He craves power and to get that, he needs to either *be* in chaos or create it himself. He could have hurt you girls today if he wanted to."

"Why didn't he?"

Melika sighed and lowered her eyes."Because he wanted me to know he's free."

"Free?" I looked over at Tip and knew she had all the answers we were waiting for.

"Yes, free. You see, Bishop kept him under her control all these years. Do not ask me how, exactly, for she would never tell me. All I know is that she has expended a great deal of energy keeping his mind locked up, but now that something has happened to her…well…the rest is quite apparent."

"She controlled him from New Orleans?"

"Yes. That is why she lives in the city and not out here with me. Up until the hurricane, he was being held at Charity Hospital in a special isolation unit with very specific rules and regulations. As long as Malecon couldn't sense any sadness or misery, his powers remained dormant. With the flooding… and whatever happened to Bishop, he obviously managed to escape."

"How did she force him into the loony bin?" Danica asked.

"Why is more important than how, Danica. Malecon tried to kill one of my charges when I first opened my home to the gifted. He has always resented me and my successes; the way I move around in a world he wants no part of. He is a dangerous, dangerous EV."

"So, what is it he wants? I mean, he's out of the nuthouse, so why stay around? Why not DD outta here?"

"Because here is where the most misery is." This came from Tip, who was looking at an invisible spot on the table. "This place is a smorgasbord of chaos for him to feed on."

"Correct. Once Malecon gets his fill, his powers grow. When that happens, he finds ways to capitalize on people's suffering."

"Capitalize? How?"

Melika shook her head sadly. "My brother is a very rich man. Before Bishop took control of him, he became rich by swooping down like a starving vulture when people least expected it. He purchased businesses, property and stocks from people who had nothing left to lose and gave them to him for a song."

"This is about *money*?" Danica asked incredulously.

"No, Danica. This is about power. In this country, power can seldom be had without money. For a man like Malecon, power gives him pawns to use in some twisted game he plays at the expense of anyone who has what he wants. He believes he is superior to the naturals. He is, by far, the most dangerous psi I have ever encountered, and in this environment, could very well be the greatest nightmare in the city."

"Would he physically hurt people?"

She nodded. "To get what he wanted. I know what he wants, and it's the land sitting under all that water."

"By the looks of the lack of aid coming in—"

Melika nodded. "You can see what's on the horizon. When all this is over, the poor will be pushed out while the big developers create a new city; a city filled with upper-class people who can afford to renovate. He will make millions from such deals, but again, it is not the money that drives him. It is the game itself, and New Orleans has just become the biggest game in the country."

"We have to stop him." Again, from Tip.

"We're *stopping* him?" Jacob Marley asked.

Melika nodded. "It isn't just how he capitalizes on the ill fortunes of others, which he does without remorse, it's what he will do now that he is able to roam free. We mustn't allow that. Too much is at stake."

We all waited, but I knew what it was.

Drawing a deep breath, she folded her hands together tightly. "He has been kept a prisoner by more than the walls of Charity. Our mother has kept his mind locked up for so long, he has had plenty of time to dream about what he would do to her if he ever tasted freedom."

"Oh no," Bailey uttered.

"Oh yes, my dear. In order to be truly free, my brother must kill Bishop."

The silence was deafening. For the longest time, no one said a word. The very idea that Malecon was matricidal stunned us all.

The first person to speak was Danica. "Wait. He wants to *kill* his own mother?"

"Not wants to, *has* to. If he doesn't, she'll contain him again. But leaving this city, he loses the power, and that's his ultimate goal. So if he's going to stay—"

"Bishop has to go."

"Precisely."

"Well, the good news is that he doesn't know where she is, right?"

Melika blinked slowly. "Not yet. That's why we must defuse him."

"Umm…I hate to ask, but is *defuse* super-speak for *destroy?* You guys are playing for keeps, right?"

"Play is the correct term, Danica," Melika replied. "Everything is a game to Malecon. His world is divided into winners and losers, black and white, life and death. That break is a chasm much like a black hole, eating everything that enters it. He is incapable of filling that void, but that doesn't prevent him from trying." Melika sighed. "I'm afraid he only grew more insistent. Danica, do you still carry that little computer with you?"

Danica produced it from her fanny pack. "Never leave home without it." Flipping it open, she waited, fingers poised over the tiny keyboard.

"If you'd be so kind as to look up Indigo Enterprises, you'll see just how lucrative a game this has been for him."

Danica quickly located the information and then whistled. "Holy crap. Not a bad day's pay." She turned the vidbook for all of us to see. "I thought you said he'd been locked up. There was a takeover not one month ago."

"Oh he has been. He also has his minions who carry out his plan when he is incapable of doing so."

Danica turned the vidbook back around. "He has holdings all over the world."

Melika nodded. "If you'd like to name them off, perhaps all of you might see a pattern."

Danica did as requested. "Indonesia, Philippines, Iran…"

"Notice those dates of when he made a financial move up the ladder?"

Danica nodded. "He's made considerable purchases after major disasters. Two in Indonesia after a quake killed over two hundred thousand people. Same with the quake in Iran that killed around thirty thousand people. Thailand…oh God, here's five for New York."

Melika looked pained. "Yes, he even managed to take advantage of people who suffered losses when the city was attacked. You see, my brother has no soul. When tragedy occurs, he is like a piranha in a pool of minnows and starts nibbling away at people's miseries. Real developers, the men with the real money never even see him coming and all the while, he is right under their noses, taking from them. Before you know it, he'll piece together a rope of transactions and sell to the highest bidder."

"Those poor people," Bailey murmured.

"Yes. Beautiful, colorful New Orleans will become the abyss of upper-middle-class whitedom, forever changing the one thing that truly makes us unique in this country. Its destruction will be complete at the hands of men like Malecon who desire nothing more than to win whatever game he is playing. Trust me. He won't leave New Orleans until he has completed those two tasks: kill our mother and destroy the character of the city that held him hostage."

"It's now *our* problem," Tip said softly. "And not just because of New Orleans and Bishop."

We all turned toward her.

"An EV is an addict…the more he gets, the more he needs, and right about now, Malecon is gorging. The greater problem is the instability of both his mind and his other powers. Because he refused to train himself, his powers are erratic at best."

"Are you saying he's insane?"

Tip shook her head. "He goes in and out."

I was reminded of Shirley, the homeless woman I had befriended three months ago. She was a clairsentient being whose powers drove her to the brink of insanity. That insanity often controlled her, and sometimes she was able to control it. But I knew what this meant for us; Malecon was even more dangerous than if he were in complete control of himself. "A crazy super on the loose poses a danger to all of us," I said softly. "To even those who are not here."

"Exactly," Melika said. "In the past…Bishop and…well… let's just say she was not alone in dealing with psionic creatures who threatened to expose us all."

We were all sitting there thinking the same thing. It only took one of us to inform the scientific community or the government that we did, indeed, exist. If that were to happen, we would be hunted down, probed, prodded and caged like rare specimens. It would be the end of our freedom and our lives.

Last month, Tip had had to deal with another TK who had decided to take his "show" on the road. It was fine as long as it was penny-ante stuff, but he started to put on such public displays, he was getting unwanted attention. Well…unwanted by the rest of us. With today's cell phone technology, it only took one person to videotape one of us doing something extraordinary, and then we'd have a lot of explaining to do. Unfortunately, we were also living in the age when everyone wanted their fifteen minutes of fame. Fame and psionic powers do not mix. The TK ended up as a video on the ever popular Web site YouTube.

When Tip tried to have a conversation with him about it, the kid gave a flick of his wrist and sent Tip crashing against a wall. Now, I've mentioned Tip's size before, so the strength in that flick told Tip that we were in trouble if we didn't rein this kid in.

But he wouldn't be collared and resented the idea that he needed to train. He wanted the limelight and the money that came with being different and had aspirations of being the next Copperfield or Angel. Of course, there already were those "magicians" who were, in fact, supernaturals, and had made a good living off making it look as if they were magicians performing sleight of hand routines. Those supers were known and trusted throughout the paranormal community, and even respected for the way in which they pulled off their careers.

What this young man wanted would have come at the expense of the rest of us, and this was evidenced by the fact that he threw Tip in front of others. Of course, no one believed it was real. They thought it was part of an act. After all, who could really knock a grown woman across the room with nothing but energy?

In the end, Tip gave Ryan a chance to do the right thing, but he didn't know what that was, so we hunted him down and gave him the same choice the rest of us have when we fall off the path: cease and desist all paranormal behavior or be banished for life. Banishment meant one of two things: the kind of life Malecon had lived, or having your brains fried from the inside and living the rest of your days as a drooling vegetable.

It's harsh, I know, but the needs of the many always outweigh the needs of the few, and it took all of us to protect our community from those of us who would destroy it from within. Ryan was one of those who didn't care, and it cost him. He chose to fight, and though he originally underestimated Tip' abilities, in round two he faced me, Tip, and Zack, a triad of powers that, when used in sync, attack mind, body and spirit all at once, which is what we did. It wasn't pretty, but we did manage to contain him without destroying him. When he realized the extent we were willing to go to put an end to his caviar dreams, he acquiesced and backed down. We keep a close eye out on him these days, but so far, he has chosen to play by the rules like the rest of us. I shudder to think of what Tip and Melika would do if he crossed that line. Tip's telepathic powers are so over-the-top, even the strongest psionic shield is incapable of holding her out completely.

Which was why her reaction about Malecon had me worried. Tip feared no supernatural…until now. I didn't need to read her to know she would kill him if given the chance.

Zack rose suddenly. "Then what are we waiting for? Let's take the SOB out."

Melika motioned for him to sit back down. "*Taking him out*, as it were, is not going to be nearly as easy as it was with Ryan. Malecon will think nothing of attacking you…of destroying each and every one of you." It was dawning on me just how little I knew about my mentor; how private she really was. I felt a little like a teenager who finally realized her parents were human.

"I didn't first feel my powers until I was almost thirteen. It's funny because I had tried to hide mine from Bishop because of her concern over Malecon. But, as you all know, she is a remarkable woman, and she allowed me the space to *hide* for almost a year. Once she realized the extent to which she would have to dampen Malecon's powers, she turned all of her attention to training me. I think that was the beginning of his hatred toward me."

"What an asshole," Zack muttered.

"He is what he is, Zachary, and it is my belief that if we do not stop him, what he *will be* is the murderer of my mother."

"And you, Melika? Would he hurt you?"

She looked at each of us before answering. "I do not know if he has it in him to kill me. Again, the man does have his standards. Killing is no fun for him. He prefers the game. And right now, that game is to find our mother and destroy her."

After we regrouped at the hotel, repairing downed shields and whatnot, we returned to the Superdome to finish our search. To no avail. No one had seen her, and so many people were looking for their loved ones it was almost impossible to get anyone to really care.

That night, we returned to the bayou with very few spoken words between us. The notion of the possibility of matricide in our ranks was as unfamiliar as the surface of Mars, and none of us knew what to do about it. We weren't used to being in a situation where we had no power, no way of immediately changing the situation that was quickly getting away from us. I wanted to call Finn and ask what the cops do about a missing person during a national disaster, but I couldn't do that without her asking too many questions even if I was an investigative reporter.

Leaning my head against Tip's shoulder, I closed my eyes and let nature heal the many psychic wounds delivered today. I was exhausted. I couldn't stop seeing the image of the guy Cinder set on fire or the one good eye staring up at the ceiling. I couldn't stop thinking about what I seemed to always force Cinder to do. Did people always die around me or get hurt in some way? It appeared so. I had to stop thinking, and the moment I did, I fell fast asleep.

When we finally stepped out of the boat, Danica asked me if I wanted to go for a walk to clear my head. Although we had been walking most of the day, I needed the fresh air and sanity of the bayou. I needed to regenerate in the only place I knew.

As we walked, I couldn't help but pick up on some of Danica's energy. It was low and pained, and she was never like that. Ever.

"You okay?" I asked as we picked our way through the trees. There were so many branches and so much moss lying on the ground, we barely felt the sogginess of the soil. I was scarcely aware of the fecund smells of the bayou.

"Yeah. I'm okay. You can stop watching me like a hawk. I know you think I should be feeling some kind of remorse, but I don't. And I won't. I'm just tired, that's all. I did what I had to do for us to be safe. It's survival of the fittest, know what I mean? What bothers me more is the fact that we're *planning* on killing her brother, and *that's* a whole different ball game."

I stopped walking, determined to breach her walls, which

wasn't hard since she was as tired as the rest of us. "I'm not talking about that, Dani. I'm talking about *you*! You blew a man's head off, for God's sake."

"Not for God's sake, Clark. For *yours*. Yours and Cinder's, and if I had to do it all over again, the results would be the same." She turned and stared hard into my eyes. "If you'd just stop for one second and consider what those fuckers wanted *to do* to us, to *Cinder*, you'd understand why I'm already over it. They were garbage. Like Mel told Cinder, it was merely taking out the trash."

I held a hand up. "Speaking of Cinder—"

"Don't. You *should have* unleashed her the first chance we had. That could have gone horribly wrong for us." Danica reached out and touched the knife mark on my throat.

"Un*leashed* her? Danica, do you hear what you're saying?"

"I hear you refusing to face the facts about Cinder. No matter how you spin this, Cinder *is* a killer and she will attack anyone or anything threatening her family. And in case you haven't noticed, that would be us. You can't stop her from doing what comes naturally."

I just stared at her. "You think killing comes naturally to a little girl?"

Danica sighed. "Didn't you hear anything Melika said about her brother? He was born *broken*. Like serial killers or other sociopaths, Malecon was fucked up in the head bone right out of the gate. I'm not saying Cinder is either fucked up or a sociopath, but I *do* think there's something inside her that enables her to turn people into crispy critters without giving it a second thought, just as there's something inside *me* that allows me to kill a man and walk away guilt-free."

I looked into Danica's eyes and felt what she said. She hadn't been top of our class for nothing. I had seen Cinder's powers first come to life when I was in danger. Cinder had calmly and coolly blasted two boats of men to smithereens, never once looking back. Did that make her a killer? A cold-blooded murderer?

"She may not mind killing people, but that doesn't mean we should allow her to do so. We have some responsibility here. She's a child, for God's sake."

"We don't *allow* her to do anything, Clark. She's an independent spirit just like you. She made her mind up long before you told her not to that she was going to blast those guys today."

I sighed. I seldom beat Danica in a debate.

Danica continued walking. "Can we move on to the *real* problem itching at you?" We came to a large clearing with boulders circling what had once been a campfire. "Tell me about this manhunt we're going on and what you aren't sharing with me."

I winced. Self-defense was one thing in the ghetto, but hunting someone down? That was a completely different game. "Given Malecon's personality and temperament, if we get into a fight with him, it looks like we'll probably have to…you know…"

"For Christ's sake, Clark, you can't even say the word. Say it with me…*kill.* Come on. We're sitting around the campfire as it were. Kill. Say it."

"Kill. There." Staring into the wet moss, I wished Cinder were here to start a fire. I wasn't cold. I just wanted the comfort; the familiarity. "Dani, we came here to help people, and all of a sudden, we're going *after* someone we might have to kill?" Sitting on one of the rocks, I felt a familiar tingle at the back of my skull. Tip was knocking. I knew it was her because Melika was smoother and less invasive than she. "I'm not ready to admit that. I just want to catch him and put him away again."

"Catch him? *Catch* him? Are you nuts? This guy would kill you all if he had the chance. You better dump the Sweet Polly Purebread routine, Clark, and face the facts. Someone's gonna have to take this guy out."

"We just need to confine him again, that's all."

"He's not a fucking genie in a bottle. He's a madman, and he wants to harm the people you love. You better step your game up, girl, because this thing here? Oh, it's on. It's so on." She looked hard at me for a few moments and then softened her voice. "Since when is shifting gears difficult for you?" Danica studied me for a moment longer before putting her hand to her mouth. "Oh God. It's Tip, isn't it? You're dealing with something other than this thing with Malecon, aren't you?"

"No."

"Liar."

I stared out at the moving water. It was so much higher than normal. "I'm a little distracted, that's all. I'm not trying to be, but—"

Danica reached for my hand. "But what? What is it?"

I looked at her. "Finn. It's Finn. Before I left she…she told me she loves me."

Danica's mouth dropped open. "Get out!"

I nodded. "It's true."

"And you're only telling me this now?" Danica jumped up and paced several steps away before returning. "Details! I want details. Where were you? What did you say? Oh my God, I can't believe you waited so long to tell me! Have I been moved to the D-list and wasn't notified?"

"Don't be a nitwit. There aren't any details, really. We were walking in Golden Gate Park and she turned and…well…it seemed to just pop out of her mouth. She looked as surprised as I was."

"So what did you say? Wait. Oh God, you didn't say it back, did you?"

I shook my head slowly. "Wouldn't that have been nice?"

Danica groaned. "You froze! You always freeze! What did you say?"

Looking over at her, I kept shaking my head. I had not been at my best. "I said *I know*."

Danica held her face in her hands. "You didn't."

I sighed hard. "I did. *Très* romantic, huh?"

"What did she say?"

This made me smile. "True to her school, she laughed."

"She *laughed*?"

"Yeah. She said she should have known better than to be the first to throw it out, but she couldn't help it. That's how she felt and it was okay if I didn't feel that way yet."

"Yet? *Do* you? Are you in love with Officer Finn?"

It felt as if the entire bayou waited for my answer. "I think I could be, yeah."

"*Could* be? It's a yes or no, goddamn it. You're an *empath*, for God's sake. How do you *feel* about her?"

I swallowed hard, as if trying to force the truth back down my throat. "I think I do love her."

"Oh wow, Clark." Danica's voice was soft and low. "Really? When did you know?"

"Honestly? Just now. I've tried not thinking about it, about her, but whenever I do, I get that warm fuzzy feeling all over like some lovelorn teen. It's sickening."

"No it isn't. It's sweet. You deserve a good gal." Danica sat on the boulder next to me and bumped shoulders. "You going to tell her?"

"I'm not ready to tell her the truth and I'm not ready to live a lie."

"You can't stay in the closet forever, little supernatural girl. If Finn's the real deal—"

"I don't know that."

"If she is…she deserves the truth. All of it." Danica tossed a rock into the river. "That's the problem, isn't it? Just how much truth to tell the good policewoman. When does it become too late? When is it too early? Questions, questions and more questions."

"Exactly."

"And then there's Tip."

"Yes. Then there's Tip." I sighed. "She probably already knows."

We sat quietly, both of us in our own thoughts, when I felt the tingle again. This time, I opened up. *"Yes?"*

"I think I may know where Bishop is."

I was on my feet in half a second. *"Where?"* I glanced over at Danica and touched my temple to let her know that I was talking to Tip.

"Best guess is on the roof of University hospital. My guess is she came to long enough to send out a general SOS. It was faint, and I can't be sure that's where she is, but it's worth a shot."

"We're on our way." I motioned for Danica to follow me as I quickly started back to the cottage. *"We leaving now, or did you want to head out early in the morning?"*

"Can't risk it. It was a general SOS. That means Malecon might have picked it up as well."

"How is she? Is she hurt? Is she—"

"We don't know anything other than she sent out a very faint, very weak signal I'm pretty sure came from the hospital."

Danica and I were practically running through the swamp. *"I'm coming with you."*

"I know. We'll leave as soon as you get back."

"Did you call Bones?"

"No time. I got something better."

"A magic carpet?"

"Something like that."

Our magic carpet was a small speedboat Bones had come across earlier in his comings and goings. He had towed it to a dock near the cottage. It was a sleek blue and white gem that skimmed swiftly across the top of the water. Even in the darkest of darks, Zack could move anything out of the path of our boat. He was amazing considering he was not at full power. None of us were, and I had a horrible feeling we needed to be, but there was barely time to repair our shields.

We left Cinder and Bailey to protect Melika, even though she continued to assure us that Malecon would never directly harm her. I had no such notion. Just the thought of that man gave me the creeps, and besides, any man who could kill his own mother was surely just as capable as doing so to his sister.

Ironically, I felt good leaving Danica and Cinder, knowing Danica would not hesitate to use Cinder's firepower if threatened. It irked me that Danica was right; that when the worst of it came, I, too, leaned on Cinder for protection. Each of us had a job to do and protecting Melika was given to the one who could do it best.

There was little for Jacob Marley to do, but his calm presence was a gift to Bailey, who was working too hard to prove herself to be an asset to the group. Of all of us, she was the weakest link and I still wondered why Melika had summoned her.

"How you holding up?" I asked Zack as he mentally shoved a large log out of the way. Katrina had scattered debris everywhere, and there were enormous moss-covered tree limbs floating in the river next to the bottles and other garbage he was having to move out of our way. Like the rest of us, he didn't have an endless supply of psionic energy. He weakened over time, and we needed him to be at his peak when we entered the city. It didn't look like that was going to happen at the rate we were moving. I wasn't the only one who noticed either.

"Take a break, Zack," Tip ordered, slowing the boat down. She knew the bayou better than anyone except Bones.

"I'm fine."

Tip slowed more. "Don't be ridiculous. Take a break. I can maneuver through this mess. Just rest a little."

Zack sat back down with me. I kept my hand in his. "I'm hangin' in there," he answered "You know, I've grown a lot since we were kids out here. I've worked some things out, getting stronger, more powerful. As much as the Big Indian used to piss me off whenever she nagged me about training harder, I've started to understand the importance of continuing education. I'm not at peak, but I'll be fine."

I hooked my arm through his and put my head on his shoulder. It was, to date, the most intimate we'd ever been. "Remember the first time we went into the city and those thugs started harassing us?"

"Don't remind me. Tip came in and saved the day." He shook his head. "Showing off my power was not one of my better moments."

"Maybe not, but I never told you I have never been afraid whenever I was with you. I wasn't afraid of gators or assholes or anyone because I always knew you'd never let any harm come to me. You were the second male I ever really felt safe with, and not just because of your powers. You're an amazingly gifted TK, Zack."

Zack smiled as he flicked more debris away with his free hand, making Tip growl. "Thanks, Echo. We've always been there for each other. Now is no exception. I won't let anything happen to you or anyone else."

I heard the hesitation in his voice. "But?"

"But I have a horrible feeling this is going to get uglier."

I'd felt it too. "You nervous?" I asked. The darkness was like a blanket all around us and I could barely make out his face now.

"Nervous? More like scared out of my wits."

"Really? Of what?" I turned to face him.

"Of not finding her alive. Bishop was the first person to understand me. She *knew* me, knew how I was feeling. Did you know she's called me every Sunday for the past six years?"

"You're kidding." I spoke with Bishop about once a month.

"Right after my mother passed away, she called. I needed that call more than anyone realized. I was so depressed. She's never stopped calling. I know it's weird, but she really helped me figure out how to exist in the world after I left here. You know, being a TK is so much more physical than the powers you and Tip possess. Something as innocent as reaching for a salt shaker became a problem. Every action poses a danger if I am not aware of what I'm doing with my energy. She taught me to be mindful of every move I make. You have no idea how exhausting that is."

He was right. I could only imagine. "I thought Bishop was mostly a clairsentient."

Zack chuckled. "Yeah, don't let that little old clairvoyant routine fool you. She makes Melika look like a minor leaguer in the power category."

I tilted my head in question. "You mean—"

"He means Bishop is far more than anything you've been led to believe." Tip came back from wherever she had been mentally.

"How much more?" I asked.

Tip shrugged as she slowed the boat down a bit during a patch of detritus-filled water. "Powers beyond anything you've seen so far. You have to remember, she grew up, for the most part, in Haiti. The Haitians don't fear women like her; they embrace them. The moment her people realized she was gifted, they sent her for formal training."

Formal training. It never dawned on me that the line of

trainers went beyond Bishop. How naïve of me to think she was the first one.

"That's why Malecon believes he must kill her. She may be the only one who poses any real threat to him. Of course..." She let her voice drift off.

"What? Of course what?"

"Of course, that means if he manages to kill her, he knows we won't stop until either he's dead...or we're dead."

I blinked. "Then we're going to war?"

Tip did not respond for a few seconds as she maneuvered the boat around what looked like a doghouse. "In a word, yes. As long as Malecon is free, we are all at risk."

"All but Mel. Why won't he kill her? I mean, if he can kill his own mother, killing her—"

Sighing, Tip slowed even more. "Mel believes he doesn't want to kill her or us. He wants to uncover us. He wants to expose us all to the government so he can make some deal to secure his own megalomaniacal future."

"Whoa, back up. He wants to *what*?" I was on my feet with Zack right beside me.

"Turn us in, Echo. Killing us would be a short-lived victory over the sister he hates, but enslaving us...giving us up...*that* would do her in. *That* would crush her spirit more than any single thing he could do, and that's what he ultimately wants. He wants her to hurt like he has and he'll use us to do it. That's why she only summoned the strongest of us who can work as a team. We must, we absolutely must, defeat him."

I licked my lips, trying to take it all in. "If what you're saying is true, he would..." I shuddered as a chill washed over me. "He would destroy all our lives."

"And every supernatural after us. He would change more than our lives and our destinies, he would change the future."

"The power of a God," I whispered.

"Bingo. He would go down in history as something greater than any explorer or scientist or—"

"How can he do that without exposing himself?"

Tip shrugged. "My people had scouts turn against us and work for the white man. Jews in the camps turned on their own kind. It happens all the time. He'll be a hero in the eyes of the naturals."

We stood in silence together, taking in the truth like a foul-smelling odor. I remembered when Melika explained the often sad life cycle of a paranormal being. First, there was the realization that you were different. Then, there came the fight for acceptance. That was usually the hardest for most of us; to know that you're set apart from everyone else whether you want to be or not. Then came training if you were lucky enough to come to Melika's. If not, then you had to learn on your own, through painful trial and error; errors that, more often than not, cost you your life. After all that, you learned how to live with it in your daily life. Some put up shields and never looked back, never using their abilities. They just pretended they didn't exist. Finally, there was what happened during the aging process. A paranormal being has more to worry about than dementia or Alzheimer's. A super who is long in the tooth runs the risk of losing control of their powers just as a natural loses many of their faculties. Some of the more powerful ones go completely insane, never to return to the real world again. Others lose control and wind up destroying themselves as well as innocent bystanders. Our future was in no way bright.

"You're going to kill him, aren't you?" I asked Tip.

Tip and Zack both nodded in unison, and I realized this was probably the first time they agreed on *anything*.

"So we are not going to put him back in a sanitarium or other holding cell?"

"No."

"Does Mel know?"

Tip looked down at me and blinked. "Know? She ordered it."

I didn't know what to say. All those euphemisms about controlling him and containing him and even destroying him hadn't really set in with me even after my conversation with Danica. I guess I hadn't wanted to hear what they had clearly alluded to. Selective hearing. That was what one of my foster mothers said I had. Maybe she was right after all. Maybe I only heard what I wanted to. "Locking him back up won't do?"

"He's done being held captive. He's like a lion who escapes

from the zoo. Malecon will never be captured alive. Not now, anyway. This is an all-or-nothing gig for him."

"And we're happy to oblige," Zack added. "Evil son of a bitch."

"Let me tell you something you might not know. You know Bishop was born on the border of Haiti and the Dominican Republic, right? She speaks Creole and French, as well as Patois, Spanish and English. Malecon is Spanish for pier, which, apparently, was where they were conceived."

"So what's Melika? The feminine form?"

Tip shook her head. "It's the feminine form of Malak, which is Arabic for angel."

"Angel, huh? Does the origin of the name signify the possible ethnicity of the father?"

"Malecon thought so. He spent three years over in the Middle East in his early twenties trying to locate his father. He never found him, of course, but the game was set. Angel versus demon. Yin and yang. Bishop always believed in the balance of the universe, and when she found out Melika was a girl, she understood that it was about that balance."

I crossed my arms over my chest. "And just how in the hell do you know all of this?" Melika was as closed a book as I'd ever seen. All the years I spent with Melika, and she'd never shared any of this with me. "Are you telling me she somehow decided to share all of these intimate details with you?"

Zack made a chuffing sound, as if mocking me. "You can be so dense sometimes."

Tip nodded slightly. "Mel didn't tell me. Bishop did. You see, Bishop worked closely with all the boys to prepare them for this day."

She may as well have slapped me. As a teenager, I barely knew Bishop. She was this little mysterious woman who seemed to know everything yet share nothing. She did help me learn how to reinforce my shields, but the truth was, she liked Danica way more than she cared for me.

"Don't look so hurt. You're strictly a defensive lineman."

I hate boy-speak. I hated it even more whenever she fell into using it. "Excuse me? Is that English?"

"You know how unpredictable and unreliable the sight is. It comes and goes like the wind. She's spent the last five years trying to get a clearer bead on this. Well, Bishop was convinced that at some point in the future, there would come a time when we'd all be in danger. She saw something, but she would never tell me what it was. She's been preparing some of us for this."

Then the lightbulb went on. "That's why Bailey is here, isn't it?"

Tip barely grinned. "You're too hard on her. She has some great skills you've yet to see, but yeah, Bishop saw she was part of the group trying to quell whatever uprising was happening. She told Mel if that day came, Bailey needed to be summoned as well."

The lightbulb burned brighter as I remembered what Danica had said about Cinder. "And does this include Cinder?"

Tip shrugged. "Bishop couldn't tell who the little girl was in her vision, but Cinder sure makes the most sense, don't you think?"

"Have you been training her to kill?"

Tip said nothing.

"Tiponi, I'm not blind. You've turned her into a killer, haven't you?"

Tip glanced over at Zack, as if the truth was too much for her to share. "That's what you've never understood about the kid; she was a killer *before* you got to her."

I hesitated, my words backed up in my mouth; she'd confirmed my darkest fear about little Cinder. "No."

"I know this isn't what you want to hear, but it's the truth. It's also not my story to share, so forgive me if I just leave it at that."

"She's just a child, Tip."

"She's the best offensive weapon we have. She's powerful, strong and relentless. None of us can kill with such ease."

"Not even you?"

She shook her head. "Not even me, and you know how powerful I am. Cinder is in a league all by herself."

I turned away, not wanting to continue this conversation. I wanted to be disgusted, to climb on some nonexistent pedestal of self-righteousness, but the bottom line was these people were my family, and if anyone threatened them, I would probably *want* Cinder to turn them into ash. I was no different than Tip or Zack in that regard. I just hated we were relying on a ten-year-old girl to do it. Turning back around, I said, "Fine. I understand, but that doesn't mean I have to like it."

"Don't assume we're overly eager to kill one of our own, Echo," Zack said, laying his hand on my shoulder. "But this asshole could ruin all of our lives. Is that what you want? You want Cinder to grow up in a cage on some army base while scientists try to figure out how to create more like her?"

I shook my head.

"Then we have no other choice but to put him down."

I hated the term, but I was getting the picture. "Doesn't he know where Mel lives?"

Tip shook her head. "He's never known where she lives. The bayou has always been her cover."

"Her cover? What does that mean?"

"There are places in the world where there's so much energy, it disrupts the normal flow. The Amazon rainforest is one such place. The bayou is another. Because of this disruption, she's out of his reach mentally. He might try to find out where she lives, but he'll never do it telepathically."

"But Bailey did. You do it."

"We're able to get *out*, to establish a line of communication. See, the bayou is a little like being in a car with tinted windows. We can see out at everything around us, but people on the outside can't get in. That's how it's always worked. It's why Bishop moved Melika out here."

I nodded. Suddenly, I felt very out of touch with the supernatural in me; a disquieting moment I swore never to feel again. "So, Mel is relatively safe at home."

"With Cinder and Bailey? Yes. Besides, Mel is no powderpuff football player. I've seen her do things that would give you nightmares for weeks. I think she's safe way out there."

"Okay, so I get why Cinder was brought here, but Bailey? Come on."

"We have a few backup plans in place. One of them involves

Bailey. She's not what you think at all, Echo. She's not some unskilled telepath."

"No? Then what is she?"

Again, they exchanged glances. Did everyone know this stuff except me? "Well…she's a shaman."

"A shaman?"

"Yeah. I know, it's weird at first, but hear me out." Tip slowed the boat down as we neared where the city roads began. "Even Mel was surprised when those powers kicked in. See, Bailey was almost eighteen when a gator came after her. A rare thing, I know, but it happened. Then, without warning, that gator turned and attacked a log lying there. It was as if there had been some sort of understanding."

"Understanding? Between Bailey and the gator?"

She nodded. "Mel wasn't sure what to do. She'd never dealt with a shaman before, never had one in the bayou with her."

I held up my hand, slightly irritated that she was right about me needing to know more about this facet of my life. Apparently, I needed to read *a lot* more. "A shaman as in a witch doctor?"

Tip grunted, her patience wearing thin like it did when I was a teenager. "In the broadest sense, a shaman has the ability to diagnose and cure suffering. Ignorant people refer to them as witch doctors, but most of today's modern shamans are linked closely to animistic regions and religions."

"So, she's a healer."

"Of sorts. That part of her skill has been underdeveloped largely in part to a lack of proper tutelage. Her greatest attribute, and one she spent the most time honing here is her empathic communication with animals."

"What Tip is saying in her typically protracted way is that Bailey is a modern day Dr. Doolittle," Zack added. "People may not like her, but animals do."

"And that's why the gator didn't attack her?"

Tip nodded. "At that moment, her shamanic powers kicked in and apparently, she told it to go away. Because those powers are largely empathic, Melika could teach her what she knew, but as for healing…that was a whole new ball game. Rarely are westerners gifted with such power. In the end, Bailey left the bayou having learned how to utilize about forty percent of her known powers."

"Couldn't you have helped her?" I asked Tip. Being of Native American descent, Tip had grown up believing in the power of animal spirits and power totems. She knew the ancient ways of dozens of cultures, most of which did not need industrialized science to tell them what was real and what wasn't.

Tip replied evenly, "Communing with the natural world is a New Age practice with very old roots. If we accept the notion that all of nature is intertwined, linked spiritually and energetically, then it's easy to see the connection we have with the whole of Mother Earth. Bailey left here with only a rudimentary knowledge of those connections. What she's done to improve that, I don't know. We haven't kept in touch."

I studied Tip a moment. Knowing her as well as I did, there was more to the *not keeping in touch* than just a lack of letter writing.

"So, she has the gift of gabbing with the animal kingdom… that's going to help us how?"

Both of them shrugged. We were nearing the submerged porch where Bones had been docking his boat, and a sense of foreboding passed over me.

"I have no idea," Tip answered. "I don't question Bishop when she tells me what to do. All I know is she told me two weeks ago to make sure Bailey was down here after the hurricane."

There was more to this story about the enigmatic shaman, but I would save the rest of my questions for later. "Well, that explains her awkwardness with people, but why didn't she say anything?"

"What's to say? It's not like people embrace her. In the human world, she's a cactus. Even other supers find her discomfitting and weird; but I've seen firsthand what she's capable of, and let me tell you this: I'm glad she's on our side."

Our side. I got goose bumps on my arms. What was happening to us? For that matter, what was happening to the US? Since 9/11, so much had changed. Now, everything was us against them, whoever *they* were. Everything was divisive. Everyone separate, no one really united.

Including supernaturals.

Here was a time when we could be getting the most use out of our powers, do the most good, and instead we were having to bring down a rogue telepath with an ax to grind. It made me angry to have my attention diverted from those in need.

"I know how you feel, kiddo, but taking him out will also help those in need. He won't stop at killing Bishop. He'll tear everything of historical value from the heart of this great place. Stopping him will stop the chain of events linked to him. You have to trust that."

"How far are we from the hospital?" I asked, wanting to end this conversation. In the dense darkness surrounding us, I had no idea where we were, exactly. Without streetlights or homes, the main source of lighting came from the luminescent glow from buildings in the distance.

"Not far. Echo, you scan for potential hostile energy. Zack, keep your fingers on the trigger. I'm going to try to pinpoint Bishop's location."

After docking the speedboat, we made our way into the city. I felt more and more uncomfortable with every step we took. The negative energy was worse than ever, the stench of rotting flesh from humans and animals alike lingered in the thick, hot air, and the putrefaction of old, mildewed food created an odor as assaulting as a hard slap in the face.

But it wasn't the smell creeping me out the most; it was the overriding sense of evil and chaos. Horrible things were being done to people because there was absolutely no order. Danger lurked around every corner. Cops were no longer upholding the law, and some of the city's poorest were taking advantage of "free" items left behind by shop owners. In the dark alleyways, I felt the sharp edge of malignancy, and for the first time, I understood how Danica could shoot a man in cold blood and just walk away.

She had been right: the man she had killed wasn't really a man; he was a nightmare in men's clothing, preying on people who had just been victimized. This was a case of the oppressed becoming the oppressors, and those thugs would have done terrible things to us…to a child. Maybe she wasn't so wrong in her way of thinking after all. How had she put it? Kill or be killed? I was beginning to feel that way down in the marrow of my bones. I didn't want to admit that my beloved home had been turned into a battlefield, but that didn't keep me from feeling it.

And boy was I feeling it.

Shuddering at the fate we had escaped, I realized Danica wasn't cold-blooded. She merely understood, better than I, that in the Superdome she had killed an animal; a vicious, soulless animal who would have continued preying on the innocent. He was roadkill. Nothing more, nothing less, and I owed her an apology.

"Keep your senses sharp, kiddo," Tip whispered as we crept through the darkness. Unlike the bayou, where you could feel a breeze, the air was still, thick and stifling. You had to watch out where you walked because of the debris washing up on the street. There were photo albums, rocking chairs, electric fans and sides of houses in front of us. In the harsh darkness, it felt like a horror movie.

"Sort of reminds me of one of those zombie movies, huh?" Zack said, feeling it too. "You know, the one where all the people run into a mall or someplace to escape the flesh-eating zo..."

"That's enough, Zack," Tip said.

We moved about in the shadows, where I actually felt more comfortable. There was danger all around us, but as long as we weren't seen, we might actually make it to the hospital unmolested. I so wanted to get there without having any contact with anyone else. It hurt my heart to think we might have to hurt these people any more than they already were.

We were dripping with sweat. We didn't have any problems until we reached the hospital, and then it was like we'd walked into Dante's *Inferno*.

"My God," Tip murmured, seeing the devastation of the hospital. It looked like...well...it looked like a hurricane struck it; or maybe a bomb. It reminded me of those pictures of Bosnia during the war where there were halves of buildings here and there.

"Please don't tell me she's in there." I didn't want to go in, but at the moment, I felt that tickling at the base of my skull;

not the knock of a telepath, but the gong of danger. Someone very powerful was trying to get inside my head, and I clamped my eyes shut and strengthened my shields. *"He's here,"* I said to Tip and Zack.

"I know." Tip stepped ahead of me. *"He's near, but that's not who I'm picking up. Oh shit."*

"What?"

"Can you feel it?" Tip suddenly spun around, facing the street. With our backs to the hospital, all three of us turned to face the street. At first, I didn't feel anything…but then…we all felt it. It was the undeniable odor of menace.

"Zack?" Tip whispered.

Zach nodded, bringing his hand up like he was going to throw a baseball. I wished like hell he was working at one hundred percent. "Ready."

Out of the darkness walked Malecon like a magician walking through the machine generated fog in Vegas. At least, I assumed he was walking. Larger than life, he seemed to float upon the very shadows we used for cover.

"You have always overestimated your own abilities and intelligences, Tip," Malecon said. I wasn't sure his mouth was even moving. "Did it not occur to you that all I need do was merely wait and follow you once you discovered her whereabouts?" Malecon was about forty feet away, yet even in the darkness, I could see his snarling mouth.

Tip walked about ten feet, bridging the gap between them. "*You* didn't follow us, Malecon, but someone did. One of your minions, perhaps?"

"Watch his hands, Echo," Zack whispered. You could cut the energy surrounding the three of us with a buzz saw. Nothing smaller.

Malecon batted Tip's question aside; ever the control freak. "So, she's in there, is she? I knew it had to have been a hospital, but this place is such a mess, I doubted she could be here and still be alive. But she *is* still alive, isn't she. It's a shame you won't be able to help her."

"Of course we're going to help her, Malecon, and there's not a damn thing you're going to do about it." Tip seemed to raise herself to a height of eight or nine feet as she spoke. She was absolutely unafraid.

"Honestly, Tiponi, do you *really* think so highly of yourself that you actually believe you and these two…amateurs can take me on? You must have gotten your self-esteem lessons from my beloved sister to believe that mishmash. Echo there, she barely acknowledges her powers, while young Zachary mismanages his all the time. It would be foolish of you to continue in this vein. It will only end poorly for all of you."

"We'll see who the amateur is, Malecon. It's been a long time since you've used your powers."

I stared out over Tip's shoulder at Malecon. He appeared more amused than offended. "Has that sister of mine finally lost her edge, Tiponi? Has she forgotten how incredibly powerful I am, and that, under these incredibly disastrous circumstances, nigh unbeatable?"

Tip shrugged. "Take your best shot, buddy, but rest assured, we *will* destroy you."

This made Malecon laugh. "Destroy me? You've been watching too much television. That's rich. Melika would never allow you to harm me. Contain me as she has, yes, but kill me off? Not hardly. There's one thing thicker than friendship, Tiponi, and it's blood. Nothing trumps twin blood."

"The only person doing any overestimating here, Malecon, is you. You way overestimate your importance in her world. We've come to put an end to you and your plans to hurt your mother."

I felt Tip change; her energy unreadable but loud nonetheless. Something else was happening here; something darker than I originally realized. I steeled myself for the moment Malecon threw his first blow.

"You're assuming this is Melika's call." Tip seemed to get bigger with every word she spoke. "Did it ever occur to you that I *do* have a mind of my own, and I have a mind to put an end to you."

I could see well enough to note the change in Malecon's expression, but he quickly recovered. "It will take more than the three of you to bring me down. You know misery makes me stronger. Look around you, Tiponi. Hell has landed in New Orleans, and it has a new name." Malecon turned and looked to his left, then to his right. From out of the darkness came a dozen or so men, mostly gangbangers, by the looks of it.

"Fortunately for you, I don't have the time to piddle with your less-than-average psionic abilities. I have to find that *dear* mother of mine and put her out of my misery." He took one step forward. "But these fine, upstanding citizens of this godforsaken city ought to be enough to keep you busy and out of my way." With the jerk of his head, the men rushed us.

Zack managed to knock two of them back, and Tip's self-proclaimed "brain squeeze" brought two more to their knees, but the other eight just ran over their compadres as if they were dead possums in the road.

"Echo?"

"On it." Closing my eyes, I concentrated all of my energy on creating a mental energy shield that repelled the first two who came in contact with it. As with all psionic energy fields, it was made from pure energy, and protected those of us surrounded by it. It had taken me years to get it to the point where it actually did some good, but it still wasn't working at top notch. I wouldn't be able to keep up for very long.

"How long?" Tip asked, dropping another to the ground. High-level telepaths like Tip can actually pierce a person's brain with enough energy to deliver a migraine-like attack ten times worse than anything the body can produce. She called it a brain squeeze because one's brain felt like it was in a vise. The pain is so harsh, it drops the person right where they stand. The victim, however, must be within a certain range and be unshielded, as our attackers were.

They may have been unshielded, but they weren't without their own offensive weapons. Before any of us could stop him, to my utter horror, one smaller black kid whipped a gun out from his waistband, aimed his gun at Tip, and fired off three rounds.

"No!" I screamed, watching helplessly as Tip's body reeled backward, slamming into the hospital wall behind us. My shield immediately collapsed as I made my way to her. She was hurt, but not dead. I would have felt a death as powerful as that one to the core of my being. What I felt from her was a searing pain in her shoulder and a huge blast of irritation. She was wounded, but alive.

"God damn it!" Zack uttered, throwing a wave of energy at the shooter that lifted the kid off his feet and slammed him into a steel pole. "Keep your shields up and around Tip, Echo! I can't—"

And that was when I heard Danica's words one last time. *Kill or be killed.* I needed a much stronger offensive weapon than I could conjure up, so I reached into my fanny pack and withdrew Dani's gun with a trembling hand. It felt cold and heavy in my hand.

"Get Tip!" I ordered, backing up and covering Zack. As Zack pulled Tip to her feet, I steadied the gun with my other hand and fired. I didn't hit anyone, but the cowards scattered for cover when it became evident we could fire back.

Looking over my shoulder, I saw Zack had one arm around Tip's waist and was moving toward the entrance of the hospital. I turned back around and squeezed off one more round for good measure. I knew it wasn't enough, but I had to buy Zack time to get Tip to safety.

"Come on, Echo! Get inside!"

"No," Tip said, pressing her hand to her bloody shoulder. "Not in the hospital. Over there. Get us over there, Zack. I'm fine." Fine meant she could move on her own, but her blood flow wasn't slowing its progress from her body. The entire front of her shirt was covered in red.

The three of us rounded a corner and made a hasty retreat through a few dark alleys before coming to a Dinky Donuts whose windows had been shattered and everything capable of being stolen had been.

"There. In there." Tip said, stepping over the broken glass. "We can make a stand in there. You'll only have to project your shield out front."

"They're gone, Tip," Zack said, clearing the floor of glass and helping Tip sit down. Pulling his shirt over his head, Zack handed it to her. "Use this."

Tip took it and pressed it against her shoulder. “They’re regrouping.”

I constructed the best shield I could across the front window we had just come through, knowing Tip was right. They hadn’t gone. They were right out there.

“I don’t get it,” Zack said. “You’re hurt. Bishop’s at the hospital where there’s bound to be supplies to patch you up, so why aren’t *we* going there?”

Before Tip could answer, a bullet ricocheted off one of the walls. My shields could stop the occasional thug, but bullets? No way.

Zack left Tip and, using both hands, managed to knock one of the guns out of a guy’s hand. This time there were seven of them, and with Tip hurt, our odds of getting out of this alive were getting slimmer by the second.

“I’m getting pretty weak here,” Zack said, pushing the gun he’d knocked away about fifty feet further from the assailant. I knew the enormous mental toll it took for him to keep this up, and once his firepower was gone, I would be all that was left to stand between them and us.

And I was merely a defensive lineman.

“Remember that zombie movie I was talking about?” Zack said, looking over at me.

Tip reached for me. “Give me the gun.” I quickly handed it to her like it was a dirty diaper. “You two go out the back. I’ll—”

“Like hell.” I said. “Since when do we abandon each other?”

“Never,” Zack said. “We’re staying, Tip.”

Tip looked at me, blinked twice, and then calmly fired two rounds over my shoulder. Now there were only six.

“I don’t get it,” Zack said. “Why do they keep coming?” He was struggling to hold one of them, but I could see he was nearly at the end of his power. “Why aren’t they freaked out by the invisible force field or—”

“These hoodlums are under his control, Zack. They probably won’t stop until…”

Another bullet shattered the glass doughnut case next to us, missing Tip's head by a foot.

She checked the clip and counted bullets before shaking her head. Grabbing me by the arm, she looked hard into my eyes. "Please, Echo. *Please.* If you never do anything else I ask, *please* save the two of you. I can hold them until you get to safety. Please."

I had never seen such fear on her face or heard the pleading in her voice. Both rocked me to the core. Laying my hand on her cheek, I gazed into her dark brown eyes. I could never leave her. I would rather die with her than live without her.

"Not gonna happen, love. Not now. Now ever."

"Please…"

Then, the strangest thing happened. It was as if someone had suddenly changed the channel of a movie I was watching. Walking right out into the middle of the fray were two little old gray-haired ladies. We went from *Night of the Living Dead* to the *Golden Girls.* The taller one, and by tall I mean five feet nothing, was wearing a pink velour sweat suit. The other one, a tad shorter and somewhat plumper, was wearing the exact same style of suit only in blue. Both were wearing matching Nike running shoes.

"What the fuck are they doing?" Zack asked.

When Tip saw them, she swore. "Shit. God damn it. Echo, give us your best primary shield you can. Zack, reinforce it with anything you have left. Then duck down behind the counter and cover your eyes."

Zack and I slammed into each other, trying so hard to act as quickly as Tip demanded so we pinballed off each other in opposite directions. I fell to the floor, and as I was getting to my feet I threw up the best shield with the remaining energy I had left. As I struggled to maintain it, a searing white flash blinded me, sending me crashing back to the ground. As I pulled myself up to the counter, the light encircled our attackers, hovered a moment, and then radiated inward in an implosion that flung me back to the ground as glass shards embedded into the walls around us. Had I not kept my shield up, we'd have become pincushions for glass needles. Instead, everything bounced off my shield like scattershot.

I waited several seconds for my vision to clear before peeking out from my relative safe zone beneath my withering shield. Every one of the hoodlums was burnt to a crisp, as were two cars also engulfed in flames.

"What the hell?" Zack growled, standing up and brushing ceiling pieces off. "Who in the hell are the grannies?" Helping Tip to her feet, Zack brushed glass off her. When she regained her balance, Tip handed the gun back to me.

"Tip?"

"They are the cavalry," she said, inhaling a shaking breath. She'd lost a lot of blood. "They came to pull our fat out of the fire. Wait here." Tip pressed Zack's shirt to her shoulder as she made her way over to the two old women who were now stepping over the glass and entering the store.

Zack glanced over at me and shrugged.

"Sorry we're late, hon," the one in the pink said. "Are y'all okay?" She actually reminded me of Betty White and every other gray-haired old lady I'd seen on TV. Her hair was a shock of white with a pink stripe, as if she had dyed it for a concert.

The one in blue looked exactly the same, only she sported a blue streak in her white hair. They could have been twins.

Tip nodded. "We're okay. Is *she*?"

"She is now, but let's not speak of it here. There's much to be done before this is all over, and we need to skedaddle before the cops get here. Come." The pink-haired one looked out at the charred bodies lying on the street and wriggled her nose. "It's never easy explaining that."

The granny in blue nodded. "Winston will take care of the cleanup." She smiled at me. "There will be time for explanations later, Echo. Right now, we have a nice, cool, penthouse up the road a ways where we can slap a Band-aid on your girlfriend and put *your* mind at ease."

"She's not my—"

"Not important," Pinky curtly replied. "I'm Rose. That's my sister, Lily. Now, if you would be so kind as to follow us. We need to step lively before the authorities get here."

We followed Rose and Lily along a labyrinthine path to a three-story penthouse near Algiers River Ferry. It was a gorgeous place that had been keenly renovated, and had suffered no ill effects from the hurricane other than a busted sign out front hanging crookedly by a single chain.

The interior of the penthouse was well-decorated, done in muted browns and golds with a slight leaning toward Edwardian-style furniture mixed with southern belle decor. It could have belonged to these two old women or someone my age. It was hard to tell.

"Come with me," Lily said to Tip, pulling her into the hallway that, presumably, led to the bathroom. "Let's see how bad that wound is and if we can't get you patched up."

Who *were* these women?

"Where are my manners?" Rose said to me and Zack. "Please, please have a seat."

"You have a beautiful home here."

Rose chuckled. "Thank you, but it isn't ours. Long story best told another day. Please, sit, sit. Can I get you some tea? Coffee, perhaps?"

"I'd love some tea," Zack said.

I wanted to kick him, and Rose must have sensed this.

"It's all right, dearie. There is nothing more that need be done tonight. All in all, it was a very successful evening."

"Successful evening?" Zack said, shaking his head. "Tip was shot and we were about to get obliterated out there."

"About to and didn't are not nearly the same thing. Besides... we had it all under con—"

"Don't you dare!" Came Lily's voice from the bathroom.

Rose chuckled. "She hates it when I tell a story without her. I'll go get that tea while she finishes patching up your girlfriend."

"She's not my..."

"Sweetie, you look hungry," she said to Zack. "I know how exhausting TKing like that can be. My first husband was a TK. Man oh man, could that boy kiss. He had these thick lips..."

"Too much information!" Lily yelled from the bathroom.

This made Rose laugh as she headed toward the kitchen.

Zack and I slowly turned to each other. "Do you have any idea?"

I shook my head. "I got nothin'. You've never met them?"

"Uh, gee, I think I'd remember meeting two super nova-throwing geriatrics."

"I heard that!" Again from Lily.

"She's got ears like a bat, that one." Rose walked back into the front parlor and handed us two warm towels before wiping her hands on her own. "I'm sure you're quite confused as to how this all went down, but it was all part of a grand plan, I assure you."

"Plan? There was a *plan*?"

Rose went back into the kitchen and returned a few minutes later with a silver tray holding five teacups. Tip reentered wearing a clean T-shirt with her arm in a sling. She was pale and unsteady on her feet, and I wondered if she was carting the bullet around inside her or if it had exited.

I rose and helped Tip sit next to me.

Lily followed her into the room wiping her hands on a towel. She did it in such a way that I realized Rose and Lily might really be twins. They sported the same white hair bob, same deep blue eyes, and same barely-there cleft chin.

"I suppose you ought to know who we are before you find out why we're here and what just happened," Rose said, picking up one of the flowery teacups. "My sister, Lily, and I were Bishop's schoolmates. We trained with her a thousand and one years ago, just like you all have trained with her daughter."

"On the bayou?" Zack asked.

"Of course." Rose sipped her tea. "Did you think Bishop learned how to control her considerable powers by herself?" Rose waved our answers away. "Of course not. Like you, we all had mentors. We all learned how to do what we do. And what Lily and I do is called cleaning."

"Cleaning?" Zack looked as confused as I felt.

"Yes, dear. Lily and I are the rest of the Cleaning Crew."

"Wait. Whoa. Back up." Zack held his hands out in supplication. "Cleaners? Who are *the rest*?"

"We'll never get through this," Tip said softly, "if you keep interrupting."

Zack leaned back slowly.

"Right, right," Rose said, sipping her tea. "First off, to answer your more pressing question, Bishop is safe now, so set your minds at ease. She was never really at that hospital. We knew Malecon would have you followed once you returned to the city. You were his best lead, and he was willing to wait it out. We just didn't keep him waiting long, that's all."

"We were decoys?" Zack asked.

"Well…yes. We needed you to keep Malecon busy thinking he was nearing his target. As long as he was focused on you, he couldn't really be looking for her."

"Then where was she?"

"That's the irony of it all." Rose chuckled more to herself. "She was at the same hospital he escaped from."

"Charity?"

"Yes. Some kind soul dropped her off after she sustained a blow to the head. She had been taken to the roof, where a couple of nurses cared for her. When the nurses decided they needed to find their own families, they left the hospital. One of them relayed to someone that they had "The Seer" up top, and it was only a matter of minutes before our eyes and ears in NOLA contacted us to let us know The Seer was hurt and needed help."

I leaned forward. "Then she's okay?" I didn't know whether to be relieved or angry.

"I didn't say that. I said she was *safe*, and for the time being, she will remain safe from the hands of her wicked son."

"You *knew* you were sending us into a dangerous arena against Malecon and you didn't warn us?"

Lily cleared her throat. "You underestimate his powers, son. Had you known you were a diversion, he would have sensed that. He is *that* powerful. We had to keep you in the dark in order to keep *him* in the dark.

Rose picked the slack. "We planned to stop Malecon's assault on you, but hadn't anticipated he would use naturals. That flummoxed us for a minute—"

"But in our younger years, we would have been all over it. We apologize for our tardiness." She looked over at Tip. "And for the wound you sustained."

"Wound?" Zack blurted. "She could have been killed! All of us—"

I laid a hand on his leg and he quieted. "We're just glad you came at all," I said. "So Malecon's plan was to have the thugs kill us while he went after Bishop?"

"Exactly. It is possible those poor people were not thinking clearly. As a telepath of his strength, it's possible he gave them some evil suggestions, maybe even played on their fears. He's quite capable of playing with the minds of the weak," Rose continued.

"Or he could have offered them pay." Lily poured herself some tea. "Either way, none of them made it out alive."

"Can you tell us more about the cleaner part?" Zack asked.

"Ah yes. I forget how young you all are. Lily and I are part of a supernatural group called Cleaners. Our job is to come in and clean up messes left by other supers so no one is the wiser. Cleaners have been around for hundreds of years. It's quite a respectable profession, really. You can't imagine how many messes we have to clean up these days now with you young people being in love with fame. Back in the day—"

"Focus in, Rose. They don't need or want a lecture about our time."

I glanced over at Tip, knowing none of this was news to her. As I stared at her, I realized just how little I knew about the community I called family. So anxious had I been to fit in to the "normal" world, I had left the bayou without giving much thought about how much more there was to know.

And there was a lot.

"You see," Lily continued for her. "As we get older, our powers become erratic and less stable. We lose the ability to sustain shields, to control our telekinetic powers—"

"In short, we have a different take on senility and dementia. Some of us finally go crazy while others become virtual hermits in order to protect those around us from powers we no longer control. Elderly naturals lose control of their bladders, we lose control of our powers."

"Then, there's those of us who do what Rose and I and The Others do."

"The Others?" Zack and I said in unison.

Rose nodded. "Yes. That's who we are. We belong to a larger group known as The Others."

Zack could contain himself no longer. "I thought you said you were *cleaners*."

"We are. That's our *job*. Our *job* is to clean, but we belong to a group of supernaturals collectively known around the world as The Others. It is a group to which Bishop also belongs. While my sister and I are cleaners because of our powers, which you got a small taste of, Bishop plays a very different role."

"And that is?"

Rose smiled. "A story for her to tell when she sees fit. Unlike many of The Others, Lily and I usually have to out ourselves because of the nature of the task at hand. We're quite a bit more visible than the Bishops of the world." Rose sipped her tea. "It's a small price to pay to save Bishop and her extended family."

My head was spinning from all the information. How had I lived for so long and never once questioned what happened to us when we got older? How self-absorbed was I? Suddenly, I felt very small.

"We take great pains to maintain separate lives in the real world. Melika is not, by any stretch of the imagination, the only mentor in the country, nor are The Others the only such group. It is just much safer for us to remain fragmented in the event that we have the sort of situation we have going on right now. Malecon cannot hurt people he cannot find or doesn't already know about, but make no mistake, there are many of us across the world whose job it is to maintain and protect the invisibility of our kind."

Zack nodded. "Makes sense."

I felt Tip starting to get weary and reached over to hold her hand. She presented me with a soft smile from her tired face, and I knew she had less than five minutes before she would collapse.

"Please rest."

"I will. I need to stay awake long enough to answer any of your questions."

"No, you don't. What questions we have, we can ask later. Please."

"Five more minutes."

I returned my attention to Lily. "If your powers are erratic," I said, "Then how—"

"Oh, *we're* different," Lily answered. "My sister and I aren't just twins. We were born conjoined. Our powers were concentrated in that one tiny body for five years. When they finally separated us, we discovered we could still use our powers as long as we were touching. It takes both of us to create the kind of heat you experienced out there." Lily chuckled. "Bishop nicknamed us Nitro and Glycerin when we were barely out of our teens. That's who we used to be."

Rose finished her tea and rose to her feet. "It has been quite some time since we have had to employ that particular power, but it was worth it. Good thing you had a strong shield, dearie, otherwise you all might be a bit on the toasty side."

"I'll say."

"What if her shield hadn't been strong enough?" Zack asked, his irritation lingering.

"Then you would have fried like the rest. It was a chance we had to take. Saving Bishop was our main concern."

"Then we were collateral damage?" Zack started to say something else, when he shot a glare over at Tip. I was pretty certain Tip had telepathically told him to back off and leave it alone, because when Zack turned back, his anger was tepid and his mouth closed.

I have to say, *I* was more than a bit bothered by the fact that we were expendable, and I was becoming more than a little frightened. I wasn't just scared for Bishop's sake any more. After all, she appeared to be in good hands with the likes of these two. No, I was more afraid of my own ignorance, of how little I knew, yet how much I *needed* to know. All that time on the bayou, all the thousands of hours I spent learning how to control my abilities, and not once had Melika ever mentioned The Others.

"Let it go, kiddo. It's a necessary evil that we must remain apart from each other. Don't you get that?"

I did, but that didn't make me feel any better. Suddenly, there were octogenarian supernaturals in control of our fate and I knew next to nothing about them.

"To answer what you both are thinking, we aren't expecting you to take Malecon down. Your job is to protect Melika."

"But she said he won't come after her."

"No, he won't kill her, if that's what you mean. You see, no matter how angry or how nuts he may be, he cannot kill his sister." Rose was still standing. "Malecon believes that, like me and Lily, his powers are *connected* to his sister. He is afraid of finding out what might happen to his own powers should he kill her. His fear of becoming a mere normal is what keeps him in check because that, my dears, would be hell on earth for a man who considers himself superior to them."

"Then why do we need to protect her if he poses no threat?"

"I didn't say he poses no threat. I merely said he would not risk his own powers by *killing* her. You see, Malecon wants to do the same to Melika as she did to him."

My hand instinctively went to my mouth. "Oh God. You mean he would have her committed?"

Rose shook her head. "That wouldn't be safe enough, nor would it hurt her enough. No, our best guess is that Malecon would find some horrifying way of keeping his sister alive while he goes on destroying those she loves. Her death would bring him no joy. The joy would be in the torment he could deliver while she was incapable of saving you all."

"And," Lily continued, "he has the financial means to sequester Melika for the rest of her life. We might not ever be able to find her, and if we did, we might never be able to reach her."

The goose bumps I felt earlier came right back and Tip squeezed my hand. *"Don't worry. We won't let that happen to her."*

"But we aren't going to let Malecon get away with that." Walking over to me, she held out her hand. I released Tip's hand and held hers. "There is a little concern we have about *you*, dearie, and Melika thought it best *we* have a chat."

"Concern about *me*?"

"Why yes. She asked if I had a moment to chat with you about Cinder, if I wouldn't mind. I don't mind, but I believe it's time for your girlfriend to go to bed."

"She's not my—"

"You go with Lily, now, Tip. I've laced your tea with a mild sedative to help you rest better. We're going to have to take care of your wound in the morning. Lily assures me you won't bleed to death, but there is no need for you to feel you have to stand guard over your girlfriend all night."

"You drugged me?" Tip blinked a couple of times and I could tell she was already feeling the drug.

Lily grinned. "Only a little. Now go. Zachary, help me get her to her room."

Zack jumped up to help Tip, leaving just Rose and me in the parlor.

"Echo, do you believe everyone has a purpose?"

I nodded. When you run through a dozen foster homes as a kid, you had to believe there was *some* reason you were alive even though no one really wanted you. "I do."

"Good. If you truly do, then what do you think is the purpose for a pyrokinetic to exist? What good do you think one can do with such a strange and difficult power?"

"I…I don't really know."

Rose came over and sat where Tip had been sitting and leaned closer to me. "We're killers, Echo. It is what we do, what we are, and what our powers are about. Why else would God give us these abilities? To roast marshmallows? To start barbeques?"

God? Was she serious? I knew of exactly zero supers who believed in a higher power, including Jacob Marley.

"Of course not. There is only one reason why Lily and I have that particular power and that's to kill people who deserve to die. That's why we're cleaners. We take out the trash. The human trash."

I was nearly speechless. "How…how many people have you—"

"Killed?" Rose leaned back. "Oh, I don't really know. Two or three dozen, maybe. I lost count ages ago, not that I ever really kept track. You sort of lose count after double digits. But this chat isn't about me and Lily. Lord knows we have hundreds of stories to tell. Maybe some other time. Right now, I want to discuss Cinder. You see, although she is very young, she knows what she is. The problem is you. *You're* not helping her make that adjustment."

"Me?"

"Yes, you. That girl adores you. You are her hero, and yet, you question who and what she is instead of accepting her at face value. You, my dear, make her doubt her very existence."

I felt my face blush. "I can't…"

"Let me finish. Cinder's purpose in this life isn't up to you. This is not your call. You are young and uninformed, and though I'm sure you believe you want what's best for the girl, the singular fact remains: *she* knows who and what she is and she needs *you* to accept her for that."

I could hardly believe my ears. I had let Cinder down in so many ways. "But Cinder is just—"

"*Lucky* is what she is. As you know, pyros seldom make it beyond their fourteenth birthdays. Without intervention of some sort, we usually roast ourselves in a fit of rage, or worse, we toast someone else. Cinder got lucky the day Big George spotted her. She got even luckier when she landed you and Danica as friends. But you're not being her friend by remaining in denial. You're not supporting her continued growth and rise in self-esteem by running around yammering that she isn't a killer. The simple truth, *she is*." Rose leaned back. You've seen her kill a man before, haven't you." It wasn't a question.

"Yes."

"Did it wreck her? Did she fall apart? Have a nervous breakdown? Scream in a rage? Cry? Did she flip out and wail that she had killed a man?"

"No. It didn't seem to faze her," I admitted.

"Exactly. Just because it would have bothered *you* doesn't mean it has to bother anyone else. You're not doing her little psyche any favors by wanting her to feel something she may never feel."

"Rose, I'm an empath. Feeling is all I know."

She patted my hand. "Right. That's *you*. That's *your* gift. She's not you…not by a long shot. She's a little girl who loves you and looks up to you and hopes you aren't ever disappointed in her. Do you have any idea how much it would crush her if she knew how judgmental you are about her use of her powers?"

"It's not judgmental. It's…"

"Yes, dearie, it most certainly is. She looks to you for acceptance and praise and all you do is harbor these judgmental feelings about her actions. You're this close to really damaging any sort of relationship you might have with the girl." Rose patted my leg. "But it's not too late. The choice is yours."

"What choice?"

"The choice of accepting the truth about her place in this world as a PK. The real truth, Echo. The honest truth. Cinder is a killer."

I looked at her. "Is Mel teaching her how to kill?"

She sighed. "You haven't heard a damn word I've said. We throw fireballs, not bullets. We can't very well wound someone with a flesh wound. It's an all-or-nothing power. Melika will teach her how to manage and maintain her skills without burning herself up, but Cinder's ultimate gift is a destructive one."

Blinking several times, I nodded slowly. I didn't want to understand, and I sure as hell didn't want to accept what she was saying, but the idea that I could be the one to ruin any sort of relationship I might have with Cinder was enough to make me take her words to heart.

Rising, Rose released my hand. "You are the yin to her yang in this battle, Echo. Your abilities are strictly defensive while hers are strictly offensive. Together, the two of you could make quite a team. That choice, as well, is up to you, but you must accept her for what she is first."

I knew seer-speak when I heard it. "Was that seen?"

She grinned. "Of course. The Others may retire from the public eye, but we always keep an eye on the young ones. Someday, you too will be an Other. Live and learn, dearie. Now, if you'll save the rest of your questions for later, I am an old woman with old bones that are aching for a bath. I think Lily and I might have blown a fuse out there."

"It was very impressive."

She smiled at me. "You should have seen us in our prime. Pretty frightening, really. Old age is a drag, dearie, but it sure felt good to let one rip."

"One more question?"

"One, and then I'm off."

"Why have you had to…kill so many people?"

She turned and half grinned at me. "For the same reason we are going to put Malecon down: he's a threat to our very existence. Anyone threatening to expose us will meet the same fate. If not from me and Lily—"

"Then from Cinder or some other cleaner."

Her grin widened. "Now you're getting it." She stopped when she reached the hall. "The first bedroom on the left is for Zack. You and your girlfriend will have the fourth room on the right. It has a nice king-size bed."

"She's not my—"

"Towels are hanging over the toilet and are in the hall closet should you need more than one. If you need anything, feel free to get up and fetch it. Lily and I both sleep pretty soundly. Good night…oh…and good job out there. We weren't the only impressive ones." She took three steps down the hall before returning. "Remember, all any of us wants is to be understood. That little girl is no exception. Give her that gift and she'll be your family for life."

I sat in the parlor for a long time thinking about what Rose had said and feeling awful because she was right. I had imposed my own sense of values and ethics on a child who was doing all she could to keep from blowing herself up. I had failed Cinder on so many levels already, it was a wonder she liked me at all.

"You going to sit there beating yourself up or are you going to come to bed."

"I am not *sleeping with you."*

"Don't be a prude. It's late. I'm tired, and you're not doing anyone any good by sitting there wondering where you've gone wrong. Come on. For once, just do as I ask without making such a big deal out of it.

It's not like I have the energy to jump your bones. I'm just about to crash. Can you believe they drugged me?"

"Yes. There's only way to get you to slow you down, babe."

"Please come to bed."

I rose and walked down the dimly lit hall to our assigned bedroom. Tip was lying all tucked in the bed looking pale and exhausted. "How you doing?" she asked.

"Me? I'm not the one who got shot." I sat on the edge of the bed. I wasn't uncomfortable being near my ex-lover and a bed. That was the one area where we had no issues. Tip was an amazingly proficient and attentive lover, but she would never presume any such sexual motives even if she hadn't lost blood. That wasn't her way.

"Merely a flesh wound," she said, mimicking Monty Python.

I looked closer at the bandage. We both knew better. She needed a doctor.

"Did it go all the way through?"

She nodded. "Lily cauterized it so I stopped bleeding, but we need to get back to the bayou so I can have it looked at."

I knew going to the hospital with a gunshot wound that had now been sealed through cauterization was out of the question, but that didn't prevent me from yearning for the chance to get her to a hospital. "The bayou? Surely we know some doctor here in town."

"Look…around you. Ain't no one here but us…chickens."

I leaned over and brushed her hair from her face. She was clammy. "You sure you're going to be okay?"

"About to drop. So, if you don't mind…turning the lights off and getting into bed…" She looked over at a granny nightgown laying at the foot of the bed. "Come on…granny, suit up."

Smiling softly, I shook my head. "Not without a shower. You sleep now. I'll try not to wake you when I get in bed."

I went into the ornate, and more than slightly gaudy white and gold bathroom, peeled off my filthy clothes, and stepped into the warm and welcoming hot shower. I let the spray massage my neck and shoulder muscles, and for the longest time, I just stood there thinking about Rose's words.

My reaction to the things Cinder was doing was not positive, and my disregard for what she had done to help us could only be described as disapproving. I was a disapproving shrew and I didn't like that self-imposed role any longer. I should have heeded Danica's words. Words from a woman who had seldom been accepted by either side of a race in her blood: she knew that pain of rejection all too well. The good news was that there was still time for me to change my evil ways. There was still time to let Cinder know I not only understood, but I accepted her for what she brought to my life and the world at large.

My life.

Down here, even amid the carnage and chaos, my life, my heart belonged here. This was home. I suppose I shouldn't have been surprised at the lessons being laid at my feet. It was almost as if I'd been in a coma for the last few years, living my life, working my job, just generally trying to be "normal."

But I wasn't. I had forgotten that...well...not actually forgotten. What I had done as a supernatural was stop learning. This trip had shown me just how much I needed to know. I was beginning to see and feel responsibilities I'd never felt before, and not just for the likes of Cinder, but for the future. I had a paranormal *future* to consider that, only a few days ago, remained buried with my past. The alarm bell was ringing and I was finally waking up.

On reflection, it didn't surprise me that I knew nothing about The Others. Like most twenty-somethings, my life revolved around me, and instead of looking outward for what I needed to learn, I had become self-absorbed to the point of blindness. Well...I wasn't blind anymore, and the need for me to move out of my party of one was crystal clear. It was time I made some greater changes than just to my wardrobe, and I would start right now.

I slipped on the granny gown and, as quietly as I could, slid between the cool sheets, hoping she was asleep.

"Long showers...usually mean...deep thoughts for you. You okay?" Tip's voice was soft, as if she was getting ready to drift off to sleep. I knew she was fighting the sedative.

"I've not been a very good empath, Tip." I reached over and

stroked her forehead. She needed sleep, not my personal issues. "But we can talk about it later. Sleep now."

In the light coming through the window, I could barely make out the outline of her rugged face. Her eyes were closed and she breathed rhythmically and deeply. "It's just time…" she said, not opening her eyes. "Not all of us…are meant to be… active in the care and protection of each other."

And that's when I realized how wrong I had been all these years about Tip's role in the world…in *our* world. I had always seen her as this interloper; this larger-than-life telepath who skulked around in the corners of our minds probing and reading thoughts she had no business reading. I'd seen her as some fanatic student, traipsing off hither and thither to spend time with indigenous people in order to learn as much as she could about their use of and understanding about psionic powers.

I had been so incredibly narrow-minded in the ways I had viewed her. "Tip—"

"Shh. I'm supposed to be sleeping." She took my stroking hand and kissed the palm. Red heat emanated from the place where her lips touched. Yes, I was a woman with a girlfriend, but this connection I had with Tip was so much deeper than anything I'd experienced with any other woman.

"The sisters think we're together," I said, withdrawing my hand.

"We're…not?"

"I'm a woman with a girlfriend, and that isn't you."

She grinned, eyes still closed. "Does *she* know she's your girlfriend?"

"Hush up and stop fighting that sedative."

She turned her head so her face was closer to mine. "If you have a girlfriend…you shouldn't be afraid…of sleeping in the same bed with me."

"I'm not afraid. I'm here, aren't I?"

Her eyes opened and I could read the last vestiges of her energy wane. "Yes…yes you are…finally."

Finally?

Her eyelids drooped slightly. "It's taken you a long time to figure this out…I thought…you were a better student than that." Sighing, she closed her eyes. "Better late than never, I suppose." And then she let go and drifted into a deep sleep.

I lay there for another half hour, unable to sleep with all the committee meetings going on in my mind, so I did what I always did whenever my mind was racing faster than I could keep up: I called Danica.

Gently sliding out of bed, I walked over to the wingback chair perched in front of the large bay window. In the distance, looking back on where the major flooding had occurred, there was an enormous darkness that had somehow managed to engulf that part of New Orleans. Reaching into the pile of dirty clothes, I grabbed my fanny pack and pulled out my vidbook.

"There you are! I was worried sick about you. Were you too tired to call with an update?" Danica had not been sleeping, and I could only wonder what she had been doing all evening. "You look like shit, Clark."

"Thanks. Sorta feel that way, too."

"Tip had been keeping us up to date, but then something happened. You guys okay?"

I nodded. As strong an empath as Melika was, reaching us when we were overwhelmed with emotions like anger and fear was virtually impossible. And while she and Tip could communicate telepathically, once she was wounded, all her energy had to be focused within to aid in recovery. It was merely one of the intricacies of being a supernatural. "We're okay. Tip was shot, but I think the bullet went cleanly through. She's drugged right now."

"Mel said as much." Danica's eyebrows raised higher than her voice.

"Malecon shot at *you*?" Suddenly, I saw Melika's face next to Danica's. "Is she is all right?" Melika asked.

I nodded. "She's okay. Drugged by the sisters, but she's lost a lot of blood. She needs to see a doctor, but—" I shook my head. "The sisters say she'll be fine."

"Who in the hell are you talking about?" Danica asked.

"I shall fill you in later, my dear," Melika said to Danica. "You are in good hands with Lily and Rose."

"Bishop is okay then? I mean, she's safe from Malecon?"

"Oh yes. Her condition is not yet known, but once it is, we'll get her the best medical attention money can buy. I trust you will return to the bayou in the morning?"

"As soon as Tip can get up and moving, yes. Is there something you need for us to do here?"

"Not at the moment. You need return so we can care for Tip's injury and make further plans for securing my brother." Melika's face relaxed. "You have done well, my dear. Get some rest. Good night." Melika's face disappeared from the screen and I was left with Danica.

"You sure you're okay, Clark? Talk to me."

"I owe you an apology," I said softly. "About Cinder. You were right. You've been right all along about her."

"That's no surprise. I'm always right. You usually just hate to admit it."

I nodded, checking to make sure I hadn't woken Tip. "Correct again."

"Yeah, it's exhausting being me, but someone has to do it." Danica studied my face in her camera. "You sure you're okay? Is there something you're not telling me?"

"Monkey mind is all. Watching Tip get shot really took the wind out of my sails. I don't know what I'd do—"

She nodded. "And you won't have to. The Big Indian is okay, right?"

I looked over at her. "She's lost a lot of blood. I wish we could get her to a doctor right now. I'd feel a whole lot better about it. Dragging her back to the bayou just feels like a stupid thing to do."

"It's no wonder your mind is spinning. Look, you can ease your mind about Cinder. She thinks you hung the moon and no matter what, that girl will forever have your back. So will I. Always."

"I know. Thank you for being here."

"I've always told you you're the most fun a straight girl can have. Oh, speaking of fun, Finn called. She stopped by the office so she could use the boys' vidbook."

My heart skipped. I hadn't even thought about calling home and checking in. As usual, I was a complete failure as a girlfriend. "What did she say?"

"I recorded it and sent it to your e-mail. When we're done, just click on the little Hollywood camera icon in the right-hand corner of your e-mail."

"Thanks."

"She's pretty smitten with you, Clark. I could read it in her eyes. Very concerned she hasn't heard from you since we arrived. Are you kidding me with that? You haven't even called to tell her you're okay?"

It hadn't even occurred to me to phone home. "I suck."

"As a girlfriend, yes you do. You always have. But, Clark, right now is not the time to beat yourself up for that. You need to be focusing on what is happening here. Finn's fine. She understands. She's used to being knee-deep in crises."

I nodded, but that didn't make me feel much better. We chatted some more, with Danica sharing with me how Bailey kept going in and out of the cottage, staying out for longer and longer periods of time. "She's weird, but the kid seems to like her."

"How's Jacob Marley?"

"That boy is having a helluva time, Clark, really. He says the ghosts of the bayou keep coming home and wanting to know what is being done to fix their homes." She shook her head sadly. "Of all the powers you guys have, his is the most fucked up."

When we signed off with promises to be careful, I clicked on the movie camera icon and waited for it to load. When it opened, there was Marist Finn's chiseled face looking back at me, her eyes filled with love and concern. I felt incredibly guilty for not having called.

"Hey, E. I was just…you know…thinking about you… wishing there was some way I could help. I don't know if you get the news there, but the entire country is outraged by what isn't happening. People everywhere are coming down to lend a hand." I hit the pause button and studied her face. Caramel colored skin, light green eyes that looked like rare marbles, and wavy brown hair all contributed to the beauty of a woman I had really come to admire. She didn't really look like a cop, her hair being longer than the military cut the men wear, but her poise and presence spoke volumes. Finn was a good cop and an even better person. I went to bed every night wondering how she would take the news that I was...different. She was in a profession, after all, where *hard* evidence was the only real evidence, and we lived in a world where who I was was only seen in science fiction movies. She lived in a tangible world where proof was everything. What would her reaction be when I was able to prove to her who I really was? Would she be angry? Afraid? Would she think I hadn't trusted her from the beginning with information so huge?

When I came down here, I came to help. I came because I was called. Now, I had a whole new world of responsibilities I hadn't had a week ago. It wasn't just Melika or Cinder anymore. There were entire communities of paranormal people I belonged to; people who had handed over their lives to protecting the generations after them. And so far, what had I done? What had I given back to a group of folks who had enabled me to return to a normal life in pursuit of normal things?

Not a damn thing.

When Rose and Lily walked out into the middle of deadly gang violence, I was in awe of their courage and dedication. I was struck by the code with which they lived—including accepting each other's powers and what those powers were meant for. I was amazed they put their own lives at risk to help people they had never met. We may have powers, but as Tip showed, we weren't invincible. They could just as easily been shot or killed, but that notion didn't stop them. They came with the sole purpose of saving us. At great risk to themselves, they calmly entered the fray and destroyed people who were trying to do the same to us.

I was ashamed now, at how little I had given back, how little I knew about my people. As I stared at the paused video of Finn, I realized that every natural who knew the truth about one of us put the rest of us in danger. This was bigger than the two of us, bigger than my desire to have her know who I was. This was bigger and more important than even love.

Ten years ago, I was given permission to tell the only person I loved, and not once did I doubt she would take that secret with her to the grave. Not once. Danica was loyal to a fault (she once punched a woman in the nose for calling me a bitch when I got the last sweater from a sales rack.) It was simply her nature.

But Finn?

I wasn't naïve enough to believe every love was the real and final deal. I didn't love her like that yet. That didn't mean I couldn't, it just meant I was realistic enough to know where I stood. Telling Finn my secret meant eventually having to answer questions about the rest of my paranormal family, and we were nowhere near that point yet. I knew she cared for me, and even loved me, but that sure as hell wasn't enough. Love, as I had discovered at an earlier age than most, was never enough.

I unpaused the video and finished watching Finn tell me to be careful and that she couldn't wait to see me. Thank God she didn't sign off with an "I love you." That would have been too much.

As I sat there in the barely light of the moon, I started writing my story for the paper. I needed to get something in, something that could, somehow, describe the horrors we had seen. I didn't want to focus on the failure of our government, because that was evident. What I wanted to do was tell the human story. I wanted to let the world know that families had been torn apart by this thing, that people had been bused out of their state, in all different directions, like a unpredictable Diaspora. I wanted San Franciscans to know how they could help. What was needed. What these people were going through.

An hour later, I finished my first installment and hit send. I loved the vidbook's many capabilities, and as I put it away in its watertight case, my hand brushed the cool metal of the gun. We had entered a war zone and I had fired my weapon, ready to take out anyone who threatened us. Just because I missed didn't mean I was any better than Danica. I had the same intention she had; kill or be killed. And I finally remembered where it was we had heard this drummed into our heads. It was an environmental science course we'd taken together at Mills. I remember the professor talking about animals in the wild having only one choice. You were either prey or predator, but no matter which you were, your choices remained constant. Only the scavenger creature fit a slightly different category. That's what we had seen when we watched those people pick apart stores and loot them: scavenging behavior. Scavengers weren't really a threat to anything living, but prey animals were.

Kill or be killed.

We were in a life-or-death struggle here, and in one instant, I chose life. If that instant were to ever reappear, I would do so again. So I guess that begged the question: does intent to kill and the actual *act* of killing mean you're a killer?

I closed my eyes. I knew the answer to that question, but whether I wanted to accept it was another task altogether. Wasn't there some other way to handle Malecon? He had been contained once, why couldn't we do so again? There had to be another way.

Rising, I yawned, stretched and walked over to study Tip's face in the moonlight. She was so handsome with her red skin and flawless complexion. Even after all we had just gone through, she looked at peace; something she seldom carried in her day-to-day life. She was exotic and gorgeous in this peace, and whenever Tip walked down the street, she turned male and female heads alike.

She still turned mine.

I think that was one of the reasons I couldn't tell Finn how I felt. Until I resolved the feelings I still carried for this woman, I couldn't return Finn's feelings for me.

Slowly, carefully getting into bed, I pulled the covers up and turned my back to her. It didn't take long for sleep to find me. When it did, visions of Cinder's fireballs danced through my head, lighting Malecon on fire, and drowning out his screams. In the dream, that was fine with me...after all…it was only a dream.

The next morning, as we prepared to return to the bayou, Rose pulled me aside and handed me an envelope to give to Melika. She shooed the others away so she could give me some parting pieces of wisdom as well.

"I know you don't know squat about me and Lily, but we know a great deal about you. It's our job to know as much about every charge under our care as we possibly can. We know about your police officer, your job, hell, even your three-legged cat." She cupped her hand around her mouth and whispered, "And we think Tiponi and you make a much cuter couple."

"We're not—"

She waved my words away like they were smoke in the air. "Cinder knows about us as well. We've actually worked with her, which is why we know so much about the way she feels for you. You are her hero. You are the first one who gave her a chance. She expects the best from you. No pressure, dearie, but we don't want you to let her down."

I nodded. "I understand. Really I do."

"Good. Because you're going to need Cinder if you want to protect Melika. Now that Bishop is safe, there's no telling what Malecon will do. It is up to you, at all costs, to make sure Melika is protected. You see, like most mothers, she is willing to sacrifice herself to save her brood. We cannot allow that to happen. The future students need her until her replacement is named, and that won't be for some time."

I nodded, feeling sick in my gut.

"And understand this: those two will give their life for you. Don't let them think you need them to. You are *not* the weakest link and do *not* need their heroics."

"I don't—"

"You have yet to tap into all of your powers, dearie. As we age, many of us gain additional powers. Some of our old powers wane while the newer powers take hold. You left the bayou believing you had learned all you could. In fact, you learned all you needed to at that time, but the new lessons are around the corner. Look for them. When something happens out of the ordinary for you, accept it as the gift it is. Accept it, nurture it, and then train it. Whatever you do, don't let them assume you need protecting. It will be dangerous for them to do so. Do you understand? You are stronger than you know."

"I think so."

"Good. We will be leaving New Orleans and joining Bishop

in the unlikely event Malecon comes after her. She will remain safely with us until he can be destroyed."

I nodded. "Thank you, Rose, for everything."

"You're very welcome. I know I've given you a great deal to think about, but Melika puts a lot of stock in you and your ability to lead through good decisions. It's easier to make good choices when one has all the information. Consider yourself informed."

After being informed, we headed back home.

When Tip, Zack and I made our way through the city and onto the speedboat, we did so with very little conversation. Tip's wound had reopened and she was bleeding through the makeshift bandage Lily had applied earlier. She would not, however, slow down. I think she was afraid of what was happening in the city and that we might suffer a second attack. We all just wanted to return to the safety of the bayou.

When we were finally back on the river, I felt all three of us sigh with relief. It was as if the river had come to our emotional rescue.

"I owe you both an apology," Tip said softly. "I had a feeling we were the red herring, but I couldn't be sure. I should have said something."

"That was why Mel didn't come with us, huh?" Zack said, driving the boat more slowly than Tip had done the day before.

"Yeah. I figured if I was right, he would be following us. I just hoped he didn't figure out why Mel wasn't with us."

"It was a good plan," Zack said. "At least we accomplished the goal of getting Bishop the hell out of Dodge. In the end, that's all that matters."

"So that leads us to Melika. You two need to understand that she is no damsel in distress, and neither am I. We may be empaths, but promise me no heroics, no gestures of knights in shining armor, no…"

"We get the point, Echo," Zack said, holding his hands up in surrender. "We're supernaturals, not superheroes."

"Exactly. So, don't act like one."

"Fine."

"Promise me."

They both nodded. "Promise," they said in unison.

I sat back, breathing a sigh of relief, and none of us spoke again until we reached Melika's.

As always, she was waiting on the dock for us, as was the rest of our group.

"Welcome back," Melika said, hugging me and Zack. Jacob Marley and Bailey reached down to assist Tip from the boat. She had gotten paler the longer we sat there, and I was just happy to have her back home where Melika could take care of her.

"It's sure good to be home," Tip said weakly.

Melika turned to her and gazed up into her face. It was an obvious read, and I was pretty sure Tip allowed her full access. She wanted to know how much pain she was in, how she was feeling about what happened out there, and her level of worry about what we needed to do next. Melika would read it all in the blink of any eye.

"We'll discuss all of that later," she said to Tip, turning away. "First things first." She nodded to me. "I want to know everything that happened. Bailey will see to Tip."

"Bailey?" I rose up. "Are you kidding me?"

Melika gave me a look that demanded I back down, which I did.

"Come on, Echo," Zack said softly. "She won't rest until she hears the whole thing with her real ears."

As we told the story of last night, Bailey gingerly undid the rest of Tip's flapping bandage and examined the wound. I watched her, not feeling jealous or envious, but out of curiosity and concern. She acted like she knew what she was doing, but I wasn't so sure.

As she examined Tip more closely, Tip winced a few times. Now that her adrenaline was leaking out, the true pain was beginning to set her teeth on edge. I didn't need to lower my shields to see how much it hurt.

"I can fix that," Bailey whispered at last, going to the sink to wash her hands. "I need a little more acacia or umbrella thorns." She wasn't really speaking to anyone, but talking out loud to herself. "My agrimony stash is low, so is my fiddle weed. If I can't find any, I'll have to make do with some substitutes." Bailey looked up at me. "It's not too bad. Bullet went all the way through the meaty part of the shoulder, but it's going to get infected if I don't get it cleaned out well. I also need to staunch the bleeding, but I'm running a little low on supplies."

"Go ahead then," Melika said, nodding with her chin. "Do you want Bones to—"

"I'll take her." The words leapt from my mouth before I had time to think about them.

Melika turned to me, surprised. "Really?"

"Sure."

Even Bailey seemed taken aback. "It could take awhile."

I smiled at her. "I have time. I can get you anywhere you need to go. Thanks to Jacob's fine tutelage, I know the waterways of the river far better than I do the streets of New Orleans. With the speedboat, we'll get there and back in no time." I knelt down next to Tip and took her hands in mine. They were ice cold. "You rest. There's nothing more you can do for now. That, my friend, is an order."

"Roger that. Hurry back."

As I turned to leave, Jacob Marley gently pulled me aside. "Can I talk to you for a sec?"

"Sure. What's up?"

"Well, there's not much time, you know? And I…I just want you to know that our time out here were the best years of my life. You were the best friend an awkward kid could have."

I grinned softly at him. "We had a lot of fun, didn't we?"

He nodded. "I don't think I ever really told you, but there were times when you literally saved my sanity. All those night sweats and hauntings when I was just a little kid." He shook his head. "You really helped keep me grounded. You're a good egg, Echo. You are one of a kind. Thank you for being my friend."

"Jacob, I didn't do anything. I just listened."

"People don't really do that anymore, Echo. You always have. You have always been there for me…and I want you to know something…" Jacob Marley looked me deep in the eyes, tears gathering in the corners of his. "I will *always* be here for you. Even when it doesn't seem possible, you have to remember that, okay?"

Throwing my arms around his neck, I hugged his slender frame tightly. "You silly boy. Of course I'll remember. I'll always remember."

He pulled away. "Promise?"

I nodded. "Promise."

As we headed down the pier, Bailey decided we ought to take the rowboat and leave the speedboat in the event Tip took a turn for the worse. I shuddered at the phrasing, but hopped into the small boat we used for scooting around the fingers of the river.

When Bailey and I got out to the water, I felt her discomfort. I couldn't blame her, really. I hadn't been particularly warm or welcoming to her.

"I appreciate this, Echo. There's a mixture of herbs and roots that are actually regenerative. It's straight out of the Amazon legends, but I've seen it work once and it's amazing. The wound practically heals before your eyes."

I pulled back evenly on the oars. "Tip told us you're a shaman."

She nodded. "I try. There's a lot more to it than a title."

"It must be more difficult than what the rest of us have."

She cocked her head. "Difficult in what way?"

"Knowledge. You must have to learn so much more extrinsic information."

She studied me a long time before replying. "It's never-ending, really. I spent a couple of summers with an ethnobotanist who was writing about the medicinal properties of plants used by the various shamans in the Amazon." She hesitated here. "I won't bore you with details. I'm sure you don't—"

I released an oar and held up a hand to stop her. "Let me back up a second before you go on. I need to apologize for being such a bitch to you. I haven't been very open or welcoming, and I apologize for that. I've been ill-mannered for no reason."

A look of utter surprise was painted on her face. "Wow. Didn't see that coming."

"It's been too long in coming, Bailey, and I really am sorry."

She looked out over the water. "I don't blame you, Echo. I think I've been a little edgy as well. I mean, none of you are my people that I trained with here. I feel a little…slighted for them. You know, like what have you guys got that we don't?" She looked back at me. "At first I thought it was because you all seemed to get along so well. You work so well as a team. I see now what that is."

I returned my hand to the oar and stroked. "And what would that be?"

She narrowed her gaze at me. "Love. You guys truly love each other. At first, it was sort of sickening, you know, the way you all were pretending to like each other and get along so well. Then I realized you really meant it and I felt like a seventh wheel." She shook her head sadly. "My time here wasn't anything like yours, and I guess I've been a little jealous."

I licked my lips and inhaled the bayou air. "It wouldn't kill us to let you into that circle, Bailey. Why don't we start over?"

She grinned. "I'd like that. I'd like that a lot." She glanced around for a few minutes, looking for the plants she needed before returning her gaze to me. "Then, can I ask you something personal?"

"Fire away."

"You really aren't in love with Tip anymore?"

I laughed. "No, I'm not. She's all yours."

Her eyes softened. "For an empath, you sure miss a lot. Her eyes never leave you, and I suspect her heart won't either. She might as well be a monk."

"In a way, she is, with all of her studying and learning. But seriously, Bailey, if you want to go aft…"

"I'm not gay, Echo. I don't have the slightest interest in Tip other than to pick her brains."

I had to laugh out loud. "You're *not* gay." I laughed again. "You're right. I *do* miss a lot. I could have sworn—"

She shrugged. "Women don't tend to see me for how I really am because they always see me as competition whether I want their hairy boyfriends or not."

Now, I really laughed. "Hairy boyfriends? That's hysterical."

"Well, if you've ever been with a man, and I strongly suspect you haven't, you'd be amazed at how much harder and hairier they are." She wriggled her nose. "Men leave hair everywhere they go, not unlike dogs."

"Ouch."

Bailey laughed. "Come on, Echo, you know as well as I do that gender doesn't matter. In the end, we all face the same tough decision: To tell or not to tell." She shook her head slowly. "And I'm not sure there will ever be anyone special enough to earn that place in my heart."

I thought of Danica and the fact that I was so very young when I told her. It could have been a very reckless decision had it been to anyone but her. "I guess Danica is the exception."

Bailey nodded. "To be honest, I'm a little envious of that…of her. How nice it would be to have someone really truly *know* me. To have a confidante you could share things with and go through the daily grind of being a super. God, how nice would that be?"

I studied her. Her long, blond hair and hippie attitude reminded me of a dryad or a nymph out here in the woods. Then, I felt it, and the emotion was overwhelming. I hadn't picked it up before, and I hadn't meant to now, but there it was, like an alarm ringing inside my skull. Bailey was lonely. Suddenly, I felt like a royal schmuck for being so mean to her. "Where are the rest of your classmates?"

Turning away, she pretended to look for her missing herb. "Most of them are dead."

"Oh. I'm sorry to hear that."

Bailey turned back to me. "It's not an easy thing being us, is it? We get here in a virtual shambles, we're scared, some of us are slightly loony, some of us can't even handle the isolation of the bayou. Then we spend anywhere from three to six years here learning how to handle our powers, thinking we are finally coming into some control. But the truth is—"

"We're only fooling ourselves."

She nodded. "I thought I had really 'graduated' from here and would be able to return to civilization to live some semblance of a normal life." She shook her head again. "But we're *not* normal, whatever that word means. That life isn't really an option for us. We're like a person encased in glass standing in the middle of a party. We may look like we're part of it, but we're not. It's foolish for me to believe I can exist in a world that would destroy me and my life if anyone ever knew what I was."

That's when I knew what had been bothering me for the last few months. I had been one of those fools. I had started believing I could tell Finn and we could just go on our merry way, pretending I didn't have the abilities I possess, pretending I fit in. But it would all be pretend, wouldn't it? It would be the elephant in the living room or the dirt swept under the rug. She would say it didn't matter, and we would move on, but how long would that last?

"When we leave here," Bailey continued, "each of us has the bare minimum to control our powers, but as we change and mature, so do our abilities. That's the one thing Melika can't predict or control. We might pick up some telepathy, we might have a vision or two, but each of us changes in our own unique way. If we're willing to learn and grow, we can even add these to our arsenal."

"Interesting word."

"Let's face it, Echo, every power we have is a potential weapon. It doesn't matter that we're here now hunting some fucking insane guy. No matter where we go or what we do, we each have, at our fingertips, the ability to change someone's life. That's a pretty amazing thing, don't you think?"

Her words rang true in my head, though my heart did not want to acknowledge their veracity. I had never thought about my skill in terms of weaponry. Even when Tip and Melika had shown me how to project my shield outward, I never thought of it as an offensive weapon. Apparently, I never thought. Period.

"Tell me about your people, Bailey."

"My classmates?" She grinned faintly and I could see traces of sadness etched on her face. "Moira was a seer. In her thirty-five short years, she had seen the deaths of her parents, her best friend, even her dog. I think the sight is one of the cruelest powers because there isn't really anything you can do to change what you see. Anyway, one night, she just hanged herself. No one knew what the last vision was that drove her over the edge, but her little nephew was hit by a car three days later. He lived, but he'll be in a wheelchair for the rest of his life."

"That's awful."

"Then there was Daniel. He was a TK who loved showing off his abilities. He was showing off for some girl, and one of the knives he was juggling fell and nicked his jugular. He died before they could stop the bleeding."

I put my hand to my mouth. She had suffered losses I couldn't even begin to think about.

"Sad. He was a really good guy, too." Bailey wiped her eyes. "And then there's John. He's a telepath…*was* a telepath. He disappeared over a year ago. Left a suicide note, but no one ever found his body. He just vanished."

"Is that all of you?"

"Oh no. There's Logan, but he's in an asylum for the criminally insane."

"What did he do?"

"That would depend on who you ask. From what I've heard, he telepathically threw a man out of a fifty-story window in Vegas. There were no prints, of course, but someone had seen him going into the man's room."

"Wow."

"When they arrested John, he was babbling on about being able to lift cars with his mind. I guess he just snapped. They had to practically muzzle him in court because he sounded like a lunatic shouting that he had superpowers."

"Why didn't The Others take him out?"

"They didn't need to. He sounded crazy, but thank God he wasn't so far gone that he showed anyone."

"And finally, there's Anna. Anna has the triad. Very powerful, very scary. She and I didn't get along at all when she was here." Heavy sigh. "My only hope for a real friend and she hated my guts."

"Why?"

Bailey sighed. "She believed she was a witch, not a psionic being. I could have handled that aspect of her powers, but killing creatures in order to make some sort of brew or potion…well… that goes against *everything* I'm about."

I know my mouth was just hanging open. "A witch? I can't imagine Melika putting up with that."

"Then you don't know her as well as you might think. Remember, Echo, people don't believe in what we can do…don't make the assumption that we're the only ones on the planet who know how to manipulate energy. Melika tried working with her, but Anna would still sneak off and kill things and make potions. In the end, Melika sent her away."

"She got the boot, eh?"

"Oh, no. Not that. She was sent to a coven. Last I heard, she is pretty high up in the order of the dark arts."

This was almost too much. "So, you believe in witchcraft?"

Bailey grinned. "I believe in just about everything, Echo, and you know why? Because the impossible has always existed. *We* exist. We always have. It just takes belief to transform the impossible to the possible."

"Let's go back to Logan. You said he's in an asylum? Is he insane?"

"Quite. He goes in and out, mostly out, unfortunately. He got lost somewhere along the way and instead of asking for help, he plummeted further and further down the rabbit hole until he was lost to us forever." She looked so sad, I knew the answer to my next question even before I asked it.

"Lovers?"

"Soul mates. He was...is an amazing man whom I will love always."

"When is the last time you saw him?"

"Three years ago. I can't stand to see him all drugged up like that. It breaks my heart to see him caged…contained. I can tell you this much, Tip is right about putting Malecon down. If I could, I'd do so for Logan, because if he ever got free—"

"What?"

She shook her head. "He'd never go back. Ever. And he'd kill anyone who tried."

My next question was more of a whisper. "Did he do it? The murder?"

She shrugged. "Probably. It was a reporter who had been investigating him…well…us, really."

I sat up. "He's *that* guy?" I remember reading about it when I was in a journalism course at Cal. It had been a big deal because the reporter had left a note for his editor that he was on a story that would change everything we thought we knew about science. Then, splat, he ended up dead.

"The one and only. Logan had been losing his grip for almost a year, becoming superparanoid people were out to get him. He even came back here for help, but nothing could keep his demons at bay. One day, he just slipped into the abyss. It broke my heart. It's still broken. I haven't been with anyone since."

"I'm really sorry."

"You know, I haven't stopped thinking about him since I arrived. He would have loved being here and doing what we're doing. His telepathic powers rival Tip's and he'd have been a great asset to our team."

We rowed in silence while Bailey scanned the area for the right plants. I pulled over a couple of times while she collected the plant parts she needed, carefully placing them in a leather pouch she wore on her belt. I was amazed at how gentle she was with each plant, tenderly placing the needed part into her bag. She was this way with everything she touched.

"Okay," she said, getting back in the boat. "That should be enough. I don't want to stay out too long. She needs the staunching herbs."

"And you learned all of this from an ethnobotonist?"

"Not from him; from the shamans and the people he was writing the book about. It's amazing the things those indigenous people can do with plants and herbs in order to heal a variety of ailments. That aspect of my power isn't completely genetic. I'd say about half of it is mental. I've learned how to be a good healer from the world's best."

I thought about how Tip traveled the world seeking knowledge from indigenous people not unlike her own. Was everyone but me enhancing both their abilities as well as their wisdom about them? I was beginning to see what a fool I had been trying desperately to fit into a world I wasn't sure I belonged in anymore. "So healing is not your primary power?"

"Hell no. When I left here, my primary power was animal telepathy. I took what I learned from Melika and tried to go to veterinary school to better utilize my power."

"What happened?"

"Science. I suck at it." She laughed. "Which is so ironic because I can name just about every plant in this bayou. Anyway, like you, I was trying to live my *regular* life when my secondary powers kicked in."

"Shamanism."

"For lack of a better word. So, Tip told you."

"Yeah."

"Well, when they kicked in, they came in harder than my animal senses. Suddenly, I started seeing the natural world in way I'd never dreamt of. My hearing became sharper, my vision more acute, in short, my senses were more like that of a creature than a human. I could smell a woman's perfume from half a football field away. I could sense when any man was hunting me. Suddenly, I was more apart from my life than part *of* it. It was so weird."

"I bet."

"So I spent the next few years learning from shamans from the Amazon basin to the jungles of Africa. I was a human sponge soaking up every bit of their knowledge and wisdom I could. At the end of three years, I could control about seventy percent of my power and could concoct over one hundred and fifty ointments and unguents to help everything from diarrhea to gunshot wounds." She smiled. "I know, seventy percent isn't great. That's why Mel sent me to Ireland to a place…well…if I tell you, I'd have to kill you. That's a story for another time. Needless to say, I have learned a helluvalot and I haven't even scratched the tip of the iceberg."

"So, you consider yourself a healer?"

She thought for a moment and then shook her head. "It's a little like your lesbian label. Once you adopt the label, that's all you are. That's how people will view you. Let's just say I have natural skills I am continually learning from and about."

I smiled softly. I was really starting to like her. "I've never met a healer."

"Because the smart ones live away from mankind. The wisest ones live in reclusion, far from the negative and destructive energy of humans. A true shaman comes when called, but lives a near-solitary life studying from and learning more about nature. It's where we feel most at home."

"So Melika summoned and you came running?"

Bailey stared at a bird perched in a tree before it took flight. Then, she leveled her gaze at me. "She didn't have to. One component of my powers is the ability to feel changes in the environment, and it kicks in prior to natural phenomena much like it does with other animals. You know, things like earthquakes, forest fires—"

"Hurricanes."

"Exactly. I was already down here when Katrina struck. I wasn't here for Melika, though. I came down to help all the displaced animals. Quite frankly, I was surprised when she called."

"Why is that?" An eagle soared overhead and Bailey shielded her eyes to see it.

"My abilities really lay outside the realm of her skills. It's not at all like regular telepathy. Animals don't understand English or any other language, so it's not like I actually hear them speaking words in the traditional sense of the word. Many anthropologists believe before we learned how to be vocal in our communication, Neanderthals were probably able to communicate like the rest of the animal kingdom. Perhaps the worst thing that has happened to mankind was the ability to communicate with each other using sound. We began relying on that until our telepathic abilities eventually faded away. That part of our brain has atrophied from disuse." She shrugged. "It's all speculative, of course, because those anthropologists don't have any test specimens. But if you think about it, what is the other ninety-three percent of our brain used for?"

"So animals don't communicate with you using words?"

She shook her head. "A dog taught in German will still do what it's told to do in another language because the animal isn't hearing the words, its picking up your vibrations and intent in pictures. The energy we exude is "heard" by the dog and it responds. There's a knowing. *That's* what telepathy really is: a certain knowing."

I was riveted. "Okay, but what about the sounds dolphins make to each other? Aren't they communicating?"

"Isn't it funny that scientist and animal behaviorists think an animal which has the power to use echo location to read things around it would still need to verbalize to his buddies? It's a silly and absurd notion. That's why they've never been able to decipher the clicks and sounds; they aren't communicating with each other that way. None of them do. Just us."

I hesitated, fascinated by the notion. "Can you show me?"

She laughed. "That's the first step, you know?"

"To what?"

"To where you're going." She looked at me softly. "You know what I'm talking about. You've been questioning your life since you got here."

"I am. At least, I think I am." I was on that path she had stepped on prior to going to the Amazon or Africa; the quest for more knowledge. It was this quest that drove Tip as well, and now completely I understood why she spent so much time away from the bayou in foreign lands. It had been a bone of contention between us when we were together; she was always off on some walkabout, but now I was beginning to understand why.

"Okay. Stop rowing for a second."

I did, and we drifted a little ways.

"See that gator?" She pointed to a twelve footer basking on the bank.

"Uh-huh."

"She's harmless. Big, yeah, but harmless." Bailey stared at the alligator a moment before the damn thing slid in the water toward us.

"Ummm, Bailey…" I had no desire to be that close to such an unpredictable creature.

"Relax, Echo. She came because I asked."

I watched as the gator floated calmly over to us until she was about three feet from the boat. She was large enough to tip us over if she wanted, and my pulse picked up a little. If an alligator is hungry enough, tipping over a small boat in order to get to 'food' was not out of the question. "Uh…can you understand them?"

"Not in the literal sense of communication. I read their energy much like you do when you're reading someone's aura. Trust me. She wouldn't come this close if she hadn't been requested to." Bailey reached into another bag hanging off her belt and held it out. It looked like a piece of jerky.

"It's beef jerky. I never leave home without it."

"Oh my God, you're not seriously going to—"

And then she did. The gator floated closer, opened its giant jaws letting Bailey drop the jerky into them. Then it turned on a dime and returned to the bank.

"That was amazing," I said, willing my heart to slow down. "Scary, but amazing."

"She's ill. The hurricane churned up a lot of things she probably shouldn't have eaten."

"Oh man, that's so weird."

"It was strange when I first knew there was something different about me. There was this white German sheppard in the neighborhood and we were all afraid of it. One day, he came running after us, and my little sister fell when trying to run away. I stepped in front of her, felt the incredible anger from the dog, and then, something changed. In my head, I yelled no at the dog. To my surprise, it stopped. As we stood there staring at each other, I knew something much bigger happened than me stopping the dog from biting us. He never chased me again, and I was never the same.

I nodded. "Not a bad power, really."

"I'm one of the lucky ones, really. It's never threatened to drive me insane or given me migraines, or hamper me with any of the other issues many of us face. All-in-all, it's been a blessing."

When I pulled up to the dock, I hoped Bailey's blessing would come in handy in healing Tip.

"How is she?" I asked Danica when she stepped onto the dock to greet us.

"Restless. Do you have anything that can put her down for a few hours? The control freak can't stand not being in the middle of all the action and it's making things worse."

Bailey smiled and nodded. "Coming right up." Before she reentered the cottage, Bailey turned to me. "Thank you for the chat, Echo. It meant a lot."

I smiled. "Back at you."

When she walked in, Danica turned to me. "You over it now?"

"Over what?"

"Your green monster."

I laughed as I secured the boat. "You know me too well, my friend."

"Yeah, I do, and I don't even have any superpowers."

I watched in silence as Bailey worked her magic with her herbal potions on Tip's wound. As she dressed it in some sort of muddy concoction, she sipped this tea Bailey had prepared in response to Danica's request of sedation.

"You spiked the tea, didn't you, Little?" Tip asked as her eyelids blinked slower and slower. "You told me it was to dull the pain, but you slipped me a mickey, damn you."

She leaned over and looked right in her face. "I lied. Of course, you won't feel any pain after you drink it. You just won't feel anything else, either."

"Damn you. We have…work to do…"

"And we'll do it," Bailey answered. "Just not right now. Has it ever occurred to you the rest of us might need to rest? Need to juice up? You're not the only super in the game, you know."

I admired her tenacity. Not many of us would have tried to speak to Tiponi Redhawk in such a harsh manner.

"How long?" She was fading fast.

Bailey looked at her watch. It was a little after five in the afternoon. "See you tomorrow morning."

Tip tried to open her eyes, but to no avail. "Damn you… Little…Never shoulda let you…two outta…" and that was all she wrote. Tip faded into the warm bosom of a sedative.

"God, I never thought she'd go down, the stubborn SOB."

I smirked. "She sure can be." Helping Bailey to her feet I asked, "Why did she keep calling you little?"

Bailey chuckled. "Nickname. Short for Dr. Doolittle. Tip would give anything to be able to do what I do. It fits more in with her heritage than it does mine."

I smiled at her. "Then she's more than stubborn. She's a geek."

Just then, Danica stuck her head in the room. "Clark, there's something here you need to see."

I left Bailey to finish up with Tip and followed Danica into the great room.

On the table sat Danica's vidbook. "Finn called while you guys were on the water. You need to see this."

Leaning over, I watched as Danica pressed play. Finn's face popped up on the screen.

"Echo—I can't just sit by here watching this insanity knowing you're somehow in the middle of it all. I've got to *do* something. So, I'm cashing in on some comp time I've got and will be catching a military transport in about a half an hour. I have no idea where you're staying or what you're doing, but I've made arrangements to help out in St. Bernard's Parish. The cops there really need some help, so my chief has okayed the trip. Man..." Finn shook her head. "What the fu-what in the hell have you gotten yourself into? Anyway, by the time you get this, I'll already be in the air. Stay safe and know this is just something I have to do. I'll be looking for you. You know where I'll be, so do the same. I...I miss you a lot. Take care, please."

"Shit, Clark. We need Deputy Dog here like we need a hole in the head." Danica turned it off and closed the vidbook.

"That's all I need is to have to be worrying about her down here."

Zack cleared his throat. "We don't have the luxury of worrying, Echo. Your girlfriend being down here changes nothing."

"She's a big girl," Jacob said softly. "Who has made the decision to come down here and help out her girlfriend. I say we leave well enough alone. We don't have time to scoot around her, Echo."

"Besides, what would you tell her? Go home? Hey, we're being attacked by a supernatural evil dude, so put your pistol away and go help the little old ladies?"

Zack shook his head. "Jacob's right. Just let it go. I'm sorry if it sounds insensitive, but we really do have bigger fish to fry. You're going to have to ignore it."

I looked over at Danica who was nodding. "We all agree."

As sweet as the gesture was, it brought forth more complications than what I had time for. It was so not the right time for my worlds to collide.

"Let it go, Clark. Keep focused."

She was right, and I knew it, but that didn't make it any easier. How was I supposed to pretend that the woman who just told me she loves me wasn't in hugging distance? How did I just walk away from that?

Before I could answer myself, Melika walked slowly down the stairs, and came over to hug me for a long time. "You feel it, too don't you?"

I nodded. She was talking about the energy in the room. It was too low for what lay ahead. We needed this rest. We needed time to regroup and form a plan.

Still hugging me, Melika sent, *Take good care of my boys, Echo. If anything should happen to me, they'll need a matriarch. Not one of them will ever follow a man. They need you. Do you understand?*

I nodded and she released me. Was this a premonition or was she just being cautious? Her words made me nervous, but her fear scared the shit out of me. I could not imagine a world without her, but then, I could not imagine a world as turned upside down as the one we were in, either. *I'm not ready to lead.*

Not to worry, my dear. I am not ready to die, but you need to prepare to lead some day. You are no longer just living your life in San Francisco, pretending you can hide your light under a bushel. You are far more powerful than that. It is time you embraced that side of you.

Melika turned from me and motioned for us to gather around. "Come outside. Cinder has started a fire in the firepit and it is time we broke out the goodies."

We all knew what that meant: S'mores with Melika's special chocolate she had flown in from Haiti. The boys practically knocked me down getting to the front door.

"Easy, boys. I swear, you're no more mature than when you were kids." She smiled, but I knew there was a hidden pain beneath that smile. She was scared for us, for Bishop, for me. Her fear leaked from her carefully guarded emotions like air from a balloon. I wondered if anyone else felt it as well. "What was the message that has you so worked up, my dear?"

"Finn is here in New Orleans."

Melika nodded solemnly. "I see. Is this going to be a problem?"

"No." I said it almost coldly. It surprised me. I meant it. "I'll be okay. I can handle this."

"Good. I need you focused. I need to know you're here one hundred percent."

"I am."

"Excellent. Then we'll share in some S'mores while we devise a plan."

I looked at her. "We have a plan?"

She smiled. "I always have a plan. Come. You'll see."

Sitting around the firepit changed our moods immensely. Cinder had started a roaring fire that might have been worrisome had the bayou not been so soggy.

Melika waited for us all to settle before beginning. "Tip is resting quietly and Bailey has assured me she will be much better by morning."

Bailey nodded. "The unguent I used was extremely powerful. It will fight any infection and help the wound heal. She's resting comfortably with the help of a mickey."

"While she recuperates, there is little the rest of you can do except strengthen your shields and make sure you are well rested." Melika motioned for the boys to begin roasting their marshmallows. One huge lesson I learned by living in the south is that manners still matter. The way we were around the table and in public was nothing at all like the way the world worked outside of the south. "Now, while you all enjoy the goodies, I'm going to go over with you what we need to do to rein my brother in."

Cinder reached for my hand. Hers was very warm, and I smiled at her, remembering all the things Rose had told me about being a pyro. "You're a good one," I whispered to Cinder, winking. She beamed.

"As much as I would like to take Malecon on here on the bayou, it is too much of a risk. This has been a safe haven for supers for a hundred years, and I'll not risk it because of a ridiculous family feud."

I felt a tingle on the back of my neck. Knock. Knock. It wasn't Tip. I wondered if it was a probe…maybe from Malecon? I threw up another shield.

"This plan is not negotiable, nor is it up for debate. The wheels are in motion and we will proceed as necessary."

"I don't like the sounds of that," Zack said, blowing on his blackened marshmallow.

"You'll like it even less when I tell you I am going with you all back into New Orleans." She held up her hand to stop our protests. "It must be done. There is one way to draw him out and that is to give him what he wants."

"Tip won't go for it," I said.

"Tip is not in charge. We do not have the luxury of waiting Malecon out. To do so would be a foolish mistake, and we cannot afford to make a mistake. Now that Bishop is safely ensconced with The Others, he will have no other alternative but to come after me. I say we bring the mountain to Mohammed in order to end this as swiftly as possible. There is much good for us to do here. We cannot drag our feet in taking care of business."

"By offering you up as sacrifice?"

"As bait. You see, there will come a point at which his strength will be superior to mine, and then it will be too late. We must find him before the chaos mounts and further bolsters his powers."

"How will we find him?"

"He'll find us. My brother is nothing if not predictable. He is furious we managed to steal Bishop right out from under his nose. He'll be looking for us…for me."

"He'll attack you even if he has to go through all of us? Why?"

"Hubris, Jacob Marley. Malecon's own superiority complex is what will, most likely, be his undoing. He does not see you as threats or he would have disposed of you in the Superdome."

"Just like that?"

She nodded. "Just like that." She waited for Zack to pull his marshmallow from the fire. "Echo, you and Zack had the good fortune of meeting The Others. I'm sure Rose explained their existence and purpose, as well as how they came to be there. What she might not have explained is how vital they are to the rest of us. The Others know things even I don't know, and things they don't wish for us to know."

"Like what?" Bailey asked.

Melika leaned forward, the shadows from the fire flickering across her face, making the tiny woman look like a warrior.

"In the Eighties, the US Army organized a special group of supers to keep an eye out on our enemies. There were rumors this project sought astral projectors to project themselves to certain coordinates on a map in order to spy on specific people and then report back. There were also unconfirmed stories of experiments on known telepaths, and whatnot, but the government was forced to shut down the project due to funding and dubious test results. In the end, the supers they *thought* they had were merely gifted naturals who had managed to fool them into believing they could actually read minds and astral project."

"How come we've never heard this?"

"No one has. It's buried deep in the vault with the thousands of other government failures. But The Others…they know the truth. They monitor our government's paranormal research and activities to make sure they don't need to step in and put an end to them."

"You mean, The Others watch them watching us?"

Melika smiled at Jacob. "No. We watch them *looking* for us. There is a big difference between the two."

"Whoa."

Melika sighed. "The Others are ever vigilant in protecting us from a government which, even now, strives to figure out a way to prove something they only suspect as being true."

"Scary," Danica replied.

"Indeed. But as long as The Others are observing, we can feel safe enough to live our lives unharrassed."

I knew what was coming and was helpless to stop it.

"The Others must be protected at all costs, though they would never admit it. They are the keepers of our key to freedom, and we cannot allow someone like Malecon to threaten their existence. If he intends to go after them, which I suspect he will, then he must be stopped."

"And that's where we put you on the hook and lure him out?"

She nodded. "Never ever forget that the needs of the many outweigh the needs of the few. If my brother fully believes I have walked into a trap, he will concentrate his energy on me and leave The Others alone. As much as this plan displeases you, it is important for you to remember protecting Bishop is our key. Protecting The Others is of utmost importance as well."

I was confused. "But Mel, Rose made it very clear our job was to keep *you* safe. She said the mentors must be pro—"

"And she was correct. But *my* safety is secondary to the well-being of The Others, especially since they now have Bishop. Remember, Malecon's money will open many doors for him. It is only a matter of time before that door opens to Bishop and The Others. We must get to him before that happens."

"And just to make sure we're all on the same page, Melika," Zack said, leaning forward. "When we get to him, we *are* going to kill him, right?"

Melika gazed into the fire for a moment before turning to fully face him. "Zack, when we have my brother cornered, the *only* option open for him is death. If we do not destroy Malecon, rest assured, he will not stop until he destroys us."

Tip's quiet breathing woke me. I had slept next to her all

night, waking every half hour for fear she could take a turn for the worse. Turned out, I needn't have worried at all. When Bailey got up to check under the bandage, the wound looked days old. It was amazing what her salve had done for Tip.

"You drugged me," Tip said groggily.

"Yeah, I did." Bailey leaned over and sniffed the wound. My stomach churned some. "No infection, which is a miracle, considering what's out there." She looked at Tip. "You needed to rest. We have a long haul ahead of us. How do you feel?"

"Stiff. Sore." She looked over at me. "'Mornin', kiddo. Can't get enough of me, eh?"

"You wish." Helping her sit up, I shoved a pillow under her back while Bailey pressed a new bandage into place.

"We ready to rumble?" Tip asked.

"We are, but you aren't." I outlined Melika's plan. She listened impassively, stoically, not unlike she does every time I tell her something she doesn't want to hear. Indians have the best poker faces in the world, and I should know; I'd lost enough money to them at poker over the years.

"Is that how Mel really wants it, or is this your spin on it?"

Bailey made a chuffing sound. "It's not about you, Captain Hero. She's the boss. If she wants to put herself on a hook and wave in the wind at her sicko brother, we have no say in it."

Tip looked from Bailey to me. "She can bait herself all she wants, but you've lost brain cells if you think I'm going to sit around here while it happens." She shook her head and tried to get up. "No way."

Bailey and I looked at each other and pushed Tip back to the pillow. Her reaction came as no surprise. Tip would be lost without Melika.

"We leave tonight," I said, holding her good shoulder to the pillow. "She thinks he won't be expecting us to make our move in the dark, especially with how dangerous it is out there now."

Tip thought about it for a few seconds. "Okay. So we leave tonight." She rotated her shoulder. "Feels pretty good. Remind me never to eat or drink anything Bailey gives me."

"She did it for your own good, and if you don't settle down and rest, I'll let her give you some more."

She knew by my tone I wasn't kidding. "Fine. But I'd like to go in and have some coffee. I take it everyone is up?" Tip wouldn't let us help her out of bed, and we both watched her carefully as she took her first steps. "Whatever was in your witch's brew seemed to really help. I feel pretty damn good."

When we walked into the great room, everyone was sitting around the table drinking coffee while Melika chopped vegetables for what looked like omelettes. "I'm fixing a big one, Tip, so sit down and relax."

"So, what's on today's agenda, then, if we aren't making our way back into the city?"

"Danica is downloading the blueprint of the Superdome and Convention Center so we can get a better lay of the land. That amazing little computer of hers sure has come in handy."

Jacob Marley peered over Danica's shoulder as she pulled up several different windows. "Is that the news?"

She nodded. "It's pretty ugly out there. No one knows what's going on, no one is getting the food and water they need, and...oh shit."

"What?" We all looked over at her. "It's Malecon. On TV!"

We all gathered behind her and looked over her shoulder. There, on the screen was Malecon being interviewed by CNN. "...and so, you're offering to pay for a fleet of luxury liners to take thousands of the homeless out of the Superdome and surrounding areas. What prompted this incredibly charitable act?"

"Look around you. These people need help, and it's incumbent upon those of us who have to help those of us who don't." He looked straight into the camera as if speaking directly to us. "The good people of the Gulf Coast need beds, food and a clean place to rest from such a devastating blow. What good is having money if you can't use it to help people in need?"

We all watched, breathless.

"Have you any idea of the cost of such a venture?" The local newswoman appeared dwarfish next to him.

"Stupid question," Zack muttered.

"Cost doesn't matter, and if the major cruise companies have any soul, they'll charge just enough to defray their operating costs. People need help. It's time for Americans to rally around and lend assistance any way we can."

"What in the hell is he up to?" Tip asked aloud.

"Shh."

"There's a rumor you have your eyes set on the mayoral seat when this is all said and done. Does that mean this is politically motivated?"

"Like you said, it is a rumor. *Now* is most definitely *not* the time for petty politics and finger-pointing, Tiffany. That's just a waste of time; time New Orleanians don't have. We need to pull together, and if anyone out there has resources, there's no better place to use them than down here in one of the greatest cities in the country." He flashed her a smile like the Cheshire cat.

Tiffany turned toward the camera. "There you have it. One more New Orleanian hero rides up on his white charger. This is Tiffany Dickenson, for CNN."

We all stared at the small screen until Danica closed it. No one wanted to be the first to speak, so we waited for Melika to say something. When she finally spoke, her voice was calm and quiet.

"It appears my brother has just put into place his own plan. I had not expected this at all."

"What's he thinking?" Tip asked.

"He has made himself known to the city so it will be harder for us to attack him. Harder to attack a hero." She shook her head. "Brilliant move, really. Now, he isn't just the savior to thousands of people, but he's a newsmaker, he's thrust himself into the limelight. He must know we intend to attack him, so he sagely surrounded himself with the entire city."

"For mayor? Hate to tell you, Mel, but that's piddly stuff."

She turned to Jacob Marley. "My brother is setting himself up in a position that will make it increasingly difficult for us to reach him and do what must be done. Trust me. He is not interested in politics. He is interested in self-preservation in the same way he used those thugs to attack you. We want heroes in this sad country of ours, and Malecon may have just made himself one. My brother has just pulled the oldest trick in the book. He's hiding in plain sight."

We arrived in the city around nine p.m. amid more of the same anarchy and chaos we'd met the day before. Things had, unbelievably, gotten worse.

"I can't believe they haven't moved those poor people out of the Superdome," Danica said, walking between me and Tip. A few rabble-rousers glanced in our direction, but we were too big a group to mess with. With Tip, Danica and Jacob all over six feet tall, they cut an imposing sight in the darkness. No one would be coming after us.

No one except Malecon.

And that was the plan.

"He's still here?" Bailey asked. Malecon's shields had protected him from probing, but we were all sure Mel knew. I suspected it was a twin thing. She had been very quiet since we left the bayou. I suppose there wasn't much to say when you were out hunting your twin brother in order to kill him.

"Oh, he's here," Melika said softly. "He's waiting for us."

"How are his powers?" Tip asked.

"Stronger than I had hoped. We mustn't make any mistakes."

We neared the entrance of the Superdome where hundreds more had spilled out onto the street. The area around the Superdome was more disgusting than before, and the stench of old urine, feces and new rot wafted out the door.

"Oh my God," Bailey said, putting her hand over her mouth and nose. "That's horrid."

"It's about to get worse," Danica said. "You won't even want to breathe in there."

Melika suddenly stopped. "We won't be going in after all. He's out here. And he is not alone."

"Think he's going to send more naturals after us?"

Melika motioned for us to walk down the darkened east side of the Dome. "They'll be coming from this direction. Try not to kill them, but keep yourselves from harm. If the police should come, you know what to do."

What to do meant get our asses out of Dodge. It was unlikely the cops would show. We hadn't seen one since we got out of the boat.

"Mel, last time we met up with some of his minions, they shot one of us," Zack said.

"Indeed. However, killing naturals who are not acting of their own free will is a violation of everything I've ever taught you."

"You don't mean he was controlling every one of those… those…"

"That is precisely what I am saying. If you weren't on the defensive so much, you might have noticed none of your attackers spoke."

I wrinkled my brow in an attempt to remember.

"She's right," Tip said. "We were so busy running for cover, we never realized they were like zombies. They weren't acting of their own volition. That means Malecon is far more powerful and even more dangerous if he is able to control the minds of the masses."

"Dangerous or not, I don't see how letting his *people* go unharmed works to our ad—"

"Cinder will take care of any bullets or other metals aimed in your direction."

"Cinder?" Zack said.

"Yes. As you trust Tip and Echo among us, so must you trust the youngest member of our family." Melika halted and turned to us, her hands out. We each took two other hands and formed a tight circle. "No matter what, you must trust and believe in each other. Do not falter, do not panic, and do not underestimate our quarry. Each of you has trained and worked hard. Now is the time you must test your mettle. All the time spent on the bayou to control your skills to the utmost comes into play now, and though I am saddened you have been placed in this position, I can think of nowhere else I would rather be than here at your side."

Closing our eyes, we each focused on the human energy field we literally drew our powers from. I could feel it coursing through my body, making me stronger, building my shields, helping me to…

"Echo! Hey Echo!"

The energy broken, we all looked at each other.

"Oh shit," Danica muttered, releasing my hand. "Not now."

I turned around to see Finn waving wildly at me. "Oh no." My stomach dropped.

"Zachary?" Melika said softly.

With a slight motion of his hand, Zack slammed a loose board from the balcony above Finn into her head. She dropped like a rock onto the dirty street before I could throw out a protective shield for her to fall on.

"What in the hell was that?" I barked at Zack.

"That was necessary," Tip replied. "We don't need that complication right now. She'll be fine."

I whirled around, ready to fire a mouthful of expletives at him. "*Fine*?"

"You should have warned her off, Echo! Couldn't you have just—"

"Enough." Melika's voice cut through the air. "Tip is correct, Echo. We do not have time to deal with your girlfriend and the complications she brings with her."

"She's not my—"

"Our adversary is rounding the corner as we speak. It was best to keep Ms. Finn out of harm's way."

"By knocking her out?"

Melika looked intently at me. "By any means necessary."

"I can't leave her out here alone. Have you any idea—"

"I've got this," Bailey said, closing her eyes. Suddenly, three German shepherds came bounding around the corner, stopping directly in front of Bailey, who opened her eyes and pointed to an unconscious Finn lying on the ground. The three dogs sat at attention on three different sides of Finn like menacing gargoyles.

"What the hell?" Danica said.

"They won't let anyone within ten yards of her. She'll be fine."

I lowered my shield and tried to read Finn, but she was unconscious. "Mel?"

"She is unconscious, Echo, but otherwise unharmed. You cannot help her and us at the same time. If you must choose—"

I shook my head. "There's no choice to make." With one last look back at a woman who had done nothing more than care about me and the safety of others, I turned away.

Maybe it wasn't even a decision as much as it was a regretful moment where Finn was in the wrong place at the wrong time. Maybe what had happened in that one moment was me recognizing my place in the world; my place with my kind. As much as my heart may have wanted to reach out to Finn, to soothe her and stay by her side, my spirit knew better.

So did Melika. "I'm sorry, my dear."

Turning away from Finn, I nodded sadly. "So am I."

Melika nodded once and turned to Danica. "Your eyes are vital, Danica. Yours and Cinder's both. You must remain focused while also seeing the larger picture. Do not concentrate on Malecon or what he is doing. The danger for the rest of us will come from someone we cannot see, some weapon we cannot control. When those weapons are produced, Cinder knows what to do." Melika knelt down and took Cinder's hands in hers. "We practiced this a lot last month. Do you remember?"

Cinder nodded.

"The key is control. Control your powers. We are not trying to kill these men, only protect ourselves. Do you understand?"

Another nod.

Melika rose. "It is time."

As Malecon's groupies rounded the corner before him, everything in my world slowed down like a filmstrip. I watched as Zack took out one attacker while Tip brought a second down.

"Gun!" Danica yelled as a third started for his gun. As he swung it out at us, Cinder pointed a single finger at the weapon making it glow a bright orange. The wielder yelped and dropped it, and, brought out of his trance, scurried away.

I was starting to build an offensive shield when I heard Danica yell gun once more.

"Gun! Oh shit. Two!"

Zack managed to knock one back, but it was the same guy Cinder had targeted, leaving the second gunman free to shoot.

Which he did.

I'd never really seen a muzzle flash, but at that millisecond, it was like seeing Cinder's fireball, only in reverse. The energy field I had been erecting jumped spastically from my mind, knocking both Danica and Cinder to the ground. That was when I heard it; a sound I had heard just the night before: the sickeningly dull thud a bullet makes upon impact with a human body.

"Jacob!" Bailey yelled as he propelled backward like a rag doll. She got to him first, but he was dead before he hit the ground. I knew because there was a void where his energy used to be the moment the bullet hit him; a big, black nothingness consumed a once bright light.

"No!" I screamed, feeling my own energy wane as his spirit left this plane—yanked from me before I could get to him, before I could say goodbye.

Cinder rose, took one look at Jacob, and threw a large fireball into the shooter's chest, incinerating him on contact. He fell to the ground in a clatter of burnt bones and singed handgun.

"Jacob?" Tip asked over her shoulder. Her eyes connected with mine and she knew. Turning back toward the fray, Tip saw Cinder raise her tiny hands once more. "Cinder, stop!" Torn between grabbing Cinder and protecting the rest of us, Tip did not decide in time.

It was too late.

As Cinder's arms went up a second time, I grabbed the back of Tip's shirt and yanked her to the ground. She let out a roar of pain when she hit the ground shoulder first. As Tip landed, I knocked Danica back down with my offensive shield and threw a protective barrier around us. It was too late to stop Cinder, and I wasn't sure any of us would if we could. One of us had been killed and all of *them* were about to pay the ultimate price.

With her palms outstretched, Cinder made the same motion Rose and Lily made, sending a wall of heat toward our attackers they couldn't see coming. Invisible to the naked eye, the heat wave emitted from Cinder's hands crossed the divide between us and instantly vaporized the men coming at us. They melted like candles in an oven. Everything in the wave's path either melted or caught on fire, and even beneath my shield, we could feel the heat's intensity.

I looked up, hoping to see Malecon caught in the heat, but I was too late to see anything other than people spontaneously combusting, cars exploding and fires igniting the wooden buildings ahead of us. In her pain, Cinder was unleashing everything she had. I wondered if the very street beneath us would melt.

"Don't fucking let up on that shield!" Danica yelled.

I struggled to maintain the energy to a high enough level to protect us from Cinder's heat. I was using a lot of energy and didn't know how much longer I could hold it.

Tip righted herself and turned to Bailey, her eyes pleading. "Jacob?"

She looked down, tears staining her face. "No." She shook her head sadly.

The pained expression etched across Tip's face was nothing compared to the anguished howl Zack bellowed as he crawled over to Jacob's lifeless body.

"Cinder, stop!" Danica yelled.

To my surprise, she did.

"We have to get out of here!" Jumping up and wrapping her arms around Cinder, Danica yelled. "Come on, people, get a move on!" Picking Cinder up, Danica ran away from the flames in the direction in which we had come.

Tip, in a show of strength that busted open her wound, lifted Jacob up and cradled him in her arms following right behind Danica. "Let's go!"

I grabbed Bailey's bloody hands and pulled her to her feet. "Come on!"

She blinked several times. "He's…he's—"

"I know. It's too late. We have to get out of here!"

Bailey looked around. "Did Mel make it? Where the hell is Melika?"

Before I could answer, a familiar presence rose from the ground and was staring at me as she rubbed the back of her head. It was Finn.

"Help me with her," I said to Bailey, who was wiping Jacob's blood off her hands and onto her shirt. Together, we grabbed Finn's arms and half carried, half dragged her away from the fire. I could see the huge lump on the back of her head, but other than that, she didn't appear harmed. Stunned, yes. Confused, most certainly, but not physically hurt.

"Echo? What's...I..."

"Not now, Finn, please. Can you walk on your own?"

"If you'd put me down, yeah."

We did.

"Echo?" Bailey's voice was soft and laced with sadness. "We *have* to go. There's no time for this. There's not much time at all."

Something shot through me, but I had no time to analyze or even feel it. We had to get out of there.

Nodding, I turned back to poor Finn. She had a scrape on her chin from the fall, but it was the look in her eyes that told me she might have seen more than she should have. Unfortunately, I had no time to explain any of this.

"Who *are* those people?" she asked, lightly touching the back of her head. "Better yet, *what* are they?"

"I can't talk now, Finn. I'm really sorry."

"Your friend. The one the huge Indian was carrying. Is he—"

"Dead? Yeah. That's why I have to go."

As I turned to leave, she grabbed my wrist. "Echo, I don't have a clue what in the hell is going on, but you need to call the cops. You can't—"

I shook her hand away. "I *need* to go with my friends. If you really care for me, Finn, you'll forget whatever you saw. They need me right now. I'm sorry."

"What kind of trouble are you in, Echo? Maybe I can help."

I wanted to hug her, to grab her arm and bring her back to the bayou with me, but I couldn't. This wasn't her battle...nor was it her life. "I wish you could, but this…this isn't something we have time to discuss."

"I'll go with you."

I shook my head. "You can't." Kissing her cheek, I managed to smile into her eyes. "Please don't follow us either. *Please.*"

Tearing myself away, I hightailed it with Bailey away from there and met up with the others who were making their way back to Rose and Lily's penthouse. Surprisingly, no one around us seemed to notice or care that we were carrying a dead man.

After all, we weren't the only ones.

Melika was not with us.

When we reached the penthouse, Tip's blue shirt was purple from Jacob Marley's blood. She waited patiently while I put towels on the floor upon which to lay Jacob Marley. No one said a word. We didn't have to. Our loss was staggering, our energy depleted, our attempt not to harm our attackers a failure.

Once we laid him down, Bailey and Zack cleaned him up. He had been shot through the chest and had bled out the entire way here. There wasn't much more blood left in him. As Bailey cleaned Jacob, and Danica held a bawling Cinder, I took Tip into the kitchen to get her bandage off so Bailey could make whatever repairs she could.

Moving like an automaton, I carefully pulled the tape from Tip's shoulder, not feeling anything except the sting in my eyes from the hot tears that would not fall. For her part, Tip stared unblinkingly at a spot on the wall. It was several minutes before either of us spoke.

"God. Damn. It," she growled, still staring. "I can't fucking believe it."

I swallowed hard, causing one tear to fall. "Mel was wrong," I said softly. "We should have killed them all right from the start." The words surprised me almost as much as they did Tip.

Finally looking at me, she shook her head sadly. "We couldn't. We had to give Mel time."

"That time cost Jacob Marley his life, Tip." I cleaned her wound and saw it had only broken open a little. That same feeling I had when talking to Finn washed over me, but I still couldn't pin it down. "And now…he's gone." I bowed my head and let the tears come. My sweet, beautiful brother was dead. As I looked back up at Tip, my lip quivered. "I …don't know how well Zack is going to do after this." Wiping my eyes, I laid my forehead against her good shoulder and sobbed. "He's…really gone."

Tip merely nodded, tears coming to her eyes. Wrapping her arms around me, she pulled me to her. "This is so fucked up."

I folded easily into her embrace, glad for the warmth and comfort; glad to have her strong arms around me so tightly I couldn't take a breath. She sobbed into my neck like I had never heard her cry before. Deep, excruciating sounds rose from the depths of a woman who had seen more than her fair share of death.

"Shh, love, I've gotcha," I whispered, softly stroking her back. I held her to me as her body wracked with sobs so hard, I could barely keep my arms around her. "I gotcha, love." Rocking us back and forth, I felt her tears slowly ebb and when she looked up at me, I knew it was only a matter of time before she shifted gears. Tip was like that. You feel what you need to then move on.

Reaching out, her fingers trailed across my eyebrow and down my cheek to the back of my neck. Pulling me to her, she kissed me softly, more tears falling as we stood there wrapped in the warmth of that shared moment.

"It could have been you," she whispered, pulling out of the kiss. "My God, I don't know what I'd have done—"

Taking her face in my hands, I kissed her again. Deeper. Harder. The kind of kiss two people share who are afraid to say with words what they really mean to each other. My hands were in her hair, hers against my back pulling me to her. Had we been alone, we'd have ended up on the floor having what Tip called "survival sex." As it was, we nearly tore each other's lips off.

When I finally pulled away, I looked into her eyes and felt

the same fear she was feeling. It could have been her lying on that floor in there. I shuddered at the thought. "I love you, you know? No matter what happens in our lives, I will always love you."

She nodded and pushed my hair behind my ear. "I know. God, do I know."

We just stood there gazing at each other, when I felt the shift in energy in the parlor.

"We have to do something, Tip. The fact that only one of us is laying on the floor out there is a miracle. We're out of our league."

She pulled away, wiping the tears from her eyes. "I thought... Mel thought...we could handle him. That Malecon wasn't that strong yet, but he is, Echo. He commandeered what amounts to an army of zombies. Do you have any idea of the mental strength it would take to do that?"

I nodded, looking in the hall closet for another shirt for her. I found a long sleeve black T-shirt and handed it to her. "He knew Melika wouldn't let us kill innocents. Because he knows her so well, he's always been a step ahead of us."

"Then we better step up our game."

I helped her pull the shirt on. "It sounds like you don't intend on following Mel's orders."

A hardened look settled deep in her eyes. "That son of a bitch is going to pay for Jacob Marley's death, and neither Melika nor God can prevent that."

"You'll have to stand in line then."

Tip and I turned to see Zack standing in the doorway. "And I'll kill anyone who tries to stop me. Even you, Echo. That bastard is going to pay, and I don't give a rat's ass who else pays in the process."

Tip started to rear up, but I put my hand on her chest to quiet her before walking over to Zack. His anger and pain penetrated my already weak shield, so I wrapped my arms around him. Together, we stood there crying for the loss of our friend, classmate and family. It was a pain I was unprepared for and the heat of it branded my soul.

"He...he...can't be gone..."

I said nothing, but just held him until he, too, was cried out.

"My God, Echo…this can't be happening."

"We're going to take care of it, Zack. I promise."

When, at last, the tears stopped, the three of us returned to the dining room, where Danica, Cinder and Bailey sat on the couch holding hands. Cinder was in the middle and she just stared down at Jacob, feeling remorse, regret and something else I couldn't name.

I could not bear to look at Jacob Marley's lifeless body, so I focused on the one who needed me most.

"How is she?"

Danica shrugged. "No better or worse than the rest of us. She's a tough kid."

Sighing, I sat on the chintz loveseat opposite them. Tip remained standing, and Zack sat on the floor next to Jacob Marley, who looked peaceful, like he was just taking a nap.

"How's your girlfriend?" Danica asked. "Bailey said she came to. Do we have even more damage control than we thought?"

"She's not my girlfriend, and she's fine."

"You left her there?"

"I had to. She's a big girl with a bump on her head. She can take care of herself."

"And she's a cop," Bailey added.

"How much did she see?" Tip asked.

"I don't know. Enough. Maybe nothing. I might be able to blame it on her nasty head wound, but I don't know." I looked down at Jacob Marley. He was so still. Looking up at Bailey, I asked, "Where do you suppose he is?"

"Hopefully kicking the shit out of all those souls who have haunted him his whole life." Zack answered, wiping snot from his nose. "Go get 'em, Jake."

"I think we ought to have a moment of silence before we sort this stupid thing out," Bailey said, looking over at Tip, who nodded. We gathered around Jacob Marley and held hands. "Remember, he probably can hear us, so say whatever it is you need to have him hear."

For the next several minutes, we held hands and sat in silence, each of us saying our goodbyes to a man we loved like a brother.

The depth of our sadness permeated the room; the quiet, was overwhelming, but it wasn't the regular quiet that bothered me. The *world* was now quieter without Jacob Marley's spirit in it. I felt the void as surely as if someone had snipped off a piece of my heart. We had come down here to help and now, we were the ones in trouble. Big trouble.

"I would like a few minutes alone with him to say my goodbyes, if no one minds," Zack said quietly.

"I think we could all use a little of that time. We'll be in the kitchen."

In the kitchen, Danica opened her vidbook to see if there was any news about our mishap. New Orleans was burning in numerous places, two of which we started, but other than that, it didn't look as if anyone was the wiser. So far.

Opening a second window, she called the boys.

"Damn, boss, we've been worried sick about you. What took you so long?" It was Roger, hair all messed up, glasses askew. He must have been napping. The boys had taken to living at the office since Danica was in such a dangerous environment. They needed to remain near all of their tech gadgets.

"We…we lost one of our party." Danica's voice cracked as she shook her head.

"Lost…as in…dead?"

She nodded, inhaled breath as if it were her courage, and asked, "Whatcha got for me?"

Before we left the bayou, we knew there was a chance we might lose Melika to her brother. In the event that that happened, and to make sure we knew her whereabouts, we taped my vidbook to the inside of her leg. Its GPS system would be traceable by the boys, and this way we would know where she was every step of the way. And wherever she was, he would be. I owed this part of the plan to Danica, whose genius status was *her* power.

We just hadn't anticipated *where* he would take her.

"Looks like…" Roger typed something into his computer. "Princess's vidbook is on the other side of the bayou. "I've got the coordinates for you."

Danica glanced over at Tip, who nodded. "Let me have them."

As Roger read the coordinates, Danica typed them into her vidbook and a map appeared on the screen. It was a detailed map of the swamp with a green flashing dot.

Tip leaned over Danica's shoulder and then shook her head. "Amazing. That bastard is hiding—"

"In plain sight," Bailey finished for him. "Just as Melika said."

"He took her there because he doesn't think we can trace her energy there."

"He'd be right," Tip said, laying her hand on Danica's shoulder. "Thank God we have the brainiac here."

"That's why we needed twenty-first century magic." Danica punched a couple more buttons. "If you can lead us through the bayou, Tip, I can take you to the exact spot where she is."

"Good. We'll leave as soon as I can take care of…of Jacob Marley."

"Uh, boss? Is there something we should know over here? You all don't look so hot from here."

"Nope. If I tell you, I'd have to kill you. And…well…let's just say I'm not kidding."

Roger nodded, but didn't crack a smile. "I see. Okay then, we'll continue to monitor the vidbook's location in the event anything hinky goes down. Don't hesitate to call us, you know? We're always here."

We could hear Carl in background, "And we aren't leavin' till you come home."

Danica nodded. "Much appreciated. You let me know the moment that thing changes direction, okay?"

"We're on top of it. Out."

Danica closed the vidbook and double-checked to make sure it was on vibrate mode. "We won't lose her, Tip. I can practically guarantee it."

She cleared her throat, shrugging. "I wish I had the words to express to you all how sorry I am that—"

"Save it," Bailey interjected. "His death is no one's fault. We knew…*Jacob Marley* knew the dangers going into this. What happened is nobody's fault."

Zack walked back into the kitchen, grim determination etched on his face. "I want a necromancer."

Everyone stared at him.

"I mean it." Zack sat at the table across from me. "I'm not just letting him go without knowing he's okay…that he's not as pissed off as I am that we coddled those motherfuckers instead of having Cinder blast the hell out of them in the first place. I want—"

"Not now." Two words were never spoken with such finality. Tip took him by the shoulders and stared into his eyes. "As much as you're hurting Zack, we must move forward with our plan. There isn't anything we can do to help Jacob Marley, and although Melika is pretty certain her brother won't kill her, I have no such illusions. We need to get to Mel and take care of business before we go chasing after ghosts."

Zack backed out of her grasp. "He is not a fucking ghost, Tip, and if you weren't so afraid of what he really was, you'd have taken the time—"

"That's enough!" I put my palms on the table and rose. "I know we're all hurt. I know we're all as pissed off as you are Zack. We made a mistake. A costly one, yes, but that's because we're human. Now, we can compound that mistake by taking it out on each other, or we can say our goodbyes to Jacob Marley and shove off for the bayou to get Melika back. What's it gonna be?"

Tip and Zack both backed down, mumbling what might have been apologies to each other.

"Good. Now, if you don't mind, I'm up. We have a job to finish and I think I know how to smoke him out." Taking the vidbook from Danica, I called Wes Bentley. At home. "Wes? It's Echo Branson."

"Are you okay? What in God's name is going on down there How come we haven't heard squat from you? I don't pay for vacations."

"This is no vacation spot, Wes. This place is a zoo."

"Ah, I see. You're wanting to come home?"

"No, sir. I need a few things."

"A few? Whatcha need?"

"Well…there's this…philanthropist who's donating quite a bit of—"

"You mean Malecon Moore? The whole country is abuzz about that guy! Don't tell me you can get an exclusive. Millions of dollars are pouring in from actors, musicians, politicians, anyone with a pot to pee in. Everyone wants to know who the hell this guy is who had the ingenius idea about the cruise ships."

"Right. What I need from you is a television connection down here. A big one. Someone with a name, and I need them to interview him at Café DuMonde."

"When?"

"No later than tomorrow before noon. I know it's short notice, but I really need you to do this. Call me when you nail the appointment."

"How will she get ahold of him? Do you have his cell number?"

"I don't, but the reporter at CNN probably does. Look, someone set up that first interview. We need a second one and we need it before noon. It is imperative you set it for as early as possible. If you can give me that, I guarantee you my story will outrun everyone else's."

There was a slight hesitation at the other end of the phone. "Ms. Branson, are you sure you aren't in any danger? You sound—"

"I'll be fine after the interview. Just please be sure to contact me once you have it all set up. I'll need to know everything."

"Not a problem. Sandy Jones owes me a few favors down there. I got her her first real television anchor job there. If she can't get ahold of this Malecon guy, no one can."

"Excellent. Look, I don't know if my cell will get a signal, so here's the number I need you to call. Ask for Roger. He'll know what to do." I gave him the number. "And thank you, sir. You won't regret it."

Closing the vidbook, I leaned back and exhaled loudly. Every bone in my body ached. "Okay. He's on it."

Tip nodded. "You've made some good connections in your short career."

"It's who you know, right?"

Everyone was silent for a moment.

"The waiting is the worst," Bailey said.

I nodded. "We won't have to wait long. Malecon jumped at the chance for the attention and adulation."

"When he leaves for the interview—"

"We get Melika back. All we have to do now is wait."

Tip and Zack looked at each other, their shared thoughts evident in their set jaws.

"And when we're done waiting?"

"Then we kill the bastard and anyone else who stands in our way."

The boat ride back was silent, with half of us asleep and the other half fighting it. I was in the fighting it half. So was Danica. "You talking to Tip?" she asked, just as I had, in fact, finished speaking telepathically with her.

"My powers rubbing off on you?"

"No thanks. You supernaturals have more problems than you can shake a wizard's wand at. I'll stay plain old brilliant me, thank you very much." She scooted closer. "So, what happened with Finn back there?"

"I think she saw."

"Saw, saw?"

I nodded.

"And you just left her there to try to figure it out on her own?"

"I had to. I can't deal with her right now, and I'm not in the mood to try to explain to her that, gee, yeah, we obliterated a dozen people, but they were scumbags, so who cares? If she saw Cinder obliterate everyone back there, it won't matter what I say. She'll see me…us…as the bad guys."

"Well…when you put it like that."

"There are more important things to worry about, anyway. How is Cinder?"

"Used up. Pretty sure she blasted those guys with every

ounce of power in her little body." Danica reached down and stroked Cinder's head. "She'll be fine. She did what she knows. It's you I'm worried about. You know exactly what leaving Finn there was about."

Sighing, I looked up at the stars and wondered if Jacob Marley were listening. "My place is here, with *this* family, solving this problem. Until we get Melika back…well…honestly, nothing else matters."

"Not even your relationship?"

I looked at her in the moonlight. "Not even that."

"You know, if she did see something, it's not like her to just let it go. She'll want answers."

"She won't get them from me. It's as simple as that."

Danica touched my shoulder. "Clark, nothing is ever that simple, and you know it."

I did, but denial is a powerful drug, and I was shooting it and smoking it. "I can't have my relationship with Finn become a complication to my life here, Dani. This is the one safe place I have."

"Who the hell do you think you're talking to, Jane? That's all relationships *are* is complication. Being single is a piece of cake. Allowing someone to participate in my neuroses, well, that's a whole new ball game. You've entered the stadium and just aren't sure you want to play."

I squeezed her hand and stood up. The speedboat was much sturdier than Bones's rickety boat. "That doesn't sound very fair, does it."

"Nothing's fair in love. You know, people say those kitschy lines because they're true. You just refuse to believe it. You're in denial if you think you aren't going to have *the talk* with her now."

"I can't think about it now. It's all I can do to keep from bawling at the thought that Jacob Marley is gone. My feelings about Finn are the least of my worries. Watching them take Jacob Marley away…" Shaking my head, I pinched the bridge of my nose to quell more tears.

We had waited at the penthouse until The Cleaners came and took Jacob Marley's body away. Tip explained to me they would handle the telling of Jacob's family. I watched them as they put him in a wheelchair and headed out to the street. Tip was willing to explain to me what would happen next, but at the time, I hadn't wanted to know. Now, as I saw my life become more and more entrenched in this, the unstable world of the paranormal, I remembered my promise to myself to learn as much as I could about the life I was letting slide past me.

Walking up to Tip who was at the wheel of the boat, I touched her forearm. "I don't need details, but just what is it The Cleaners will do with Jacob Marley?"

"They'll take him someplace where he's likely to have been shot by random violence and leave him there. They'll be the ones to discover him, to make sure that his remains are taken care of. Don't worry. They're very good at what they do."

"How do they do it? How do they get in and out of places?"

"The elderly are invisible in this country, kiddo. No one sees or cares when an older person goes somewhere they're not supposed to be. It's a lot easier than you realize. I remember this one time, one of us was in jail, and The Others needed to get her out. No one paid any attention when a little old *confused* lady walked right on in the main compound. They're amazingly good."

"Why didn't I ever know they existed?"

"The Others have always existed. You never knew because you never really cared to know much beyond what your own powers could do. And I'm not calling you selfish or self-absorbed. Most of you come to Melika at a time in your lives when you think the world revolves around you. Then you get here, and it sort of does for a number of years. We just sit back and wait until you're in a place in your life when you're ready for the knowledge."

"Does that mean the boys know?"

Tip nodded. "Zack has been taking instruction from a Master TK for the last nine months."

"That explains his increase in strength. I've never seen him have such power."

"Among other things."

"And Jacob Marley? Did he know?"

Tip sighed. "Necromancers are such a different breed from the rest of us. The energy they deal with is residual energy from the living. It's not something the rest of us use or even remotely understand. While he could have been a gifted necromancer, Jacob Marley preferred to pretend it wasn't much a part of his real life. He battled demons for so long, he was exhausted."

I knew Tip well enough to know a deflection when I saw one. "You didn't answer the question. There's something I don't know, isn't there?"

She sighed. "There's a lot you don't know, and it isn't my place to tell you. You have questions about Jacob Marley or anyone else, you need to go to Melika. She'll tell you if she thinks you're ready."

"Damn it, Tip, I'm not a little girl anymore. I don't enjoy being pinballed between you and Melika."

She reached for my hand and held it. Hers was very warm. "I am well aware of that. Look, just because you've had an awakening doesn't mean everyone is obligated to tell you anything. Welcome to the party."

An awakening. What an odd and yet appropriate term. "Is that what it's called? Is that what's happening to me?"

"I don't know." She turned to me. "What's happening to you?"

I pulled away and stared out at the darkness. The bayou was so dark at night, it seeped into your spirit like a dark fog settling in. "I…don't know. I just…I've never felt so ignorant about something that is such a big part of my life."

"And now, you feel like a sponge and you just can't cram enough wisdom into your being?" She chuffed. "That's an awakening, and yours is full-bloom."

I blinked several times. There's something comforting about knowing that there's a *name* for the things that ail us. Whether it's a disease or a mental condition, I think people need to know that somewhere along the line, so many others have gone through it that it received a name.

"It could have come at a better time," I grumbled.

"It comes when it comes, and usually it comes under duress. Do you honestly think Malecon is the first super to lose his mind and go after things that aren't his? This isn't my first hunt, and I suspect it won't be the last. Remember when I was in Australia a few months ago?"

I nodded. "You were with the Aborigines."

"I was hunting another guy down just like Malecon. Another telekinetic wanted to show the world what he could do, wanted to invite scientists from all over the world to watch him perform and ask questions, even study his behavior. That's one of my jobs, Echo. All this time, you thought I just cruised around the world studying with ancient tribal people and gaining all their wisdom…but there's so much more to my job than that."

I was stunned. I had never known Tip to lie to me. One, because lying to an empath is really, really hard, and two, because she wasn't the lying type. Now, here I stood, questioning everything I thought I knew—which turned out to be *not much*.

"You're a…a…"

"A hunter? Yeah. That's what I do. That's my role in our little fucked-up community. I travel around the world taking out those of us who are a threat to the rest of us. And no, I don't go around killing them. There are other means, other ways to get our point across."

Words evaded my lips. I couldn't believe all of this had happened practically under my nose. "When we were together—"

"I was a hunter."

"And Zack? Is that what he's training for?"

"Not mine to tell. I told you—"

"Ask Melika." I nodded slowly.

"I know this is a shock. It always is. I never wanted to lie to you, and believe me, it wasn't easy, but that's the code we live by. We all understand that not everyone will want to participate in the health and well being of our community. Most of us take our gifts, leave the bayou, and try to live as normally as we can in a world that thinks we exist only on television. And there's nothing wrong with that. Don't get me wrong. There are times when I would have loved pretending to be normal, but I can't. I have…well…too much responsibility to just walk away."

Okay, my head was spinning. It was like being proud that you drop a hundred-dollar bill in the tithe plate at church, only to discover that everyone around you dropped thousands. "Wait…please…this is all so fast—"

She reached for my hand again. "There's no slow way for me to tell you. Now that you know, now that you *want* to know more, you'll start remembering things…times when something didn't add up, but you let it slide by anyway. You know, most of us see only what we want to see in life. Well, when you look at a building, you see the *whole* building…not just a door and then a window. I'm showing you the whole building, kiddo, and I'm sorry if it's a bit overwhelming."

"Overwhelming is an understatement. I can't believe I never knew you were lying."

"Sure you do. Why do you think we're not together? Something kept not adding up in your mind, and you didn't know what to do about it. You like to fake yourself into believing that it has to do with me reading you all the time, but that's just not true. You broke up with me because deep inside, you knew I was lying about something, but you just didn't know what it was."

I opened my mouth to respond, when Danica did it for me. "Bingo!"

I turned and hushed her. "You aren't supposed to be listening."

"Umm…it's a small boat and I'm bored silly? Pretend I'm not here. Sounds like pretending is something you've been really good at."

Tip sighed. "It's not her fault, Danica. They all do it. Every single one them who walks through Melika's doors wants desperately to fit in. What they don't know is that there's a whole world, a whole big family just like them waiting for them to come be a small piece of a larger puzzle, but you have to have an awakening first. You have to know where you want to belong."

I turned back to Tip. "So this family, this community. What do they do? Big George is a spotter, Rose and Lily are cleaners, you're a hunter, what else is there? Doormen? Hang gliders? Partridge in a pear tree?"

She sighed again. "You think it's easy covering up fifteen charred bodies and a block of burned buildings? Do you have any idea how many of us it takes to get a mess like that straightened out so there's a logical explanation for what happened? It takes a lot of hard work and dedicated supers to help us remain invisible so all of us can live in peace. What they are and what they do is something you'll have to get from Melika, not me. I'm in no position to tell you anything more than I already have."

"So what you're saying is now that I've suddenly pulled my head out of my ass and realize I am trying so hard to pretend I'm normal, my real life is flashing before my eyes. Is that it?"

"You know, Clark, for a woman as smart as you, sometimes, you just can't see the big picture. This *is* your real life. Hell, maybe it always has been. When you turned your back on Finn, you made a much bigger decision than whether or not your relationship took precedence. You walked away from your pretend life and started hitching a ride to your real one."

I looked at Tip, who was nodding. "She's right. This doesn't mean you can't still go back and live that life, which I suspect you will. It just means your real life will now include a quest for further paranormal knowledge and wisdom. It means you might start training the dormant powers each of us carry. It means acknowledging to yourself that who you are *is* what you are. It's not so bad."

Not so bad?

A woman had come to New Orleans to help me, to be closer to me, and I had just left her standing there with a sack full of unanswered questions and a knot on the back of her head. Not so bad? I had left my life in San Francisco thinking I knew who I was and what I wanted out of life, and I would return a woman who knew absolutely nothing about anything.

Nothing about anything. To say I was shaken up a bit was an understatement.

"Cheer up, Clark. This is how it's meant to be. What don't you get about it?"

Tip released my hand. "Dani's not a super and yet, even

she gets Cinder's role better than you. You have some pie-eyed Pollyanna view of that little girl that has no place in our world, and *she* has no place in yours. In your world, Cinder would be a freak trying to contain her powers every time she is in a stressful situation. In your world, it's only a matter of time before she is put away in some institution—or worse—because of her abilities. But in our world, she is someone special, someone who will have a job to do. You don't have to like it, but you need to accept it."

"I'm trying."

"Because there's so much more you have no idea about. Cinder is just the beginning of the people you are going to meet and know, but you have to truly accept what Melika is doing for her."

"Is that going to be her role…her *job*? Are we taking a little girl and giving her the power of life and death?"

Tip shook her head. "We already have."

I stood next to her, filtering all of the comebacks I wanted to say but wouldn't. I couldn't be mad at her. She was just preparing me for whatever it was Melika was going to teach me.

"Just know that whatever happens with Malecon extends far beyond the bayou, far outside your current realm of understanding."

"You mean, like, why aren't there others out here helping us with this? If he's such a big threat, why don't we have all the best psionics in the country out here to battle him?"

"Valid question. The short response is this: we're the first line of defense. There are others, of course, waiting on the sidelines to step in should we fail. We don't always send in the same people. People still have their lives to live. But trust me. If we fail, there will be others after us who will stop him."

"Gee, somehow, that's not very comforting."

"I know this is all way too much way too fast, but you need to be ready. Mel would have…well, she *wanted* you to really be ready when the time was right. Well, the time is right now, and I'm sorry it came when it did. Awakenings happen when they happen. There's no control over them."

Nodding, I went back and sat next to Danica, who reached

over and held my hand. Apparently, I was in that place where a lot of hand-holding was necessary. It sure felt necessary. I had never been so lost or out of whack in my adult life, and it was disconcerting.

"It's okay, Clark," Danica whispered. "Just think of it as a new adventure in the annals of your life."

"Adventures like this one? I think I'll pass."

"Well, if you do get a cool job, promise me one thing."

I turned to her. "And what is that?"

"That I get to be your geeky sidekick."

"You want tights and a cape too?"

Danica laughed. "Just the cape. Tights are so…Robin."

When we finally docked the boat at our predesigned location far down the river, it was almost midnight and we were aching from the long ride. The small shack we repaired to was cobwebby and filled with empty jars lining an old, rickety bookcase. There were three cots with plastic sheets covering them, and shelves filled with mystery meat such as Spam and those little canned weenies. Five plastic lawn chairs were strewn about the small room.

Zack and Tip had no problem digging into such yummy delights, but the rest of us begged off, choosing instead to munch on a candy bar from the airport that Danica had in her fanny pack. We hadn't thought to bring any food from the penthouse. I suppose none of us were really thinking too clearly after the death of Jacob Marley. Already, the void he'd left was like a gaping wound, and I wondered if he was with us, watching us, urging us to go forward with all of this. Again, I had studied virtually nothing of what it meant to be a necromancer. I knew he managed to communicate with the newly deceased, but that was about all I knew. I had no idea what happened after death or whether or not a necro could see and hear what was happening in real life.

Sitting in one of the five plastic lawn chairs, I thought about my conversation with Tip. I was filled with questions about the life I had been leading and the one now before me; the one without Jacob Marley in it; the one where I had some major decisions to make.

I knew I was having this awakening, and it felt like a runaway train without a conductor. I had no idea how to turn it around and get it on the right tracks. I knew I wanted to; I just had no idea how to get started.

"How are you doing?" Danica asked, flopping into the chair next to mine. Bailey had gone outside to commune with nature or something, and Cinder had crashed almost immediately on one of the cots.

"I've been better."

She nodded and flipped open the vidbook. Roger's face appeared instantly. "Hey boss. The guys and I have been at this all night and I think we've got a pretty decent map of the area for you."

"Bring it."

A yellow bar appeared on the screen and slowly filled with purple as she uploaded his map. When it appeared, Danica smiled. "Remind me to give you guys a raise."

"I will. Look, near as I can tell, the layout of that particular section of the swamp has a longish sandbar-like thing. See it?"

Danica studied the map. "Yeah."

"One way around that sandbar only, but there are any number of places to go once you get around it. The thing is, once you start down that part of the river, you'll be boxed in on two sides. It doesn't make any sense to hide in that location."

I felt Zack next to me and smelled the odor of mystery meat. "Why would he put himself in such a vulnerable position?"

Tip joined us, smelling of the same faux meat scent. "Because he's not expecting to be vulnerable. He's not expecting us to follow. He knows we can't locate Melika out here using our powers."

"He didn't count on Danica's little friend. He's overconfident and believes he is safe out here."

"Yeah," Danica said. "That superiority complex is gonna get him sooner or later. He's not expecting us."

"What if he is?"

We all turned around to find Bailey standing at the door. "If this guy is as cunning as you think he is, maybe he does, in fact, expect us to follow her. Because if you ask me…that…" She pointed to the screen. "Looks and feels like an ambush to me."

Zack studied it a second and turned to Tip. "She has a point."

Tip shrugged. "Doesn't matter if Melika is sitting on a floating minefield. We are going after her *tomorrow*."

I looked up at her and that was when I knew: Tiponi thought Mel was already dead. "Tip…"

She held her hand up and rose to her full height. "That's final. You all can stay here if you want, but—"

"Nobody is leaving anyone. We just—"

Suddenly, Roger's voice cut through the tension. "Yo, peeps! There's a call from princess's boss, Mr. Bent Westly!" Roger put a cell to his ear and listened. "He says eight a.m. at Du Monde. Sharp."

I sent a silent prayer of thanks to my boss.

"Thank you, Roger," Danica said. "You guys are awesome."

"One last thing, boss."

"Yes?"

"That place you're in is a maze, but there's just one way in and the same way out once you get by the sandbar. I know you think we're just a bunch of propeller heads here, but we've played enough video games to know that whoever you're following, knows you're following."

Danica forced a smile. "Thank you, Roger. I'll keep that in mind." Danica closed the vidbook. "Well, boys and girls, that gentleman is only the second smartest person I know. If he thinks this is a setup, I'd bet a year's supply of toilet paper he's right. Malecon is setting a trap."

"Shh," Bailey said, putting her finger to her lips. "He's here."

We all jumped like we'd been shocked. "Here? Now? What?"

"Not Malecon. Bones. Bones is here."

We all peeked out the window, and sure enough, there he was, only this time he wasn't in his rickety old boat, but another speedboat much like ours.

"How does he always know?" Danica asked.

"He's a receiver," Zack replied. "He can hear us, but can't project. He can't send thoughts."

"But I thought outside of here was a *no read your energy* zone."

Tip nodded. "It is. No one knows how or why Bones is the only person on the water who can get through the energy patterns, but he can. He always has. Who knows why?"

"I know." Bailey's voice was quiet as we all turned to her. "He's a creature of the bayou. Have you ever noticed that he never, not once, has been attacked by any of the gators? The infamous gator getter is for looks. Bones is as in tune with the bayou as Trump is to real estate. Like a spider that feels the vibration of the web from one end, Bones feels whenever anything is on the water. That's the best way I can describe it…well that…and the fact that he and Melika are tight. Bones isn't about to let her go without a fight."

"Frankly," Danica said, "I don't care *what* he is. I'm just glad he got a new ride."

Bones waved at us as he stood on the dock. "I come wid de bedder boat."

"Apparently," Danica mumbled. "You comin' inside, Bones?"

He shook his head. I wasn't surprised, I'd never seen the man indoors. Ever. "Nah. Bones stay wid de boats. When you riddy, we go. Faster."

We left him with the boats and returned inside, where Cinder still lay asleep on the cot.

"What are we going to do?" I asked Tip.

"Rest up, everybody," Tip said. "We leave at six thirty. He should be gone by then if he's going to make an eight a.m. interview."

"What makes you so sure he won't take her with him?" I asked.

Tip shook his head. "He brought her here so we couldn't locate her. Bringing her into the city would be a dumb move. No, whatever he has planned will have to wait until his fifteen minutes of fame are up."

I had to agree, though I was still surprised this was where he chose to bring her. Out here, he had no minions to command, no armies to manipulate. So, there had to be another reason why he brought her here. Had he already prepared a place for her? Was she already dead? Neither Tip nor I had been able to get a read on her thoughts. I was pretty sure that Malecon would have had to drug her, which would explain why none of us could reach her. From within the bayou, our powers were on an even playing ground. It was different if you were on the outside peeking in.

Rest didn't come easily for any of us, but I managed to nod off a couple of times before Tip gently shook me awake. "It's time," she whispered.

When we moved out to the dock, Bones was standing at the ready. Did that man ever sleep?

We separated as prearranged into the two boats. Danica, Cinder and Bones in one, Tip, Bailey, Zack and I in the other. The morning air was already warm and the humidity damp on my face.

"*Is she alive?*" I asked Tip.

"*I don't know. I haven't been able to pick anything up. How about you?*"

"*Same. I can't feel her anywhere, but that's how it was with Bishop.*"

We were only out about thirty minutes when suddenly, she cut the engines.

"What's going on?" Zack asked. "Why are we stopping?"

Tip pointed to Bones boat in front of ours. It had come to a stop and Bones was craning his neck, as if listening for something.

Bailey closed her eyes, and craned her neck as well. They could have been mirror images. "Something's not right."

"What is it? What are you seeing?"

"It's not what I see…it's what I don't see…or feel. Animals which would normally be here are not. Something has scared them away."

Looking beyond our boats, I saw the sandbar Roger told us about. We were about twenty yards away.

Bones pulled his boat alongside ours. "Someding idn't right." He shook his head. "De water too still. De creatures too quiet."

Tip nodded slowly. "Bailey says the same. Then we'll go inland. Stay off the back, watch where we walk, and…listen to Bailey."

Carefully, all of us except Bones got out of the boats. We were utterly silent as we moved away from the boats. Even though the land made slogging noises as we maneuvered through it, we were quieter than I thought a group this large could be.

I kept my eyes trained on Bailey, who kept cocking her head and stopping to listen. It was unnerving not to hear whatever it was she was hearing, and she was definitely hearing something.

She held her hand up in a fist.

We all stopped.

"Someone was here. Recently." She listened some more. "This is a trap."

Zack looked around in a three-hundred-sixty-degree circle. "You sure?"

"Yes. How close are we to where Melika is being held?"

Danica consulted the GPS on the vidbook. "Not far. Maybe two hundred yards in this direction."

Bailey turned to Tip. "At the risk of sounding racist, how good are you at tracking?"

She looked intently at Bailey. "I'm a hunter, Bailey. Tracking is what I do best."

"Then we're looking for footprints or anything out of place, anything manmade."

Tip nodded. "The rest of you stay here."

It took her less than two minutes to find human footprints, which she followed to a stake connected to a line of monofilament. I watched in fascination as she followed the line to where it was rigged.

"Bingo," Tip said, kneeling down to take a closer look. The nearly invisible fishing line appeared to extend out over the water less than twenty-five yards from where we had stopped.

"Roger was right. The channel is rigged to blow. He was using the inlet as a receiver for the other leg of filament."

"Then he has help," Zack offered. "He couldn't have done this alone."

"Maybe. Hard to say."

"We tripping it?" Bailey asked.

We all looked at her.

"If we want him to think his trap was sprung, then we need to trip it…make the bastard think he got us. This is all about him getting us, isn't it?"

I nodded. So did everyone else.

"I suppose we ought to."

Danica held her hand up. "Wait." Opening the vidbook, she waited until Roger answered. His hair was all askew and he wasn't wearing his trademark black-rimmed glasses. "Yo, boss. Looks like…" He put his glasses on and turned from the monitor to study his computer screen. "Like you're almost there. How come you stopped?"

"I'll show you." Danica turned the vidbook toward the stake so Roger could see why we had stopped.

"Oh. Man. Boss. You just gotta blow it." He turned again and studied the map on his computer. "Yeah, the pathway is narrow enough that he could blow it in two places to make sure the boat didn't get through. You'll need to detonate it since there's no way around it. Whatever you do, don't mess with the stake. As a matter of fact, back away."

We all did.

"What's wrong with the stake?"

"The Vietnamese were geniuses when it came to setting trips. Our guys thought it was the pulling of the wire that tripped the explosives. They were wrong. *Any* movement of the monofilament will set it off."

Danica nodded. "Thanks."

"Boss?"

"Yeah?"

"Be careful."

Danica closed the vidbook. "Well boys and girls, there you have it."

Tip looked over at the speedboats. "We're going to have to trip the damn thing."

"Not using those, we aren't." Zack said. "Get the boats and everyone else to safety. I'll trip them telekinetically."

Tip shook her head. "I don't think so."

Zack cocked his head at Tip. "I appreciate your concern, big girl, but we don't have a lot of time or options here. I know what I'm doing, and I'm going to blow that thing up." To my surprise, he turned to me. "Unless Echo disagrees."

I looked from Tip to Zack and back. "Zack's right. We are out of time and options. But if he's tripping it, I'm helping."

Tip turned to me. "Out of the—"

"I have the best defensive shield, Tip. You said so yourself." I crossed my arms over my chest. "Now get out of here and let me and Zack do what we have to."

Tip hesitated a moment, but Danica grabbed her arm. "She's right. We don't have time to stand around arguing. Go for it, Clark."

Zack and I waited until the two boats backed away from the danger zone. I shuddered at the thought of what might have happened if Bones hadn't alerted us.

"Can you do this kneeling down?" I asked Zack. "My shield is stronger the closer to the ground it is."

"Not a problem. Let me know when you're ready."

It didn't take me but a few seconds. "Ready."

Zack brought his arm up as if he were pushing someone away. In a deafening explosion, three bombs blew geysers of water shooting straight up in the air. The plumes of water rocketed twenty, twenty-five feet in the air, spraying everything in a hundred-foot radius. My shield kept us safe as well as dry, and I lowered it as soon as the water landed.

"That would have been rather unpleasant," Zack said as I helped him to his feet.

When we got back to the boats, Danica was just putting the vidbook in her fanny pack as she withdrew her gun. "Try to blow us up, eh? Rotten motherfucker."

Tip shook her head, shooshing my protest. "Everyone uses whatever form of protection they have, including guns." Tip stopped and closed her eyes. "I'm picking up two other energies nearby. Echo?"

I lowered my shield. “Yes. They’re faint, though. Very faint. Why is that?”

“You can be sure it’s Malecon’s doing,” Tip answered.

“Well, there goes our element of surprise,” Zack said as he climbed back into the boat.

Tip nodded. “You think? I’ll bet they’ll be even more surprised to see us now.”

Unfortunately for us, we were the ones who were surprised.

Danica had her vidbook back out once we started down the river again. She was carefully directing us closer to where Melika’s signal came from. “She should be right over there, beyond those trees.”

Bailey held up her fist for us to stop. Squinting through the trees, she nodded. “I see a shed of some sort. Could be a house.”

I’d learned long ago that something that looked like a shed on the river could, in fact, be someone’s home. Quietly, we climbed from the boats, taking cover behind a small grouping of trees.

“No one else around?” Zack asked out loud to anyone capable of detecting energies.

Tip and I shook our heads.

“They aren’t here, but that doesn’t mean they aren’t on their way back from somewhere. Come on.” Tip started to lead the charge the rest of the way, when Bailey stopped her.

“Not so fast. People who can rig those kinds of explosives probably have other ways of detoning devices as well. We don’t need your leg chopped off by a bear trap.”

Tip glanced over at me, and I nodded. “We wait and go in quietly and cautiously.”

What bothered her most was having to work in a group situation. She was used to hunting solo and we were definitely cramping her style.

The shed was a worn, wooden structure that had seen better

days about a decade or so ago. There was a single window, but the broken glass had long been absorbed by the swamp, and the window opening had been boarded up. A wooden door with a brand-new padlock faced south, and there didn't appear to be any other way in. It resembled many of the sheds where drug runners used to hide out, cut their drugs or rest before continuing on.

"Let Zack do it," Bailey whispered.

Zack shook his head. "I'd have better luck just busting the door down."

Tip pursed her lips. "I have the feeling that's precisely what he wants us to do." Turning to Cinder, Tip knelt before her. "Can you direct just enough heat at the lock to open it?"

"Tip, she doesn't have that kind of control yet," I said.

But Cinder nodded.

"Just the lock. If you miss and hit the building, that thing will go up in flames in a heartbeat, so make sure, okay?"

Cinder stepped away from her and she motioned for all of us to get back. I erected yet another field of protection and prayed that Cinder could find her range and accuracy.

"The moment the lock opens, Zack, I want you to open the door from here. Don't blast it open, mind you. If Melika is in there, we don't want to pepper her with splinters."

"Roger that."

Cinder raised one arm and, with only her index finger, pointed to the lock. From twenty feet away, she managed to hit the lock dead center with enough heat that it fell open, and Zack ripped it loose from the wooden frame. The door then opened slowly at first, coming to a complete stop only when wide open. From where we were, it didn't look like anyone was in there. I could see gardening shears, glass jars, binoculars and assorted other paraphernalia that screamed drug stopover, but no Melika.

Tip looked at Danica. "Are we in the right place?"

"We're right on top of it," she answered, holding the vidbook out to show her.

One by one, we all moved closer to the door, until we were standing on the front porch.

"Shit," Danica said, peering over Tip's shoulders.

Lying on the dirty bench next to a pair of rusted pliers was my vidbook.

"It *was* another trap," I murmured.

"It might still be," Zack announced. "He could have rigged this place to blow as well."

Tip nodded and made Danica, Bailey and Cinder slowly back out. "No use in all of us being blown to hell in a handbasket."

I nodded and held my breath as the three of them backed out to where we had stood seconds ago. "He seems to be one upping us," I said, reaching for the vidbook. As I did, a powerful blast knocked me against the wall, my shoulder slamming hard.

"Don't!" came Zack's voice as I crashed to the floor.

Tip reached me and helped me to my feet, and I could hear Zack apologizing profusely for sending the energy blast to save me. "I'm sorry, Echo," he said, helping Tip help me up. "The shed isn't wired, but the vidbook is. See the monofilament?"

We all turned to look at the small fishing line attached to my vidbook. "That must be his plan B, in case we escaped the first blast."

Tip nodded. "We've got to go to our own plan B now. He seems to be calling all the shots and it's really beginning to piss me off. Let's leave that here. Without a blast, he'll assume we never made it this far."

"You think he's getting past our shields?"

Tip shrugged. "If he is, we're royally screwed."

They both stared at me, and I knew what they were thinking. "You think the weakest shields are Dani's."

Neither said anything. They didn't have to. They were both right. "Damn it."

Tip shook her head. "If he's been reading Danica's thoughts, that means he's still here in the bayou. We can turn that to our advantage, though. We need to replace what Danica is thinking with a trap of our own. We need to let Malecon think he's at least killed you. If she can't do that, I'm afraid we're going to have to knock her out."

Sucking in a breath, I nodded. "And then what?"

"Then we go after the two people we felt in the swamp.

One of them may know where Melika is, and we have ways of making them tell us."

"Are they supers?" Zack asked.

I couldn't be sure, but Tip was. "Not supers like us. Half-witted henchmen with no real skills except in forearms and bomb building." Tip motioned for us to leave.

I left the shed carefully rubbing my shoulder. I didn't relish the idea of having to knock my best friend out, but there was no doubt her shields would be the weakest. Although I had trained her long ago in order to prevent me from accidentally reading her, it had been a long time since we'd worked on strengthening that defense. It was an oversight that would not happen again.

'Well?" Danica said, her hand wrapped around her gun.

"How would you feel about being knocked out?"

"Come again?"

I explained the situation, with Danica nodding the entire time. "Makes sense. It doesn't mean I like it, but it makes sense."

"We'll leave you with Bones so you'll be safe."

"Is it going to mess up my hair?"

I smiled. "You're in the friggin' swamp and you're worried about your hair?" Before she could answer, Tip tapped her on the back of her head with her fist. Okay, so she did more than tap her, but she went down like she'd been hit with a baseball bat.

Picking her up, Tip gently set her on one of the cushions in Bones' boat. "Take good care of her, Bones, or we'll both be answering to Echo."

"I protect her wid my life."

Cinder climbed up next to Danica and put Dani's head in her lap. I knew it was hard on her to see Danica helpless. Hell, it was hard on me.

"Let's find them and see what we can see," I said.

Tip closed her eyes and tried locating the two men. "One's near the first set of explosives, and the other is on foot." She turned to me. "You guys take the boat. See if you can't get back to the one near the explosives before he leaves the area."

"What are you going to do?"

"I'm going to track down the motherfucker who's still on land. Remember, we want them alive if we can. But don't expect them to know anything." With that, she took off.

Bailey looked at me. "Let's give them a reason to stay."

I grinned. "I can do that."

Returning to the shed, we backed up about twenty paces so I could still see the vidbook laying on the counter. Inhaling deeply, I held my breath and sent the strongest energy wave I could in the direction of the vidbook. It must have been enough to jar the monofilament because the next thing I knew, the shed blew into a million tiny toothpicks.

"That ought to do it," Bailey said. "If Malecon is as thorough as it appears, he'll send his goons back here to look for body parts. You ready?"

I was already on my way back to the boat.

"How far can you extend your offensive shield?" she asked me, hopping into the boat right after me.

"I can go about thirty feet. After that, it's pretty useless. What did you have in mind?"

Getting behind the wheel, Bones started up the boat.

"Wait a second." Bailey closed her eyes, her lips moving silently. When she opened them, she nodded. "His boat is stopped. All we need to do is get to him before he can get to us or the finger where the bombs went off. Right now, Malecon does not know what has happened to us. We could be dead, we could still be alive. We need to keep him guessing for as long as we can."

I nodded. "Then we're still in the game." Reaching for Cinder, I helped her slide out from under Danica's head.

"Don't leave her, Echo."

"She's going to be fine, Cinder. Bones will make sure of that."

"Oh yes we are," Bailey said, grinning. "His boat has been stopped and he can't check out the explosion area to see if we suffered any casualties unless he gets out. Unfortunately, that means we can't use our boat."

"Why not?"

Bailey pointed to the water as a gator quickly swam by. "We've got allies in the water and taking our boat is too dangerous to them."

I stared at her. "Are you telling me *they* stopped his boat?"

Bailey nodded as she reached into Danica's fanny pack and retrieved the vidbook. Then, she handed it to me. "Come on. We don't have much time."

Zack looked to me. "What do you want me to do?"

"Stay here and protect Bones and Dani."

Just then, a shot rang out. "He's shooting at the gators! Come on!"

I helped Cinder over the side of the boat, her eyes never leaving Dani. "We have to leave her, hon, but she'll be safe with Bones. Right Bones?"

"Day don't get her, leedle one. Now go. You too, Zack."

We leapt from the boat, landing with a splat on the muddy riverbank.

"It's too dense for us to get through," I said, barely able to keep up with Bailey. Cinder's little legs seemed more adaptable to the soggy marsh, as she pushed them faster and faster.

All of a sudden, one of the biggest alligators I'd ever seen on land jumped in front of us and started carving a path for us to follow. I knew they were quite fast on land, but had seldom seen them do anything except bask in the sun.

"Keep going!" Bailey yelled. "He's on our side!"

Turning to Cinder, I grabbed her hand and pulled her along. She didn't seem the least bit afraid of the enormous alligator cutting a wide swath for us. I, on the other hand, was freaking out.

As we pushed ahead, more shots rang out. "Don't worry," Bailey said. She wasn't even out of breath. "They're just keeping him busy."

In under two minutes, we'd managed to cross the finger and had a visual of the man and the boat. When we were within my thirty-foot distance, we stopped to catch our breath. He was too busy worrying about alligators to see us.

"If I…knock him…into the river." I said, hands on knees, bent over like an asthma patient trying to suck in oxygen. "How will we keep the alligators from eating him?" I watched as our guide joined his six buddies in the water. They had somehow managed to create a dam with their bodies so the only way the boat could make it by them was to go over them, and the driver had opted against that. It must have been quite a shock to see six alligators head to tail in the river.

"He's panicking," I said. "And scared to death."

Bailey nodded. "The Creoles are most afraid of the gators. He'll keep shooting until he doesn't have any ammo left. Once he's out, he's all yours. When you hear that clicking sound, knock him out of the boat."

I nodded and edged closer. When his last pull of the trigger yielded an ominous and empty click, I rose up and pushed my force field toward him with all my might. He almost lost his balance completely, and probably would have managed to regain it, had the big daddy of gators not rammed the boat with his enormous snout, sending the Creole into the water.

Before I knew what was happening, Bailey flew by me to the riverbank, and Cinder stood next to me panting and reaching for my wrist.

"What is it?" I asked.

Cinder held up five fingers, each one with a little flame burning at the tips. Then, she closed each finger, one by one until they were all snuffed out. "*Melika says gators are dangerous.*"

"They are, but this time, we have to trust Bailey."

"*I trust Bailey…but the gators? No way.*"

Rising, I looked into the river to see the Creole flailing haplessly in the water as five gators hovered just beneath the surface showing ten unblinking, bulbous eyes. Big Daddy, it appeared, had better things to do and was nowhere in sight.

"Swim over this way," Bailey commanded the Creole. "They will only attack you if you have a weapon. Do you have a weapon?"

"Help me! P-please!"

"Calm down. They'll only hurt you if you don't cooperate. Are you going to cooperate or am I going to let my friends tear your arms and legs from your body?"

"Yes! Yes, I will. P-please! Just get them away!"

"Swim over here. You'll be fine."

Looking around at every set of beastly eyes gazing at him, he slowly dog paddled through the water until he was close enough to stand on the muddy bottom. When he was waist deep, Bailey held her hand up. "That's plenty far enough."

"No, no it is not! They can still get me."

"They'll get you on land too, which they're about to do if you don't stop moving."

He looked around and realized that the gators had all moved to the bank, and two of them were already over the edge. Each alligator was within one powerful tail-thrust from him.

"How did you—"

"Not important," Bailey said as Cinder and I came up next to her. "We need answers right here and right now, and no second chances." Bailey looked to the gator closest to the Creole, and it jumped out of the water and snapped its great jaws.

"Wait! Wait! Okay!" He held his hands up in a gesture of surrender.

Bailey stood about ten feet from him, far enough out of reach that he could not reach her before one of the gators got to him. "Where is she?"

"Who?"

Bailey turned to me, and I shook my head. He wasn't lying. He had no idea what she was talking about. I know lying the way naturals know the scent of skunk, and this man did not have any pieces to our puzzle.

Opening my fanny pack, I pulled the vidbook out and flipped it open. "Here's the deal. You're going to call your boss and tell him all but one of us is dead. Tell him it's the black woman. Tell him we dropped her off before getting ourselves blown up. Tell him you've seen her making her way through the swamp, but you can't get a bead on her. Do you need me to repeat that?"

He shook his head.

"Repeat what she just told you," Bailey ordered.

The Creole tried, but he missed the part about Danica running through the swamp. It was obviously hard for him to concentrate with all those alligators waiting on his every move.

"And if you have any doubt that your life is in danger,"

Bailey turned to Cinder. "Don't hit him with it, Cinder. Just give him something to think about."

Cinder nodded and tossed a small fireball about five feet over his head. He started to dive back into the water, but decided to face possible burns rather than probable bites.

"*Good job,*" I said. "*Can you reach Dani?*" My telepathic abilities were long range only with Tip, and short range usually sucked the life out of my mental abilities. I had to keep them short and simple.

"*Yes. She woke up a few minutes ago. She has a headache.*"

"*Tell her to stay there. That we're coming back to get her, and she needs to sing the Brady Bunch theme song in her head.*"

"*The Brady Bunch?*"

"*Yes. She'll know what I'm talking about.*"

"One last thing before you talk to your boss. Do you know what the death roll is?" Bailey didn't wait for an answer. "It is what a gator does once it clamps its big, gnarly jaws on its prey. Then it drags you into the river rolling over and over and over again until the prey drowns. The death roll usually breaks many of your bones before you eventually inhale water and die a horrifying death. But do you know what five gators would do to you? They will each take an appendage and shake you like a rag doll until you are ripped open. That, my little Creole friend, is what will happen to you if you so much as deviate one little bit from what she told you to say. You don't answer his questions, you don't even listen to anything he has to say. You just say what she told you and hang up. One uh-uh, one no, one yes, one grunt, and your body will be in five pieces before you can say Five Easy Pieces." Bailey snapped her fingers to make her point.

"I-if I do all this, will you let me live?"

Bailey looked over at me and I nodded.

"*He's bad and needs to be dead.*"

"*We're not always judge and jury, Cinder.*"

"*Well, I vote we kill him.*"

"*I'm sure you do. Did you reach Dani?*"

"*Yes. She's groggy, but she said the Brady Bunch was the perfect song. She's singing it now. You guys are dumb.*"

I smiled. "*Yeah, what else is new?*" After someone regains consciousness, it is far more difficult for a telepath to get an accurate read because your brain waves have been disrupted. By keeping a song going in a loop, as it were, she made it difficult for Malecon to read her. Hence, the *Brady Bunch* theme.

"Repeat it one more time." When he did, I finally held the phone for him.

The Creole looked at it a moment before punching the numbers with one hand. The vidbook did not register caller ID. "It's me," the Creole said. He delivered the rest in a monotone voice. Then, his eyes grew wide. Malecon had asked him something. I stepped next to him and listened as Malecon repeated his question. Then, I pulled away and nodded; the Creole mimicked this and then answered in the affirmative. When the Creole hung up, I took the phone from him and backed away.

"He's on his way back here," I said, walking away from him. I have to admit, I was sure glad those gators were on our side. They were creeping me out.

"We gotta get back," Bailey said, moving up the bank.

I started to follow her, then turned back. "How much was he paying you?"

The Creole blinked several times. 'Wh-what?"

"How much?"

"Ten…ten thousand dollars. T-twenty for the little girl."

I looked over at Bailey, and something happened. Some emotion, some connection, some*thing* happened that brought us together on the same plane, on the same page, with the same agenda. I wasn't expecting it, and wasn't really ready for it, but the thought that this man put a value on Cinder's head at twenty thousand dollars made something snap inside me, and I made a decision I was sure would change my life forever.

Still staring at Bailey, I gritted my teeth and said curtly, "Do it." Just as Danica had done with Cinder, I had given Bailey permission to do what I could not.

Instead of turning to see the gators, Bailey took Cinder's hand and led her away. "Consider it done. Come on."

I started up the bank, but turned to look back when I heard the first gator lunge.

"No! You said…" he yelled before being pulled into a frothy broil of scaly water.

"I lied," I said softly, watching as the water turned a reddish purple. It was the most gruesome display of animal power I had ever witnessed. Ever.

And I watched.

I watched because I had, in effect, ordered his death. I was no better and no worse than Danica or Cinder or any one of us who killed out of necessity. This wasn't necessary as much as it was desire. I desired him dead. I had made the call, and Bailey had let me because she knew, in the end, that it was my decision to make.

Turning away and following Bailey and Cinder, I felt no regret. No remorse. I felt nothing. What had Rose said about taking out the trash? It was the perfect description for what was happening to us all as we dealt with the refuse Katrina had brought with her.

We had simply taken out the trash.

As we made our way back to the boat, I felt a small tingle at the base of my skull. It was the familiar touch of Tip's mind.

We took care of our guy and we're all okay. How about you?"

"Same. Did you get anything?"

"He's coming back. Coming after Danica, who he thinks is still alive."

There was a pause as she contemplated the fact that I had just opted to use my best friend as bait. *"You sure you want to do that?"*

"Are you kidding? She'll dig it. She walks the walk of the ghetto girl, Tip. She'll be fine."

"Meet you back at the boat then…oh… and kiddo? It's not so bad taking the life of a parasite, is it?"

"No, Tip. No, it's not. Anything on Melika?"

"Nada. I'll meet you at the boat."

"Nothing on Mel yet," I said to Bailey and Cinder, "but Tip blasted her quarry as well."

"So, what now?"

"Now we wait. It's not like we can really go after him until we know where Mel is."

"And there's no way Tip can read his mind?"

"My guess is that Malecon is as afraid of letting his shields down as we are. I doubt Tip can make a dent. We're just going to have to find another way."

By the time we arrived back at the boat, Zack had found one.

Danica was nursing the back of her head. "Tell the Big Indian I owe her one when she least expects it. Bitch."

"Sorry, Dani. It had to be done."

"Yeah, yeah, I'm just sore to realize I'm the weakest link. So, am I next on the chopping block or what?"

I looked at her. I was beginning to think being a friend of mine was more dangerous than I was worth. "We're just about out of options, so, yeah, in a way, you are."

"Hey, as long as I can stop that goddamned Brady tune, I'll dig to hell if that's what you want me to do." She smiled at me. "Stop worrying so much, Clark. It'll give you wrinkles. No one ever said being the sidekick of a supernatural was going to be easy."

"You don't have to do this."

"Sure I do. You and I both know I'm the only one he can read. If using me as bait will bring the mountain to us, I say let's go for it."

I put one arm around her and pulled her to me. "I won't let anything happen to you."

She grinned. "You sure as shit better not. I have a whole world I want to see." Looking around, Danica asked, How's Firefly?"

"She's good. Quite a bit of help."

"Did she—"

Bailey shook her head. "No, she did not kill those men. I did. Well…I did by proxy."

Danica nodded, still rubbing her sore neck. "Good. If you need her to, you guys know you can count on me."

When Tip and Zack showed up, they were up to their armpits in mud and muck.

"Have a little trouble?" Danica asked Tip, eyeing her dirty legs.

"Not at all. He wasn't going to give anything up, so…we took care of him."

"You said Zack had an idea." I sidled up next to Tip and felt her heightened state of awareness. The woman was a Native American through and through, and could track, hunt and fish with nothing more than her bare hands. She was ready and eager for anything Zack wanted to throw at her.

I could feel the drop in Zack's energy. He must have used some when trying to convince the thug to talk. "My thinking is like this: We can be pretty sure that Malecon hasn't killed her, but since none of us can contact her, we have to assume he's got her drugged or something else that prevents her energy from leaking out to us."

"That's a tall assumption. So far, Malecon has just about outwitted and outplayed us at every turn. It's possible she's not even in the city."

Zack shook his head. "Not this one. I think he truly believes Mel is part of his power. He'll keep her alive as long as he thinks he would be weaker or even impotent if she were dead. I think the key to this lays with Mel. She's waiting for us to figure out how to reach her, and I think I've figured it out." He looked at me for a sign of support. "We need a necromancer."

Tip shook her head. "I thought you just said—"

"I did. I don't want a necro for *her.* I want a necro for Jacob Marley."

We all just stood there.

"I don't get it," Danica said at last. "Jacob's dead. How can he help?"

Zack sighed. "Jacob's been seeing Bishop a couple of times a month for the past year and a half. He made me swear I'd never tell anyone…until the time was right. I think that time is now. I think Jacob is sitting there pissed off we haven't figured out that *he* is still part of our team."

Bailey leaned forward. "You think Jacob *knew* he was going to die?"

"Yes." That curt answer came from me. "I'm pretty sure he did." I relayed the conversation I had had with Jacob the day Bailey and I went looking for herbs. When I finished, Zack had tears in his eyes. "Jacob may not have known it was his time, but he knew something was up. He gave me the same speech about seven months ago." He shook his head. "I just thought he was getting all soft on me."

I nodded. "I'm pretty sure he knew. He and Bishop both knew."

"That's why he was seeing someone. He was trying to figure out whatever it is we need him to do."

"He wants us to *do* something," Bailey added. "The poor schmuck is hovering around in the land of the dead waiting for us to figure it out? Well, we figured it out, so let's get a God-damned necro here!"

Tip turned to me. "Can you get ahold of Rupert?"

Rupert was one of the best in the business, but he was back in California.

"Here." Dani handed me her vidbook. Rupert had fallen in love with the computer the first time it saved our hides. As a result, Dani had one made especially for him so he could keep track of stock quotes, horse races, the Americas Cup, all the little hobbies of the ultrarich. He never left home without the thing. I could only hope that was still the case.

It was.

He answered on the first ring, his healthy head of white hair, à la Phil Donahue, coming first into view followed by the bluest eyes I'd ever seen. Sporting a perennial tan from being on the bay all the time, he had aged well for a man who regularly spoke to spirits from the deck of his yacht.

"If it isn't my favorite reporter. How the hell are you, Echo?" Rupert's grin was infectious, and I could only wish I didn't look as worn and harried as I felt.

"I've been better, Rupert. I need your help again, I'm afraid."

"This must be about Melika's disappearance. Everyone is talking about it."

"Everyone?"

He chuckled. "All the dead folks. They take a vested interest, you know?"

"That's exactly why I need you."

"Darlin' the last time I helped you with a story, it cost me twenty-two grand to repair my yacht. You're an expensive date, Echo Branson, but you're also stinkin' cute. What can I do for you this time?"

"My friend, Jacob Marley, was killed yesterday. I…need to contact him."

Rupert blinked several times. "You want me to contact Jacob Marley? It's not as easy as it…" He stopped and tilted his head. "Uh…looks like you won't have to go very far." Rupert turned from the screen and muttered something at the wall.

"He's *there*?"

"Oh yeah, he's here. And he doesn't seem very happy."

I felt Zack get closer to me so he could see the screen. "Now? He's with you right now?"

"Hang on, hang on." Rupert returned his attention to the screen. "To be honest, someone's been rapping their spiritual knuckles on the door of my psyche for the last twenty-something hours, but that's not uncommon in the world of a necro, as you know. I've just been a little preoccupied with this one female spirit who refuses to do anything more than stay in her home and scare the crap out of everyone, so I apologize for not realizing who it was trying to contact me." Rupert turned once again. "Yes, yes, Jacob, I'm sure there's urgent business to attend to." He looked back at us. "I swear to God, the dead are in more of a hurry than the living. Okay…tell me what's going on. He's jabbering on like a parrot on speed."

When Rupert paused to listen to more of Jacob's ranting, Zack whispered in my ear. "Necromancers unnerve me."

Danica, who was listening to him, said, "I find it totally bizarre you people freak each other out. You're *all* screwed up."

"Don't go getting your hopes up that Jacob Marley can help. This could be nothing." Tip offered up.

"Oh, no, Tip," Rupert said evenly. "This is a lot more than nothing." Rupert paused again before chuckling. "I know." To us he said, "First off, he wants Zack to know that he's pissed as hell it took you so long to figure it out. If he would have known how dim you were, he'd have drawn you a map."

Zack grinned. "Tell him I was too busy grieving over his lame ass dead body."

Rupert relayed the message, then listened again. "He said there's no time for that. He wants to explain everything to me and I'll get right back to you. Don't go anywhere."

The vidbook signed off and we all just stared at it.

"Well, that's just fucking weird," Danica said. "So Jacob's been, like, busting Rupert's balls, but Rupert ignored him all this time? Why is that?"

"You have no idea how many of the dead seek out the necromancers in this world. Some have unfinished business, some don't believe they're dead. If Rupert answered every spirit who came knocking, he wouldn't have any time for his own life."

Danica shook her head. "Like I said…"

"I can't even believe Bishop showed him his death. It's so unlike her, you know? She *never* shows death."

"I think," I began, turning to face Zack. "She couldn't really help us with *this* without showing him *that*."

"Echo is right. Bishop is all about protecting us…caring for the future. My guess is she figured Jacob didn't have to die in vain…that his death could actually mean something."

Bailey shook her head. "Meddling in the future? That's just not like her."

Tip looked at me. "Not unless she saw something else."

"Like the death of her daughter?" I finished for her. "That would certainly make breaking the cardinal rule easier."

"Whoa. Hold on a sec, will you?" Danica demanded. "For those of us who take the short bus, are you saying she *knew* he was going to die and so she prepared him for what's coming down the chute where Mel is concerned?"

Zack shrugged. "It's one explanation."

The vidbook vibrated in Danica's hand. "Well, boys and

girls, we're about to find out." Flipping it open, Danica smiled at Rupert. "Did ET phone home?"

Rupert did not find her amusing. "His first words were, *what in the hell took them so long?* If that answers your question. Seems Jacob has just been hovering around waiting for you."

"It wouldn't have taken so long if he'd have just told us before he—"

Rupert held a hand up to stop Zack. "He said you'd say that. The last thing he promised Bishop was he wouldn't tell any of you he was going to die. As for the future, and Bishop and Melika, he said her vision wasn't clear. Just that something ominous was going to happen and he needed to be prepared." Rupert looked down at his notes. "Apparently, Bishop wasn't sure if what she saw had anything to do with Katrina or not. She just knew when all was said and done, Jacob wasn't going to be with you, but he would still be needed. She told him where to go for the training he would need. You see, the newly dead have these sort of way stations they need to go through before they can actually contact the living. Your Jacob Marley seems to have found some way to circumvent those."

Zack clapped his hands together. "All right! Now *that's* what I'm talking about!"

"Can't you just tell us if Melika is dead or not?" Tip asked tersely.

"He said you would be impatient. No. She's not dead, but that's not why you need him." Rupert turned to the wall once more and listened. "Yes, yes, she is." With a slight smile, Rupert continued. "He's asked you all to suspend your comments until I am through. Time is not on our side." Rupert nodded again. "When Bishop saw what she saw, she started working with Jacob, but not in the ways you might imagine. Jacob, as you know, is an unwilling necromancer. He preferred not to engage with the many spirits appearing to him on a daily basis. Can't say I blame the boy. Their presence is a persistent state of being for our kind. He would rather not be in this position, but Bishop summoned him and he came."

"Of course he did. It's what we do."

"Apparently, there's...something else you do as well."

Rupert rubbed his face. "There is no easy way to tell you this except to just come out with it: Bishop taught Jacob the power of possession."

We said nothing. What was there to say? For one being to actually possess the mind or body of another was the stuff of urban legends even in our supernatural world. It wasn't something we did, were taught, or even gave any thought to. You just didn't. Naturals were not to be made puppets just because we could.

But then, Jacob was no longer human, natural or otherwise.

"Yeah, I was pretty amazed when he told me too. Possession isn't…well…you all know our position on that score. At the time of their training, Bishop could not tell him who it was, exactly, that he would need to possess, only that it was a skill he needed to learn. He worked on it tirelessly, knowing there would come that day when he would have to die in order for him to exercise the knowledge he'd gained. That day is now, I'm afraid, and his target—"

"Melika…" I murmured.

"Yes. If Jacob can possess her, even for a few seconds, he can take a look around and see where it is Malecon is holding her. If she is unconscious or sedated, there's a good possibility he'll be able to get in, get the information you need, and get out. It's a long shot, but Jacob thinks he can do it."

"And you say he knows what he's doing?"

Rupert nodded. "Possession is a little like the first time you try to control a marionette puppet. The wires get all tangled and the puppet usually crashes to the floor, so in all likelihood, Jacob could hurt Melika if he did anything more than see what she sees. It takes a lot of practice to work an unfamiliar body. Whoever was training him gave him a thirty-second window. Jacob will possess her, find out where she is, tell me, I'll call you, and hopefully, we can get Melika and end this mess."

Tip looked at me. "Malecon is here, in the bayou."

"Then I suggest," Rupert interjected, "that we let Jacob do what he needs to do and then get back to you."

"Fine."

"There is one thing, however. Jacob is a…shall we call him a virgin in this dark art? We have no way of knowing how the actual possession might affect him even as a spirit. They are not invulnerable, you know?"

Danica shook her head. "No, we don't know." She looked at me. "At least I don't."

Rupert leaned forward. "Spirits can do a lot of the same things the living can. They get lost, they become dizzy or disoriented, they wander off to places and never return. I, personally, have only dealt with possessions from this side of the great divide. I have no idea how it will affect Jacob, if at all. So…if there's something you need to tell him…something you'd like him to know, now is the time, because I can't guarantee we'll ever hear from him again."

"You mean it might not work?"

"Precisely. Not only might it not work, but Jacob could wind up in some other alternate state. It's just an unknown area even to necromancers. We call it death after death."

Danica turned and handed the vidbook to Zack. "Go for it."

Gently taking the vidbook, Zack peered into the screen, his eyes welling up once more. "Tell him…tell him I can't believe he didn't give us the chance to say goodbye. Tell him…we really miss him. Tell him…I'll find him on the other side when it's my turn to join him. And…thank you, Rupert, for giving me the chance to say goodbye. It…it means a lot." Handing the vidbook back to Danica, Zack turned away.

"All right then. I'll be in touch." The vidbook went silent. So did we.

When someone finally spoke up, it was Danica. "Wow. Possession, huh? You mean, like *The Exorcist*? I thought I'd seen it all hanging out with you guys, but this…this takes the cake."

Tip nodded. "Here's the short version while we wait for Rupert. There are several kinds of possession. The church has priests whose sole occupation is to cast out demonic possessions. This is obviously not that."

"Whoa, whoa, wait a second."

"No, Danica, those exorcisms don't work. The church, with

all of its crosses and holy water, is full of crap when it comes to exorcizing a spirit. None of that works. Ever."

Danica shook her head. "You guys are getting creepier by the second."

"There are possessions that a handful of supers can do while still alive. Most of them are sequestered away from the population as being too unstable. There are possessions where—"

I reached out to touch Tip's wrist. "She doesn't need a history lesson, Tip." I looked down at my watch. "Any chance you think Mel is with Malecon?"

Tip shook her head. "He's put her somewhere; somewhere safe. He knows we're gunning for him. He won't put her in the line of fire."

"What about the interview?" Bailey asked. "Did he make it there?"

Taking the vidbook, I opened a different window and called Wes. I got his secretary.

"Echo! Good to hear from you. Your first two installments are outstanding. We're getting great feedback."

"Thanks. Is Wes around?"

"No, but he did leave a message for you. He said something happened to your eight o'clock interview. Oh…here it is. Yes. The man, Mal something, gave the interview over the phone. Nothing Sandy tried could get him to come in. He's sorry."

"Thank you." Closing the window, I handed the vidbook back to Danica. "Damn it."

"That means he's out here."

"That means," I said, shaking my head. "That it's the other way around: *he* is gunning for *us*."

The vidbook started vibrating less than five minutes after Rupert had signed off. I didn't know if this was a good thing or not.

"Well?" Danica said, when she opened the window up.

Rupert looked grim. "Jacob was able to get inside Melika's

head all right, but it was almost too brief a moment and he wasn't sure he saw what he saw. He said it didn't really make any sense to him." Rupert consulted his notes. "He said there is an alley near the Superdome where five dead elderly are parked in wheelchairs. Each of them has a name pinned to them and there's a plastic binder of some sort in the lap of one of them. He thinks he saw all of this from the window of a small room right beyond them." Rupert's eyes looked sad. "It was a little more than Jacob could take, I'm afraid."

"At least she's still alive."

He nodded. "But for how long is anyone's guess. According to Jacob, Malecon has injected her with something that's making her heartbeat slow way down, and she's clammy all over. Jacob said it felt like she was weakening every second he was in her."

"That's his insurance," Tip growled. "That way, Melika makes a better pawn."

"Pawn? For what?"

"For us," I answered. "She's his escape route. If everything goes wrong, he can still pull that ace out knowing we will acquiesce to whatever he wants as long as she remains unharmed. That's why she's still alive."

"One last thing," Rupert jumped in. "Jacob thinks there's a guard of some sort posted at the door. He couldn't be sure, being as new as he is to the task of possession. He just thinks Melika is in a bad way, so you must hurry." Rupert held up a pencil sketch of where Jacob had told him Melika was being held. "Here's my rendition of what Jacob told me. I hope it makes some sense to you."

Tip leaned over and studied the drawing. "I know where that is."

Rupert nodded. "He said you would. He also said…and he's not sure, mind you, that he thinks she may have or is going to have a heart attack. You mustn't delay in getting to her. Time is of the essence."

Bailey turned to me and nodded. It was time to stop talking and act. "Thank you so much, Rupert."

"Let me know if you need me…er…us. Apparently, we're a team now." Rupert forced a grin and signed off.

"We'll never get to her in time," Tip said.

"What about The Others?"

She shook her head. "The closest ones live in Baton Rouge, and the second string is being briefed there. Even Rose and Lily have returned home. What we need—"

"Is Finn," I said calmly.

Everyone turned.

"Hear me out."

"Wait." Bailey took Danica's hand. "She need not hear this. Her shields are down. Malecon doesn't need to know everything we know. Not yet."

Danica nodded and walked far enough away that she couldn't hear us.

"You want Finn to help?" Tip asked.

I nodded. "She's been working near the Superdome every day since she got here. She can get to Melika now and get her to medical attention as a cop faster than anyone else, including a super."

Tip nodded. "Make the call."

"She doesn't know the area."

"She doesn't need to. She's working with NOLA PD. They'll take her where she needs to go." I took the vidbook and pressed the *phone only* button. Finn was on the other end before the first ring had finished.

"Where are you?" she asked. "I've been worried sick about you."

"Long story."

"Yeah, I've got a few of those coming my way. What's up?"

I could hear Tip's instructions in my head and I repeated those verbatim to Finn, who looked tired. "There's an elderly Haitian woman, about sixty years old, long black hair, in a wheelchair in a storeroom at the back alley on the east side of the Superdome. I need you to go get her and get her medical attention as soon as possible. She may have already had a heart attack and is probably wearing a toe tag or something like it."

"Wait. Where are *you*?"

"Doesn't matter. Please. This really *is* a life-and-death one, Finn. She's…she's like my mother. I need—" Tears filled my eyes as I choked up.

"Say no more. I'll grab a bunch of guys and get to her ASAP."

"One more thing. There could be a guy guarding her…so be careful."

"I don't want to know how you know all this, do I?"

"No. Not right now."

"Fine. Look, I'm gonna put on one of the NOLA cops so you can give directions. Tell him where to go and what you need, and we'll be there in a heartbeat."

I wanted to cry. There was hope after all. I handed the vidbook to Tip, who gave the cop precise directions as to where to find her, and when she finished, waved Danica back over and handed her the vidbook. Danica slipped it back into my fanny pack. "Looks like we have reason to be glad your girlfriend came to town."

"She's not my—"

"Shh." Bailey's voice silenced us. No one said a word or moved until she whispered to Danica, "Your shields are down, right?"

Danica nodded. "Yep, and if that little tickling at the base of my skull isn't our boy, then someone is flirting with me."

"Excellent."

Her shields down meant Malecon could find her easily.

"I can sense the discomfort of the animals along the river," Bailey said. "Even they have a sense of foreboding about Malecon's presence. He's here."

I turned to Danica. "You don't have to do this, you know."

"Actually, Clark, I do. Let's put this guy to bed so we can get back to helping those who really need it."

I smiled warmly at her. "Thank you, Dani."

"Hey, thank me later when you buy me a Hurricane at the only bar in town that's still standing. I don't do goodbyes, Clark, so don't start now. Let's kill the goddamned megalomaniac. I'm tired of running around this swamp."

"What do you want me to do?"

"Run. Get halfway between our boat and theirs, but keep your eyes on their boat," Tip simply said. "We'll spread out around you, close enough for us to be able to take him down.

That's crucial." Then, to Bones, she said, "Take the boat somewhere he won't be able to find you. Don't go far, but far enough he doesn't run the risk of seeing you. Echo, you need to stay with the boat. Bailey?"

"I'm working on it."

Danica turned to me. "Malecon can't…you know…do what she does, can he?"

I shrugged. "Honestly? I have no idea."

"Then you're gonna see one fast black chick trucking through this swamp." Danica turned to Tip. "I'm trusting you to make sure I don't get eaten."

Tip nodded. "I know I speak for us all when I say thank you for this."

"You know where to find me if you lose me."

"We won't lose you."

Danica turned to me and for the first time in our friendship, I felt fear from her. "Don't leave me hanging, Clark."

"Never."

"Here goes nothing." Wheeling around, Danica sprinted away from us. "Just don't leave me hanging!"

"Hear dat?" Bones asked as we all watched Danica run.

I listened, but heard nothing.

"More dan one boat come. Get in!"

Scrambling, Zack, Bailey and Cinder were barely in when Bones started the boat and gave it full throttle. I have no idea how Tip got on board, as Bailey's knee rammed into my back, my foot hit Zack's butt, and all three of us rolled against the back of the boat as Bones hit the gas again.

"Go! Go! Go!" Tip yelled, hanging on to the silver railing. "And don't lose sight of her!"

When I was finally able to right myself and look up, Bones was taking us into a very shallow part of the river; a place where no one but a very skilled bayou boatman would ever dare take a boat.

"He brought backup!" Zack yelled above the engine. "The bastard brought backup!"

Tip locked eyes with me. So far, nothing had gone our way. Nothing. And now, I had left my best friend powerless against a man who would have, and might have killed his own mother.

"Tip—" My voice was thin and weak.

"Don't worry. We're not going to leave her on her own." Tip scanned the swamp and nodded when her eyes caught Danica's still running form.

"Here!" Tip ordered. "Stop here!"

Bones pushed the throttle up and we chugged to the side. "Der are only two boats commen from dat direction." Bones pointed to the west. If Danica kept running, she would run right into them.

"Shit!" Zack yelled, jumping out of the boat and landing with a splat on the ground. "I'm going after her."

"No," Tip said. "She's still got to lure them into thinking she's the only one left."

I didn't want to, but I had to agree. "We've got no other choice. Once Mel comes to, Malecon will know, and he'll go back after her. We have to end this here and now."

"Let's take care of one boat at a time," Zack said.

Tip nodded. "Echo, can you pick anything up from them?"

I closed my eyes and concentrated, but felt nothing. "Too far away."

"Dey commen close now. Look." Bones pointed into the shallows about two hundred yards away from us. We were well hidden among the trees, and there was a straight shot between us; the only problem was Dani was in the middle, slowing down as she picked her way through the muck, but it was clear by their movements they had spotted her. Cutting their engines, they drifted to the bank about seventy-five yards from Danica, who had stopped running, when the engines were cut and leaned over, hands on knees.

"*What now?*" Danica thought.

"*Don't move any closer. They've already spotted you.*"

"*Joy. Is my cavalry on its way?*"

"*You betcha.*" Suddenly, I got an image, a short flash that turned my blood cold. "They have rifles."

"Damn it," Zack said. "How many?"

"Two men, two rifles," Tip said.

Zack turned to run, but Tip jumped out and was at his side. "Not yet. You want to get us all killed?"

"As opposed to the only one of us incapable of defense? They'll pick her off like a sitting duck."

I, too, was out of the boat, with Cinder right behind. Only Bailey stood motionless, her hands at her side, her eyes closed.

I looked over at Cinder, whose hands were beginning to get that glow that said fireballs were on their way. Kneeling down, I took her face in my hands. "Do *not* start firing away, Cinder. No matter what happens this time, you must have self-control. Danica *needs* you to follow the rules this time. Do you understand?"

Cinder stared hard into my face and nodded slowly.

"Wait." It was Bailey. "Those rifles are different. Yeah." She nodded and closed her eyes again. "They're…tranquilizer guns?" Opening her eyes, she cocked her head sideways. "That doesn't seem right. Why would they want Danica alive?"

Tip and Zack stared at her.

"What?" she asked, shrugging. "What good is it to have shamanic powers if you can't tap into an eagle or hawk every now and then? I *saw* tranquilizer guns. I've dealt with enough animals at the zoo to know what a tranq gun looks like, and that's what they're holding."

"He wants her alive." I shook my head. "What could he possibly want from her?"

"Collateral." Tip said the word so softly, I barely caught it. "He doesn't trust that we're dead. If he gets her, he practically guarantees we'll back off and do whatever he wants. If he has both Melika and Danica, he knows he owns us."

"If Malecon isn't on *that* boat, that means he's more than likely on the other. We have to be able to get to these two men before they can warn him. We have to take them out silently and swiftly. Malecon wants her alive. Let's keep it that way." Tip knelt beside me, creating a pool the muck flowed into. "They'll shoot her the moment they see her. You know that, don't you?"

I nodded and swallowed the lump in my throat. "Just make sure that's all they do. Death, Danica can handle. Being… sexually assaulted would destroy her completely."

"I won't let that happen, kiddo. I promise."

Oh, if only Tip's promises meant anything.

From our place in the shallows, I was pretty sure the other boat could not see us, but that didn't make this any easier on me. Knowing I had just sent my best friend toward the enemy was like a dagger in my heart, and I felt awful for having agreed to it.

"They've got tranquilizer guns, Dani."

"Oh goody. So, what do you want me to do?"

"Stay where you are and wave your hands to get their attention. You need to act like you believe you're going to be saved."

"I sure as hell better be. Just answer me this…do those darts hurt?"

"I have no idea."

"You should have lied and assured me they don't."

"I've never lied to you."

"Start now."

"Okay. No they don't."

"Then one last question: are we going to get out of this alive?"

"Yes."

"Is that a lie?"

I grinned. Even in danger, she was a fresh mouth. *"Have I ever let you down?"*

"No."

"Then I won't start now. See you in a few."

I shielded my eyes from the sun and held my breath as Danica started waving her hands, signaling to the boat.

"It's a good plan," Bailey whispered softly, as we carefully made our way through the brush and closer to Danica. "You're a good leader. You may not believe it, and you might not think you're ready for it, but it's true. Trust your instincts, Echo. You're spot on."

Trust my instincts? That was easier said than done. So far, it didn't feel as if I had done anything right. So far, I'd left the woman I was dating to pick up after the grisly aftermath of one of Cinder's supernovas, I'd watched one of my best friends die, and I'd sent the other into the jaws of the beast chasing us.

Trust *my* instincts?

If I were Bailey, I'd run as far and as fast away from me as she could. "Bailey..." Before I could finish, there came a soft thwupping sound followed by a slight grunt from Danica. "*You lied, Clark. It stings like a son of a...*"

If my heart ached before, it was surely breaking now as Danica looked down at her thigh and slowly pulled out a yellow feathered dart. "*Fuckin' A, Clark...*" And then she went down on her knees. I could feel her struggling to fight off the effects of whatever drug was coursing through her.

From our place behind the trees, Bailey, Cinder and I watched as one of the two men leapt from the boat and carefully picked his way toward Danica's now still form. Malecon was definitely not in this boat, but that didn't make it any easier to just stand there and watch as my best friend lay helpless.

To my left, Cinder waited, palms open at her side facing Danica. She could create a fireball as quickly as I could make a fist, and I hoped she wouldn't have to.

"Easy, Cinder," Bailey whispered as the three of us watched the shooter climb out of the boat and look around. His weapon hung loosely from his shoulder, and he reached into his belt and pulled out a handgun. I felt his trepidation and nerves. He was unfamiliar with the bayou. They could never have found Danica on their own unless someone other than Malecon knew the way.

"They're not supers," I whispered to Bailey.

"I know."

Cinder looked up at me and I shook my head. "*Not until I tell you.*" I turned my attention back to Danica and sucked in my breath. The shooter was looking everywhere, sweeping left and right with his gun. He wasn't just afraid, he was terrified that a gator might be near; so near, in fact, he never even glanced ahead in our direction.

When he reached Danica, he pushed her with the toe of his boot. She did not budge. He tried a little harder, and still, nothing. Jamming his gun into the belt of his pants, he knelt down and rolled her over. That was when every alarm I had started ringing loudly in my head. When he ran his hand over her breast, it took everything I had not to tell Cinder to blast him.

"Fucker," Bailey murmured.

Apparently, the driver thought the same thing, because he started yelling and gesturing for the man to knock it off and get a move on; which he did. Slinging Danica over his shoulder like a sack of potatoes, he started slogging his way back to the boat. Danica is not a petite six foot gal by any means, and he really struggled beneath her weight to maintain his balance.

As he worked to keep his footing, he did not see Tip and Zack in the water behind the now driverless boat. Tip had pulled the driver out of the boat so quickly, he barely made a splash. I did not see what she had done with the driver, but I had a good idea the swamp was the last thing that man would ever see.

When the shooter was about twenty feet from the boat, Tip came around the back of it, and with nothing but a thought, brought the man sinking to his knees. As he was getting ready to drop Danica, Zack used his powers to keep her steady until he could get close enough to grab her.

"Thank God," I murmured.

The three of us waited until Tip whistled before we came out. *"Only two."*

Cinder ran ahead of us, but Bailey and I scouted around to make sure everything was still safe.

With Danica safely in Zack's arms, and the shooter now laying face down with blood coming from his ears, the six of us made our way back to Bones' boat, which had just pulled alongside the speedboat.

"She be good here," Bones said, laying a life jacket down for Danica's head. "Bones don't let nuddin near her, Miss Echo."

I smiled and thanked him. "Nonetheless, she's done her bit for us, and we'll not use her again, so I'm leaving Cinder with you."

I knelt down and took Cinder's hands. "Protect Danica and Bones at all costs, okay? That means don't hesitate, don't wonder if you'll get in trouble. Just do it."

She nodded, her eyes on fire.

"Good. Let's finish this," I said to Tip.

As we left the boat and headed back to the speedboat, Bailey turned to me. "You know she'll blast anything that gets close, right? She's pretty fond of your friend."

I glanced over my shoulder at Bones and Cinder. "So am I. That's why I left her."

Bailey nodded. "Well, I'm up."

Leaving us, Bailey headed inland, walking unafraid among the wild, her gaze sweeping back and forth along the ground. It surprised me that I not only liked her, I respected her tremendous ability.

As Tip, Zack and I approached the boat, I stepped over the shooter and pulled the gun from his belt. "He looks dead," I said, knowing he wasn't. Dead people have no emotional energy.

Tip nodded. "In five minutes, he'll wish he was." Picking him up, Tip ripped the shooter's belt from his pants and secured his hands behind his back. Picking him up under his armpits, Tip and Zack dragged him to the boat and heaved him in.

After helping me into the now crowded boat, I watched as Tip splashed water on the shooter's face. "Wake up, asshole."

The Creole sputtered and let the expletives fly until an invisible force slapped his face. His eyes grew wide as he looked around to see who had hit him.

"Let's see if this bad boy can't loosen his tongue," Bailey said, appearing as if from thin air. I used to think there was no one better at creeping around than the Big Indian, but I'd have to say that Bailey gave her a run for her money.

"Oh shit," I said, backing away from her so fast, I nearly fell out of the boat.

Wrapped around her neck was an enormous black and gray snake. It was a million miles long and looked pissed as all hell.

Tip and Zack both gave her a wide berth as she climbed the ladder into the boat. "Keep that thing away from me," Zack said, backing as far away as the small boat would allow.

Bailey grinned. "Be nice and maybe I will." Kneeling in front of the shooter, Bailey looked at Zack and nodded. Suddenly, the shooter's head appeared as if it were being held in an invisible vise. His eyes were frantic as he struggled against Zack's unseen force.

"Don't even think about yelling," Bailey purred as the snake slithered from her neck to her forearm. "Yell and he gets you. Swear, and he gets you. Move, and he gets you. Get it? Do anything other than what I tell you, and you'll be seeing this snake from the inside. Understand?" She smiled a smile that sent chills through the marrow of my bones, and at that moment I wasn't sure who the shooter feared more; her or the snake now coiled around her arm like a bracelet.

"Okay, we're all tired, wet and ready for this nightmare to be over. My friend here is a western cottonmouth, the most poisonous snake in North America. It is incredibly toxic, and when it bites you, the death is not a smooth one. So, I'm going to ask you one question at a time. Think really hard before answering because the first time you lie to me is the last breath you'll take. Are we clear so far?"

His eyes were enormous and he tried nodding.

"I'll take that as a yes. Now, remember, the truth will set you free. A lie will set my friend here free. It's your call." Bailey looked at him and then to me. I nodded. He would tell her what we wanted to know without much problem.

"Question number one: where is Malecon?"

The shooter tried to see out of the far corner of his eyes, but since his head was unmoving, he didn't get far. "In de udder boat. At de end of de river. He wade for us to bring de girl."

I stepped next to Bailey, who seemed to be holding the snake in check, but for how long, I had no idea. I hated snakes. All of them. But I hated the snake who shot my best friend more than all the others put together. "What does he want with her?"

"He…he mentioned a trade."

We all stared at each other. Now *that* was unexpected. "For whom?"

He tried to shrug. "I'm just de hired mon. So…" His eyes looked frantically around for the driver. "Where is de udder?"

"Worry about yourself for now. You have no idea who he wanted to exchange her for?"

Again, he tried shaking his head.

I looked over at Tip. "*Who else does he want? Bishop?*"

"*He thinks he has Melika, so he wouldn't be trading for her. He must want Bishop as well.*"

Bailey rose. "We need anything else from this hoodlum?"

I looked at Tip, who shook her head. "We have Dani. Bishop is safe, and Mel will be shortly. The only thing we have to do now is take Malecon out."

"Home turf," Zack announced out of nowhere. "The bastard is going to have to confront us on our home turf."

I watched as Bailey released the snake into the water and it sidewinded away. "We can leave him out here. They won't let him make a move until it gets dark."

Tip nodded. "Strip him down. I don't want him to have anything he could use to signal Malecon with." At the name, a cell phone vibrated itself across the deck of the boat. I reached down and grabbed it.

"You tell him you have the girl. That's it. If you can do that, we'll let you live. If you say anything else other than that, she'll haul that snake right back into this boat. *Capische*?"

"Yes."

I flipped the phone open and held it to his ear. He said, "I have de girl." And then I threw the phone into the river. "Good choice."

Tip started the engine as Zack and Bailey undressed the shooter. "Trade Dani for Bishop?" I asked softly.

He nodded. "I know. Leaves one to wonder why he didn't trade Mel for her. Could he really be so evil as to want both his mother and sister dead?"

Tip just looked at me out of the corner of his eye. "Here comes Bones."

Bones pulled alongside the speedboat. "Der's a buzzin' commen from Miss Danica."

Cinder was holding the buzzing vidbook and handed it to me as soon as Bones could bring us close enough.

Seeing it was just the phone, I pressed phone only and held it to my ear.

It was Finn.

"Got to her in the nick of time," she said above the din in

the background. "They're running tests on her, and are pretty sure she was poisoned or drugged. They just don't know with what, but they think we got to her in time."

I had to really work hard to maintain my calm and composure. "Honestly?"

"I wish I could tell you more, but we'll have to wait until they've finished the tests. Are you on your way?"

I so wished I could tell her the truth. "We're working on it."

"Echo, I wish you'd let me in. Let me help."

"Oh, Finn, you have been more help than you could ever imagine. I can't begin to thank you enough for saving Melika."

"Saving her from whom? What's going on?"

This was one of those pinnacle moments that define a relationship. Did I have the right to pull her any further into my own personal madness or did I push her away to keep not only her safe, but my secrets safe as well?

The choice didn't really exist.

"Thank you. That's all I can say right now, is thank you."

"I'll call if anything changes with your friend."

My eyes teared up. "I have to go."

"Echo…"

But I had hung up and was facing Tip, who already knew by my reaction that our mentor was still alive. "Poison or drugs. She'll let us know when she's out of the woods." Placing the vidbook back in the watertight section of my fanny pack, I sighed with relief.

Tip nodded gravely. "Then it's time." To Bones she said, "Stay here, Bones. We're going to take this boat and finish this once and for all."

Zack and Bailey had just released the naked shooter and told him to stay where he was. "If you're still there when we get back, guess what? We'll even give you a ride back into town. If you've decided against that option, then you're on your own here in the swamp without clothes or a weapon. It's entirely up to you."

The Creole swore in the language most of us had a rudimentary knowledge of, but who could blame him?

"We're taking this goddamned boat right at him," Tip growled, grabbing the wheel. "Hang onto something. Bones, no matter what, you get those two to safety."

He nodded and stood more erect. "Der safe wid me."

Cinder came to the edge of Bones boat and I went to the edge of ours. "You know what to do," I said softly.

She nodded and held out the palm of her hand. In it was a fireball that suddenly took the shape of a man. The flaming man stood there a moment before she crushed it in her tiny fist.

"That's right. No mercy. If he gets past us…"

Cinder shook her head. *"He won't."*

I grinned, wishing I had a child's faith. "You're right. See you in a little bit."

As we pulled away, I couldn't look back.

"You're doing the right thing, Echo. Dani and Bones need protection and—"

"And this isn't her battle to fight," Zack added.

"Slow down," I ordered, seeing Bailey wincing at some power I could not see nor hear.

Tip cut the engines by half.

"What is it?" I asked.

"He's waiting on the shore at the mouth of the river."

"Waiting?"

She nodded. "They seem to think he's…afraid."

"Afraid?" Zack asked.

And that was when I knew. I should have known all along, but it never dawned on me…never occurred to me. "Oh my God, Malecon is afraid of the bayou. That's why he sent his flunkies out to do a job he could easily have done anywhere else. Think about it: Dani's a city girl wandering in the swamp. How much larger a target could she have been, but still, he didn't finish the job. There's only one reason, and that's fear."

"What's he afraid of?" Zack asked.

I looked over at Bailey, who grinned and said, "He has very little power here."

I nodded, feeling my hopes rise. "The bayou is full of life. Strong, pulsing, vibrant, verdant life. There's no chaos, no turmoil."

Tip was nodding. "You're right. The bayou is all about life and peacefulness, nature at its finest."

"And that means he has nothing to draw on. He's going to have to conserve his energy if he stands a chance at taking all of us on."

"And he thinks we're dead. He's not ready for what's in this boat."

The four of us nodded. It was just the opening we needed. "He made a mistake coming here. He made a mistake thinking we're dead. He's finally making mistakes."

"He won't be alone," Bailey said. "He'll have at least one other with him."

Zack nodded. "This is my turn, Tip."

Tip started to argue. "Are you kidding me?"

I stepped in between them, recognizing, for the first time, my true destiny. "That's enough. Zack's right, Tip. This is his turn. You take out anyone closest to the back of the boat. They won't have shields, so you should be able to disable one or two rather quickly. I'll take anyone toward the front of the boat, maybe force them into the water. Zack's powers need to bind Malecon as best he can until all of us can focus our powers on him. Once any crew are out of the game, we give Malecon everything we've got. He can't possibly be strong enough to keep the three of us out."

Tip blinked several times before nodding. "Fine. I've got the back." Tip did not look at me as she pushed the throttle down. "But we're going straight at him, kiddo, so you better work on getting some shields up in a hurry."

As we rounded a corner that nearly tossed us all out of the boat, I looked up to find Malecon looking at us through a pair of binoculars. With a wave of his free hand, he sent a wall of water at our starboard side that hit us with such ferocity, Bailey and I fell back against the back of the boat.

"Hold on!" Tip yelled, struggling with the boat. Without my shield, and with Zack desperately trying to hang on, we took gunshots to the port and forward bow of the boat. Zack threw a force field out, but Malecon counteracted it with another wave of his hand. He may have been able to stop Zack's wall, but he couldn't take us both on, so I forced a wall of energy toward the shooter on the right, knocking him into the water.

"Now!" I yelled as we sped by Malecon and his crew. Zack came right back at the second shooter just as Malecon tried to halt the force of my energy shield. The second shooter plunged into the water as well, but not before Malecon sent another wave at our side, knocking Bailey out of the boat.

"Bailey!" I cried, and started after her.

Tip grabbed me and threw me at the wheel moments before diving into the water after her. With the wheel in my hands, I slowed the boat down, made a slow U-turn, and tried to use the boat for protective cover around the area Tip and Bailey went in.

"Echo!" Zack yelled, but he was too late. The bolt of energy Malecon threw at us knocked us out of our boat.

I watched our speedboat carom under the pier and smash into the shore, running aground on the sand. Neither Tip nor Bailey were anywhere in sight. "Tip!"

Neither Tip nor Bailey were anywhere in sight. "Tip!"

A thwupping sound landed near me and I realized I was being shot at. Going back under, I swam toward the cement pier which was about fifty yards from where Malecon stood.

"Stay under," Tip ordered.

"I can't." River water in the south is murky at best; you can't see anything right in front of your face. But after a hurricane, it takes days for the silt to settle back down to the bottom. Even with my eyes open and the sun out, I was swimming in virtual darkness. *"I didn't get a good breath and I can't see for shit!"*

"Fine. I'll count to three, we both come out of the water and hit whoever's got a gun. Take a good breath and get back down."

"How many are there?"

"Three plus Malecon. Ready? One…two…three."

Thrusting with all my might, I propelled out of the water and directed my shield toward the gunman closest to me. As I pushed out, I saw Tip and Zack doing the same, and the gunman would have fallen off the boat had Malecon not intervened and grabbed him.

Inhaling a deep breath, I went back down in the water and continued to make my way toward the only structure that could stop a bullet. It was one of the hardest, scariest moments of my life as I could hear the patter of bullets as they kerplunked into the water around me.

When they paused for a moment, a hand reached out and plucked me from the water. It was Zack, and he was pushing me toward the small clutch of trees about half a football field away from where Malecon stood.

"There," Malecon waved, pointing toward us. The gunman raised his rifle and pelted the trees around us. The sound of bullets thudding into trees is one I shall never forget.

"Where are they?" I asked.

"Can't find them. I only found you because I saw you come out of the water." More bullets zinged around us. "Get down!"

I fell on my butt and pressed my back against the tree.

"Can't you find him?"

I shook my head. "Not if he's doing more than one power. No." The dirt around us flew up as the bullets sprayed everywhere. "We have to get that shooter out of the way!"

And before I could move, Tip rose out of the water like a phoenix rising. As the gunman swung his rifle around, he suddenly dropped it, grabbed his head, and fell to his knees.

"Now!" I shouted to Zack, who came around the tree running as fast as he could. I hadn't expected him to leave the safety of the trees, but when he saw Tip was completely vulnerable, I knew why Zack left. If he couldn't distract or take down the second gunman, Tip was as good as dead.

That wasn't something I was going to stand behind a tree and watch.

Following on Zack's heels, I was amazed at the sheer power of his energy. The wall of energy emanating from his outstretched hands bowled over everything that lay in his path. In three seconds, his energy reached the second gunman, knocking him into the water, and pushing Malecon off balance.

From behind Zack, I raced along the soggy edges frantically searching for Bailey, whom I had not seen surface. "Bailey!" I cried, cupping my hands to my mouth. If she answered my call,

I did not hear it, because a large rock slammed into my left shoulder, knocking me back into the surf.

Feeling like a hot sword had been thrust into my scapula, I scrambled out of the surf and back onto the bank in time to see Malecon flick his wrist, sending a boulder the size of a basketball flying toward Zack's head. Had I not resurfaced where I did, I would not have had time to deflect the stone. As it was, I was only marginally successful; instead of crushing Zack's head, it merely clipped the top of it.

He went down like the proverbial ton.

"Zack!" When I reached him, I threw a protective barrier around us in time to deflect another flurry of items telekinetically thrown at us by Malecon. I knew Tip must have engaged the first gunman because no gunfire could be heard.

"Go…" Zack whispered. He was bleeding pretty badly from his temple, and I knew the instant his consciousness left him. "…Please…"

"Leave him," Tip ordered.

Leaving Zack on the bank, I dodged a second missile by diving behind a tree. This was getting to be too much. Our energy was not endless, and I could feel Tip's weakening. Why couldn't we take down one man?

I knew I had to go back out to get Zack. Although he appeared dead, I knew he wasn't. I couldn't risk him coming to at an inopportune moment. I couldn't risk the shooter taking a free shot at him. Counting to three, I rushed out from behind the tree, but what I saw stopped me dead in my tracks.

Tip was levitating her body out of the water. She was no more than twenty feet from Malecon, who had his hands raised as if to push Tip away. Tip stood with her arms to her sides, glaring at the man before her. Energy crackled around them as both mentally pushed theirs at the other.

"Come at me Tiponi Redhawk with your petty mind games, and it will give me great pleasure to kill your little girlfriend before crushing your mind."

Did he mean me? For a moment, I was too startled to move; not just because of what I was seeing, but the fact that Malecon was going to go after *me* instead of taking Tip on. Then, with a backhanded slap, Malecon's energy ripped into Tip, knocking her off her energy and sending her plunging back into the water.

"No!" I cried, running toward the bank. I needed to get to Tip before she drowned...before... Fear coursed through me, blinding my senses, and before I knew it, I ran headfirst into a barrier of energy. Like a person walking into a sliding glass door, I hit it and bounced off, landing dazed on the wet ground.

Malecon laughed derisively.

He was enjoying this; toying with us, his earlier fear replaced by overconfidence.

"Of course I'm enjoying it, you unwanted little street urchin. Did you really think you could take me on with your mediocre skills and petty powers? Have you so little respect for my sister and mother you don't realize the full extent of *my* powers? You should have done more homework, children."

I slowly rose, my own fear replaced by something I'd only felt once in my life; cold, murderous rage. "Have *you* any respect for *them* at all?" Ignoring my aching shoulder, I stood erect and slowly started toward him. "They're your *family* for God's sake."

"Family is just a pretty synonym for cage, little one, but I wouldn't expect *you* to know that, seeing as no one but my pathetic sister ever wanted you."

I hesitated a second.

"Yes, *I've* done my homework on you all, Jane Doe, and I know more about you than you know about yourself. I expected you to at least be a worthy opponent, seeing as my sister and mother think so highly of you, but you are not even mildly interesting. You don't even know what you could have truly accomplished in this life had you lived long enough."

I was unafraid of him now. If I was going to join Jacob Marley, I would do so standing on my feet, fighting for the lives of the ones I loved.

Finding my way around the energy field, I kept walking toward him. Because of my emotional bond with Tip, I knew she was not drowned, but merely shaken up. Wherever Tip was, I needed to give her time; time I was willing to die for if need be. "I'm going to live a lot longer than you think, Malecon." Without moving a muscle, I sent an energy field at him, but he managed to shove it away like it was nothing more than wind.

"Don't make me laugh, Echo. If you were even remotely amusing, I'd let you live." He turned to one gunman trying to get to his feet. "Leave her. I'll take care of this nuisance myself."

I watched his hand move and ducked just before a piece of driftwood flew over my head. He was weakening. There wasn't enough negative energy for him to continue with this fight much longer. If I could distract his mental powers long enough to build up my own, I might stand a chance. *We* might actually make it through this.

"Melika is safe and alive," I said, rising shakily.

His poker face and calm demeanor did not kick in fast enough to hide his surprise.

"Yeah, you screwed that up too."

"You lie."

"Do I?" I felt Tip's energy reinforce, but Zack was still out cold. "We rescued her from that storeroom you had her in by the Superdome. Does that sound like a lie? You drugged her. Is that a lie? You weren't trying to kill her, but you might have. Is that a lie? Mel is safe. Bishop is safe, and all you've got to show for your lame return to real life is—"

He came at me with both hands flying and everything he had. Rocks, driftwood, dirt, branches, if it was on the ground, it was coming at me. He was giving me everything he had; that was when I knew for certain his powers were waning. He should have just knocked me back, but moving a target my size took a great deal more energy and concentration; neither of which he possessed at the moment.

I had a chance.

Concentrating on my shield, which was the only thing between me and the rocks he was hurling, I advanced slowly, waiting for it to crack. I had few reserves left and the sharp throbbing pain in my shoulder was making it difficult to hold my concentration. This was my last card to play. If Tip didn't get here soon, I was dead girl walking.

"Where. Is. She?" He shouted, stopping the barrage to hear an answer that never came. Suddenly, the boat Malecon was on tipped hard to one side as Tip hauled herself completely out of the water in one smooth motion and wrapped her arms around Malecon, slamming them both to the deck.

"Kill her!" Malecon yelled just before hitting the deck with a grunt.

The first gunman was making his way toward me, without his weapon. My defense of Malecon's missiles left my powers weakened, and before I could knock him back, he was on me in an instant, his hands around my neck. I knew right then that one of two things was going to happen: he would either kill me, or he would draw Tip away from Malecon in order to save me.

I hadn't counted on there being a third choice.

From behind the line of trees came a thunderous crashing of the underbrush that made my attacker look up. So did I, and the next thing I saw was an enormous, black, feral boar charging us. Foam dripped from its mouth as it lowered its head, his large tusk ripping into my screaming attacker who flew off me, landing with a thud, his side sliced open. He landed a good ten feet from me, blood gushing from the ugliest wound I had ever seen. Blood sprayed everywhere as I scrambled away from both man and beast.

The wild pig was on him in an instant, driven by a blood frenzy that made feral pigs one of the most dangerous creatures in the bayou. They ate everything man ate…including man. They were known to have eaten lambs or calves without leaving any physical evidence they had done so. They were vicious killers with jaws that could crush bones.

This one was eating a screaming man alive.

As I scrambled backward and away from them, a pair of hands reached down and pulled me to my feet. "Come on!" Bailey yelled, pulling me to my feet. "Don't look. Just give us a shield or something."

"Shoot it!" my attacker screamed at the other gunman, who fumbled with his rifle, unsure of where the greater danger lay: Tip as she grappled with Malecon, or the boar, who might very well charge him.

The boar's meal was screaming now, being scarfed on by the boar, red foam oozing from its mouth as it dug in.

We both ran back to the safety of the trees with me trying to construct something, anything, that would protect us. Like Malecon, I was running low on power, and having my neck in a man's vise-like grip hadn't helped.

"We have to help Tip," I said with a raspy voice.

Bailey peered out from behind the trees. "There's one more shooter still in the game."

I looked out and saw Tip struggling fiercely with Malecon. For a man his age, he was defending himself well against a woman Tip's size, and Malecon was using the last of his mental powers to drain Tip of hers.

"You get Zack," I said, seeing his head move slightly. We couldn't afford for him to come to and try to reenter the fray. He would be a sitting duck for the last shooter, who now swung his gun toward the boat, his buddy already dead from being eviscerated, his guts being consumed by the boar.

"I'll get the shooter."

Bailey took off and so did I. I imagined commandeering a wild boar had pretty much used up her energy, and if we didn't end this right now, we weren't going to be on the winning end. It was only a matter of who had the most power at the end of the battle.

As the final living gunman raised his rifle, Malecon flicked his hand at Bailey, sending her to the ground. "Shoot her!" To my horror, with one squeeze of the trigger, the gunman shot Tip, sending her reeling off the boat and back onto the bank.

"No!" I screamed, seeing her body land with a sickening thump on the damp ground below.

Something happened to me in that moment…something that would bring back to me all the words and clues and hints Melika had been dropping to me about my powers all these years. Everything she had ever said to me about me being stronger than I realized came to fruition at that moment. Seeing Tip hurt or possibly killed filled me with an energy I had never felt before. It was not the same kind of human energy field I tapped into whenever creating my shields or reading other's emotions.

No, this energy came from the darkest place in my soul.

It was like a hot flash starting in the pit of my stomach and extending outward to my limbs, like an electrical signal which had been turned on and all systems were go. Well…all but one system: my moral compass was broken, and I knew, as I ran toward him, that I was going to kill him. No hesitation, no thought, nothing but a blood lust transcending everything else. At that moment, I was no different from the boar now chowing down on the gunman's face.

I was like that feral boar, bearing down on a man who was slowly swinging his rifle toward me just as I was only a few yards away. I saw no danger, experienced no fear, I felt nothing but a burning rage and desire to end this man's life.

Stopping in my tracks, I did just that.

Putting my arms out like Jesus on the cross, I brought my hands together in a loud clap in front of me. Like a concussion grenade, the force knocked his brains around inside his skull. He dropped his rifle and sunk back into the shallows, face first in the water.

And, like the wild pig, I was on him in an instant. Grabbing his rifle, I turned it around so I was holding the muzzle, and, with the power of deep-seated darkness running through me, I crushed his skull with the butt of the rifle. It caved in like a watermelon with a thickening crunch.

I had no time to feel anything, nor am I sure I would have even if I could. Something had tapped into a corner of my soul that was ancient, powerful and menacing, and I was barely aware of myself inside this rampaging evil, and had no desire to stop it. All I wanted was blood and death, and I would have continued to smash his head in if I hadn't felt an emotion of Malecon's seep into my soul.

He was going to make a run for it.

Malecon had started his engine and had already swung the boat around so it was now facing the only avenue of escape.

I quickly flipped the rifle back around and shouldered the weapon. I had only shot a gun once in my life and that was when Finn had taken me to the gun range when I expressed my fear about the sidearm she always had with her. Unafraid, I closed one eye, took aim and fired off a round. The butt of the rifle smashed itself into a shoulder that no longer felt any pain. The only emotion in my soul was vengeance, and it was all-consuming, even as I missed.

Remembering Finn's words the first time she had taken me to the shooting range, I held my breath and this time, slowly squeezed the trigger.

I missed Malecon, who was leaping for the water, but I hit the boat's gas tank, and the ensuing explosion blew the entire thing fifty feet in the air, sending flaming boat pieces scattered around the bayou. Orange and yellow flames licked the air as black and gray smoke billowed thickly above the water. The boat was nothing more than flaming splinters.

When the pieces all landed, there was nothing but smoldering debris floating on the water. I stared at it through cold, uncaring eyes, then there was movement from the corner of my eye.

Swinging the rifle around, I saw the only remaining gunman clawing the ground as he tried to escape. His left leg appeared broken and he had no weapon. In ten long strides, I was standing in front of him, rifle poised at the base of his skull. At that moment, I was judge, jury, and executioner without one moral fiber to be found.

"Please..."

Cold blood ran through my veins along with something I couldn't name and hadn't known still existed within me. "Please what?" a voice said. If it was mine, I did not recognize it. I did not recognize the woman standing with a rifle pointed at a man's head.

"Please don't kill me."

I cocked my head. "But you would have killed us."

He looked up at me, making the mistake of looking into eyes I'm sure must have appeared slightly insane. I knew the answer. He knew the answer. We all knew the answer. What none of us knew was that whatever energy had risen from the depths of my despair at seeing Tip shot had consumed me entirely. Without a second thought, I squeezed the trigger.

"I thought so."

"Echo…"

The voice in my head made me stare at what I had done. In my hands was a rifle that now wore the gore from a man I had shot at point-blank range and from the other whose head I had bashed in. Blinking rapidly, I felt the rage begin to subside; my awareness slowly regaining, and the black energy bled slowly from my being.

"Echo?"

Dropping the gun, I turned and ran to Tip. She was lying on her side holding her collarbone. Blood seeped from between her fingers, but she was alive. I wondered what it would take to actually kill this woman.

Kneeling down, I pulled her hand away. The bullet had nicked her collarbone and gone through the top part of her shoulder. Pulling off my shirt, I pressed it to the wound and placed her hand back on it. "Keep applying pressure," I ordered, standing back up to see Bailey running toward us. "Zack?"

"He's going to be okay. Head wounds bleed like a mother, but I patched him up with this." In her hand was some sort of greenish goo. "Let me see that."

Tip pulled my bloody shirt away, and Bailey ripped Tip's T-shirt open. "This will slow the bleeding," she said, smearing a big glob of the stuff on Tip's wound.

"Holy shit!"

"Oh yeah…forgot to mention it might sting." Bailey turned to me. "You okay?"

I nodded, unsure if that was the truth.

She studied me a second. "No, really. You…uh…"

"I know. I'm fine. Let's get out of here."

Bailey and I helped Tip to the boat. As I put her good arm around my neck, I saw the bruises and scratches on her neck where Malecon had managed to attack. The fucker fought like a girl.

"Malecon?" Tip asked, looking at the still fiery pieces of the boat. "Any sign of him?"

"We need to get you and Zack to a hospital."

Tip balked. "No. We have to know…You need to find him, Echo. Feel him. Is he alive?"

"The boat blew to hell and back, Tip," Bailey said. "Which is probably where he is right about now."

Tip shook her head. "Echo?"

Closing my eyes, I tried to find Malecon's energy. I was too weak to even find my own. "I got nothin', Tip. I'm sorry."

"We can go..." Tip said, her voice losing strength. "We have to..."

"Get you to the hospital, like Echo said."

After we got Tip settled in, we went back for Zack. As we neared him, I stepped over the body of the man whose head I blew off. My stomach jumped and threatened to empty itself then and there, but I fought off the wave of nausea. I couldn't believe what I had done.

Zack was still on the soggy ground, but was sitting up and holding the green goo to his head with an enormous leaf.

"Let me see," Bailey ordered, pulling his hand away. Blood was all over Zack's throat, shoulders and hair. "It's a bad gash. Twenty, maybe thirty stitches. We have to get you out of here, pronto." She looked in Zack's eyes. "You there?"

He looked at her and nodded, but he wasn't. When she turned to me, I shook my head. "He's up, but nobody's home."

It took a little more work to get Zack into the boat, as his legs weren't fully functioning because his brain was on auto pilot. A concussion, I was sure, but we managed to get him up and over the side without doing much more damage to him.

Once in the boat, Bailey reached into one of her pouches and pulled out an orange and brown leaf. She stuck it in her mouth, chewed it for a moment and then spit it out in her hand before pressing against Zack's head. "Move us, Echo."

I jumped behind the wheel, my eyes seeing, for the first time, the remains of the man attacked by the boar. There wasn't much left.

"Don't look at it, Echo," Bailey commanded. "It's the grossest thing you'll ever see. The boar is the most vicious creature in the bayou." She shook her head. "Those tusks...like daggers. It took me awhile to find one."

I tried to look away, but not before I saw that the pig had eaten the entire center of the man, leaving him now in two pieces;

one of which the boar was still consuming. "That's horrific," I said, starting the engine and swinging the boat around. In the distance, I heard another boat. It would be Bones, I was sure, coming to see what the explosion was about. If Danica had come out of her tranquilized stupor, she would have demanded that he bring them to the fight.

I put the boat in neutral and waited. If the boat wasn't Bones' boat, I wanted to be ready. I wished I hadn't left the rifle on the pier, and wondered if I had time to get back to it. Both Bailey and I were tapped out, and whatever had overtaken me was clearly not something I could call up at will.

And I was really glad about that.

"Can you see him?" Tip asked from her place on the deck of the boat. "Is there a body?"

I shaded my eyes from the sun and scoured the debris. Lots of boat parts floated by us, but nothing of human remains. "I don't see anything."

Tip struggled to get up. "We have…to…"

Bailey gently eased her back to the deck. "Get up again, and I'll hit you over the head like you hit Danica. My unguent will help as long as you don't keep breaking its seal. So sit still."

"You don't understand—"

"Of course I do. You need to see a body. We need to get you both to a hospital. Guess what? We win." Bailey folded her arms and stood over Tip, challenging her. She did not have the strength to battle Bailey's will.

As I heard the boat getting closer, I tried reading the energy coming toward us, but I had nothing. Nada. Nitch. Nil. I was energetically bankrupt. Instead, I reached into my fanny pack for the vidbook. At least, if anything were to happen to us now, the boys would be able to locate our bodies.

As I pulled it out, I saw the vidphone had a message. I pressed play and held the phone to my ear.

"It's Finn." I tasted my fear. "The good news is Melika is out of the woods, though no one is quite sure how. Some doctor nobody knew came in, spent five minutes with her, and when she left, Melika's heart rate was normal and all her vitals good." She paused here and I knew she was struggling with all the emotions of the day…emotions and questions that might not ever be answered. "The doctor who came in…sort of…well… disappeared right after. No one has seen her since, but I doubt that surprises you any, huh?" Another pause. "Anyway, she's going to be fine. I'm going over to help with the clearing out of the Superdome. I guess they're sending these people to Houston. It's all fucked up, but they need some sort of order so I'm going to lend assistance. I'll come back to check on her when I can." Another pause. I knew she was struggling with everything she had seen, but she didn't have the words. "Take care of yourself, and please let me know when you get this message. If you need anything else. Anything. Call."

I turned to Tip. "Melika is out of the woods. She's going to be okay."

Relief flooded her face and she closed her eyes and sank against the side of the boat.

"Echo?" Bailey said, staring at the boat that had just rounded a corner about a hundred yards away.

I shook my head. "I got nuthin'," I said as I placed the vidbook back in my fanny pack. As I did, my hand grazed something cold and metallic. Danica's gun. Pulling it from the pack, I held it up for Bailey to see. "I take that back. I have this."

Bailey quickly switched places with me, and took the wheel while I settled the gun on a stable surface and aimed with one eye. It took an eternity for the boat to reach us.

"Go for the driver," Bailey said. "If you miss, I'm going to use the only other weapon we have."

I nodded. "Ram 'em?"

"Absolutely." Bailey gazed intently at the side of my face. "We save them at all costs, right?"

Without looking at her I nodded. "Right."

"If I haven't already told you, I think you rock."

I barely grinned. "Right back atcha."

For a tense moment, we waited as the boat neared, and then I saw her; dark skin, regally tall, standing on the bow of the boat; I released my death grip on the butt of the gun.

"It's them," I said, shoving the revolver back into my fanny pack and heaving a loud sigh. When Bones pulled up next to us,

Cinder jumped from their boat to ours, hugging me tightly.

"We tried reaching you telepathically, Clark, but you never answered." Danica surveyed the wreckage just behind us before looking down at Tip and Zack. "Shit. Are they okay?"

I nodded. "We need to get to a hospital, and they'll be fine."

Danica nodded to the pieces floating by. "What about *him*?"

Bailey and I looked at each other and shrugged. "Dust in the wind, I guess."

Danica nodded again and Cinder pulled away, studying me. "I'm okay, Cinder, really. So is Mel. Finn left me a message on the vidbook."

Cinder clapped.

Danica studied me closely from her position on the bow. "You sure your okay?"

I nodded.

"Bones gid you to de Red Cross faster. You follow me der."

I nodded and got back behind the wheel. "Cinder, hon, Bones and I are going to switch boats, okay? You come back over in this boat with me." She did as I asked and hopped back in the boat with Danica.

"We're right on your tail, Bones."

He nodded and pulled in front of us.

"Uh, Clark?" Danica said as I started to follow behind him. "Do I want to know why there's a giant pig eating a man?"

I shook my head. "Probably not."

"Bailey?"

I nodded.

"Damn. She's good."

I couldn't have agreed more. "In another hour, the swamp will swallow up anything that remains. You'll never know we were here."

Danica touched my shoulder, and I winced. "Let's just get the fuck out of here."

And so we did.

We spent the next hour and a half at the Red Cross station getting Zack and Tip sewn up. They were both incredibly antsy and wanting to get to the hospital tent where Finn had dropped Melika off. I called her back once we reached shore and got the information about her whereabouts, since there were several makeshift hospitals dotting the city.

Tip's injury required ten stitches while Zack needed twenty-five. Both stoically stared ahead while being attended to, giving vague answers to doctors and nurses too tired to be doing what they were doing. Bailey hovered a bit, sensing their urgency to get a move on. Once I sat down my shoulder began throbbing, so I had a doctor look at it. He handed me three Advil and told me not to call him in the morning. It was a bruise and nothing more. He was trying to be good-natured about it, but I saw his weary countenance and felt his hopeless spirit. I took the Advil and waited for Tip to finish up.

"They really ought to rest before leaving," the redheaded doctor said. He looked like Howdy Doody's cousin. "You know, I'm supposed to report all gunshot wounds."

I nodded. "I know. We can wait here all day for cops who have better things to do, or you can trust me when I tell you that wild horses aren't about to keep that very large Indian in here. Your call."

We left shortly after.

When we arrived at the tented hospital facility, Melika was sitting up in bed, eyes closed, hands folded on her lap. She looked tiny on the cot, an enormous pillow behind her head. It was the first time I had seen her look anything but strong and powerful.

She smiled as we all gathered in the little area cordoned off by nothing more than a white plastic curtain. When we were all in, her smile instantly vanished and she opened her eyes. "Oh no." Melika bowed her head. "I had so hoped…" Looking back up at us, she had tears in her eyes. "I had hoped seeing Jacob's death had been a dream." Slowly shaking her head, she realized what none of us had wanted to tell her. "Then he *did* come to me." The emerald green eyes suddenly held a fire. "Damn her."

"Ma'am?" Tip said.

"Bishop. Damn her. She knew." Melika waved the answer away, knowing the truth before any of us spoke it. "Never mind. I know she did. I knew that old woman was up to something." Melika shook her head and then waved her hand like she was clearing the air of cigarette smoke. "She and I will have our go 'round later. How are the rest of you?"

Tip started toward her bed, then stopped and turned to me. The combined emotions of fear and pain wrapped themselves so tightly around her heart, she was overcome by emotion.

"The rest of us managed to survive," I said, stepping next to her. "Zack and Tip took some damage, but Bailey, Cinder and I are good. How are *you* feeling?"

She closed her eyes, a warm grin spreading across her face. "Being alive is a wonderful thing." Melika breathed so slowly that I thought she might have fallen asleep. "Not asleep, my dear. Just resting. Just at peace knowing you are all safe and this whole ugly affair is over." She looked over at Tip and grinned softly. "No, Tip, I have not lost my powers. They are incredibly weak, however, and I do not imagine I could do much outside of this room. But what I *can* read is all of your tremendous sorrow over the loss of Jacob." She looked over at Zack. "And for that, I am so very sorry." Holding her arms open, Melika waited for Cinder, who hugged her tightly. "I am so very proud of you," she whispered into Cinder's hair. "Of all of you."

Tip glanced over at me and I nodded. "Mel—"

"I know, my dear. You cannot locate Malecon. Neither can I. Whether he is dead or unconscious is beyond my powers right now, so there is nothing more for us to do than wait until I am full strength. Do not worry so, my dears. We are all safe now, and should my brother still live, he will be hunted down again the moment he surfaces." She closed her eyes again, and for the first time in my life, seemed old and fragile.

"We haven't heard anything about Bishop."

Melika laid her head back down and made shooing motions with a hand. "I am utterly exhausted, and the five of you need food and...well...baths!"

We all took our turns hugging her and started for the door when she said, "Tip, stay."

I ushered everyone out and sent Danica and Cinder to locate some food, leaving me, Bailey and Zack to sit in uncomfortable plastic chairs to wait for Tip, who came out a few minutes later.

"You feeling okay?" I asked Tip, eyeing one of the few empty cots. I decided not to wait for an answer. "Come here. Just lay down for a few." To my surprise, she didn't argue, but lay down with her head on a pillow and closed her eyes. I stroked her forehead softly, feeling the exhaustion and emotional drain she was experiencing at knowing she would eventually have to deal with Jacob's death.

"Just for a minute," she murmured.

"Sure. Just a few minutes." I looked over at Bailey, who had her head against the wall and her eyes closed. The doctor who sewed Zack up said whatever she had used to close his wound probably saved his life. "Just rest, Zack." I watched as he slipped into a quick sleep. Then I returned to Bailey, whom I thought was asleep as well.

"How's your shoulder feeling?"

"Sore," I replied, sitting next to her. Her eyes were still closed. "You know...what you did out there was pretty amazing."

"Thanks. I've spent a lot of time working on it." She sighed. "Which is what I imagine you'll be doing for the next few years."

I closed my eyes and leaned my head back like hers. "Is it that obvious?"

"We change. It's your time. That's all. Don't let it freak you out, Echo. You're ready."

My time. My time for what? To deal with the reality of my life? To finally understand that I wasn't normal and therefore a normal life wasn't really an option? "God, Bailey, there's so much I don't know, so many things I wish I understood." I turned to her. "Do we all go through this...this..."

"Awakening? Yes. Some of us choose to ignore it, some of us try to fight it, but in the end, we all wind up at the same crossroad." She opened her eyes and turned to me. "You know,

Echo, I've watched you now for several days, and it amazes me how you are in awe of what the rest of us can do, yet, you don't give yourself that same respect." She reached over and held my hand. "*You* are more amazing than all of us, but you don't seem to see that. You've been trained by the best empath in the world, yet you don't realize all of the gifts under your tree. You're an incredible empath, Echo, but there's so much more. Do yourself and the rest of us a favor and don't ignore it or fight it." She squeezed my hand before letting go. "We need you."

I cocked my head. "I don't understand. Need me for what?"

Bailey smiled and shook her head. "You really don't see it, do you? We need you to lead us."

My mouth fell open. "Lead? But…Melika…"

"Is getting old. She knows it is only a matter of time before she hands the reins over to someone else. Who do you think that someone is going to be? Tip? Not hardly. She is a hunter. It's what she does best, and there are few of us who could fill her shoes. But teach?" She grinned. "I think not."

I blinked several times. "Teach? I…I don't know anything about…"

"Not now you don't. But it's time for you to learn. That's what I mean by it's your time. You can either keep trying to live a pretend normal life, or you can accept your fate."

Before she could continue, Danica and Cinder came back bearing beignets, coffee and other sticky goodies. "Sugar ought to get us all going until we can get some good food in our bellies," she explained, handing a coffee to me.

"You look better," I said, taking the coffee. It felt like forever since we'd left the cottage.

"Good-looking doctors are like their own drug." She pulled a slip of paper from her pocket and waved. "This is a prescription."

I took it and looked at. There was a phone number on it. I laughed. "Leave it to you." I pulled Cinder over and whispered, "Why don't you hop up there with Zack and take a rest?"

Like Zack, she did not fight, but carefully lay next to Zack. She was asleep in two seconds.

"Take a load off," Bailey said, standing and stretching. "I've got to hit the bathroom." Pushing the chair toward Danica, she turned to me. "Think about it, Echo."

When she left, Danica sat next to me. "Think about what?"

Sighing, I told her about the Awakening, but did not mention anything about teaching or Melika. Danica looked at me hard in the face, almost as if she were reading me; she knew me well enough to know something else was going on.

"What are you leaving out?"

Shrugging, I sipped my coffee. It felt so good going down. "Remember when I was bashing Todd's head in with my math book?"

"Never can forget it."

"Something came over me at that moment, and for all these years, I thought it was merely the onset of my powers."

Danica faced me. "And?"

I shook my head. "It was more than that. There was a…a rage…do you remember?"

"That it took three of us to pull you off? Hell yes. Why?"

"I…I wanted to kill him. I was *trying* to kill him. I *would have* killed him if you hadn't managed to get me away from him."

"Yeah, so?"

"So the desire to kill has nothing to do with my empathic abilities."

Danica nodded slowly. "Clark, killing someone is easier than people think. You can regret it all you want, but when it comes down to them and us, something kicks in that makes us able to kill."

"Something…yes." I stared out at the bustling street. "Something happened inside me on that day, Dani. The same thing happened to me out there on the river. Something… something happened…like a switch clicked on."

"You did what you had to do, just like Cinder and I did in the Superdome."

I shook my head. "It's not about *what* I had to do that's bothering me, Dani, it's what came over me…deep down inside me…that scares me. It's like a darkness that comes to life within me, taking over, filling me with this almost psychopathic rage."

"Not you, Clark. There's nothing psycho about you in the least. Don't overanalyze what you had to do. Survival instincts are deeply embedded in all of us, supers and naturals alike. Yours kicked in, that's all. Don't beat yourself up for it." She pulled my borrowed shirt away from my neck. "The fucker left fingerprints on your neck. I say, go little piggie."

I shook my head. "Gross."

"But true. Did Bailey sic that thing on him?"

I nodded and took a bite from the beignet.

"You know, she's all right."

"Yes, she is." I sipped more coffee. "But so are you. Thank you for coming and being part of my insanity."

She grinned softly. "Clark, I've been part of your insanity for as long as I can remember. I would have been really pissed if I missed this one."

"Your vidbooks saved the day again. You know that, don't you?"

She blew out a breath. "Absolutely. They're so cool, I don't know if I want to share them with the general public."

We sat in silence drinking our coffee when she chuckled. "You shot a rifle, huh? Clark, you hate guns."

"Yeah, well, that's what I'm talking about. Something deep inside me came out."

"Rambo?"

"Funny."

She took my hand. "You're changing, huh?"

I couldn't look at her. "Yes. Yes, I am."

She nodded slowly. "Have your feelings changed as well?"

"You mean, for Finn?"

"Finn, Tip, whoever."

I thought a long time before answering. "Would you think I was copping out if I said I think I need to be alone?"

"Dumping Finn won't make what she saw go away, Clark. You're going to have to deal with it some day. After all, she deserves an answer, you know what I mean?"

I nodded. "I know, but not here and not now. Can I run away from home?"

"No. This time, you gotta deal."

I knew she would say that. In all our years together, we never let each other run from a fight or skirt around an obstacle. "I'm going to have to end it with her, huh?"

She squeezed my hand like Bailey had done and then reached in the bag for a beignet. "There's no gray in this one, I'm afraid. She deserves to know what she's getting into if you're going to continue seeing her. If you can't tell her the truth—"

"Then I need to let her go."

She smiled, beignet powder on her upper lip. "She won't go away that easily, Jane. The girl's got it bad for you. She knows she saw something that didn't add up. She saved a drugged Haitian woman, and she's going to want answers."

"Answers I can't give her right now."

She turned to me, and I wiped the powdered sugar from her face. "Then you have your answer."

I stared at her, loving her more at this moment than any other. They say a true friend offers you honesty when you least want it or need it. I don't know who *they* are, but I'm pretty sure they must have met Danica. "So much has changed since we arrived. A few days ago, I was a solo supernatural living my pretend normal life secure in the knowledge that I could make it happen and keep the two worlds from colliding. I thought I could use my powers to make people's lives better."

"And now?"

"Now, I realize that I have a responsibility to my people first and my personal life second. I guess I have a lot of re-evaluating to do."

She smiled at me. "You done good, Clark, really. I know that you haven't even begun to scratch the surface of everything that has happened here, of what it means to be you now, but you will. Give it a rest for now."

I watched a doctor bend over Zack's sleeping form. He shook his head before wandering back out to us.

"Are you with that young man in there?"

Uh-oh. "Yes."

"When did he get those stitches?"

"Yesterday," I lied, not sure why.

He nodded. "Oh. Okay."

"Why?"

"They look good."

When the doctor walked away, Danica cocked her head in question.

"Bailey used some of her green goo. It has some sort of healing property. He's healed pretty quickly."

"Speaking of super healers, what happened to Melika? I mean…how—"

"My guess is The Others. Finn said a doctor came in, spent a few minutes with her, and when she came out, Melika was much better."

"They're kind of like ghosts, huh?"

I nodded. "Pretty much." I slumped in exhaustion. I had never been this tired in my life. I had overextended my powers on a level I hadn't previously known existed. My throat was sore, my shoulder was throbbing and my head was pounding.

But I was alive and so were all the people I loved.

Well…almost all.

When Bailey returned, she knelt in front of me. "Close your eyes."

I did, only slightly afraid I would fall asleep right then and there.

She placed her palms on either temple. "Relax. Take deep breaths. Think of something cool and soft…something—"

I didn't hear the rest. Images of cuddling on the couch with Finn wafted across my mind's eye. She was such a good person…a woman we owed for getting to Melika in time. She was someone I might be able to trust…someone…

Suddenly, my headache was gone and when I opened my eyes, I had no idea how long I had been like that, but Zack was now sitting across from me in a third chair. "Damn, Bailey, you're really something."

She was sitting next to Zack. "You know Echo, not all of us see the cursed side of our powers. I'm one of those. There never has been anything I've regretted about being who I am. I'm very lucky."

Zack and I looked at each other. "Yeah, you are."

Danica came back from checking on Cinder. I must have been out longer than I realized. "So, what now?" she asked.

Bailey and Zack waited for me to respond. "I say we take Melika home where she belongs. Zack, you and Cinder can stay at the cottage, just in case we haven't seen the last of Malecon's henchmen."

"What about the rest of us?"

Sipping my now lukewarm coffee, I nodded. "We finish what we came here to do: help people."

Bailey nodded. "I'm with you. I don't have anywhere I need to be, and there are still plenty of people who need assistance. Besides, I'm not going anywhere until we make sure Bishop's okay. How come no one has contacted us?"

"Because they wanted us to focus on Malecon and Melika." This came from Tip, who was standing in the doorway of Melika's cubicle. "Bishop is in a pretty weakened state right now. They...they're not sure she's going to make it. The Others are doing everything they can."

What energy I had left me like the vestiges of air in a balloon. "Where is she?"

Tip shook her head. "I don't know. They won't tell me. She could be anywhere." Tip reached down and took me by the hand, pulling me to my feet. "She wants to see you."

I pulled the plastic door back and walked in.

"Come. Sit," Melika ordered. In her makeshift hospital bed she looked tiny but indomitable.

I did as she said. "You look tired."

She grinned. "As do you, my dear, but you prevailed, didn't you? As I knew you would."

I bowed my head. "I suppose so. I am so sorry about Jacob."

"I know you are. So am I. I should have taken better care of my brother before Katrina hit, but who could have imagined—"

"Bishop did."

She reached for my hand. "Bishop needed to forget what she saw and let Destiny play its course."

"Jacob's death?"

"All of this. Bishop is an amazing woman with incredible skills, but even she could not have stopped my brother. She saw that. She saw Jacob's death. She saw…she saw the changes that are going to happen in your life...to all of ours."

I nodded, not really knowing what to say.

"You met Rose and Lily. You now know something of The Others."

"Yes, ma'am."

"You know, they are a little like the beings on Mt Olympus; they see from afar, rarely getting involved unless they have to. They are powerful and yet, somewhat removed." Melika took my hand. "Bishop is now one of them."

"What? You mean…she's left NOLA for good?"

She nodded. "And because she is one of them, it is now time for her to remove herself from the dangers of this world and take her place among them…if she survives, of course." Her voice was calm, as if she were discussing a stranger and not her own mother.

"Won't you miss her? I mean…she's your mother."

She laughed. "Of course I will. But becoming an Other isn't like going to a retirement home. There's no visiting. One does not drop in and out. They remain isolated for a reason."

"Because of the unpredictability of their powers?"

"That and more. Naturals have all sorts of mental issues as they get older. We are only slightly different in that we respond to those changes differently. Age sometimes pushes us into making wrong choices."

I frowned, an ugly feeling bubbling in my gut. "What are you not saying?"

"I'm saying I should not be alive." She held her hand up to stop my questions. "Bishop did something inexcusable with her powers when she saw Jacob Marley's death and intervened to save me; it is entirely possible she changed the outcome of this. Had she not taught Jacob how to do a possession, or sent him to a mentor, I would most likely be dead."

"Then she *did* change the future."

Melika shook her head. "There are innumerable futures, my dear. She could not and did not change Jacob's fate, but she surely did mine. I should be dead. That does not mean the rest of you wouldn't have still succeeded in containing Malecon. Your lives may yet be altered by her decision to use Jacob's death to prevent mine."

"She wouldn't do that."

"Oh, but she did. You see, when Jacob came into my consciousness, he and I shared everything that remained in his. I know everything they did to prepare him for that moment. I know she hid her actions from me, knowing I would never allow it. And although she never saw *my* death, you and I both know that without Jacob's intervention, I would have died in that storeroom."

"But that wasn't Malecon's intent, was it? We thought he was afraid of harming you."

Melika shook her head. "No. He was never going to kill me, but the drug he injected acted like a toxin when mixed with the heart medication I'm on. Malecon did not know I have been having heart issues, so he could not have known the drug he injected should have killed me."

I licked my lips. My head was beginning to spin. "Heart medication?"

She squeezed my hand. "I am getting old, my dear. I have heart murmurs and arthritis. There is nothing fun about getting old. Trust me."

"Are you okay though? I mean, you don't have anything life threatening, right?"

"Correct."

My heart felt heavy. "So they've taken Bishop away?"

She smiled. "It isn't like a prison sentence, my dear. She is quite old and they will take good care of her."

"Is there something else?" It's difficult for an empath to fool another empath.

"Abuse of her powers is enough. The Others could have sent a Cleaner. They still might choose to do so. We cannot allow others to play Goddess, my dear, and though I am glad to be alive, Bishop rolled the dice with her own life when she decided to show Jacob how to possess. As you know, this is strictly forbidden. In saving my life, she willingly gave up the right to her own."

"They wouldn't—"

She shrugged. "Let us hope they let an old woman live out the rest of her years in peace."

"You make it sound like they put us out to pasture."

She grinned. "That is precisely what they do. It is what I will do someday. You see, my dear, after carrying around this energy, after dealing with all of this power, after spending our lives erecting walls, keeping people out, letting people in, all any of us wants to do is live a life where none of that is a concern any more. It's Bishop's turn to rest. She deserves it."

"But you just said—"

"I said they *might*. She is not out of the woods, as they say, and it might very well be that they decide to let her go home."

"Home...heaven?"

She chuckled. "Or something. When you reach my age, death is not always something to fear. You'd be surprised at how many of us actually embrace it when it comes."

I sighed. "If she could save you, how come she couldn't save Jacob?"

She looked at me with pride in her eyes. "*That* is why I called you in here. I know how much you all loved and cared for Jacob Marley. He was a wonderful little boy and even more beautiful young man. You see, Jacob would not allow it. He...I know this will be hard to accept, but he *wanted* to go."

I felt my throat constrict. "What?"

Melika patted my hand. "He never told any of you because he knew you all would move heaven and earth to help him, but Jacob was slowly going mad. Bishop and I did everything we could for the poor boy, but as you know, madness is so often the fate of so many necromancers. All those voices in their heads, all those spirits constantly bothering them, wanting answers they don't have or can't give. For the last three years he was being haunted by someone...someone evil and dark; someone he could not shake."

"Couldn't The Others help him?"

Melika shook her head. "They don't interfere, my dear, unless the situation is dire or it appears we will be discovered. Once he knew there was a danger to his family—to us—he refused any help. He felt he would be more use to us all dead than alive." She sighed sadly and looked away. "Unfortunately, he was right." She turned back to me. "So Bishop decided since he was willing to go, she would use that to our advantage in order to save her daughter's life."

I heaved a huge sigh. Had I any energy left, I would have started crying. As it was, I just sat there in the sadness of the loss of my dear friend, at how close we came to losing him for nothing. "Jacob sacrificed himself for you."

"Jacob was tired of battling his demons. He did not wish to alter his fate…only mine."

I nodded. "Good thing Finn was here. I was so surprised when she—" I hesitated, seeing the look in Melika's eyes.

Melika looked at me unblinkingly, waiting for the lightbulb to go on.

"Wait. Was Finn—"

"Lured here?" She nodded slowly. "I'm afraid so. While I was never privy to all the machinations Bishop put into place, I do know from Jacob's memories that he made sure Finn received some well-timed prompts. I do not know the ins and outs of it from Jacob's position, but let's just say your friend did not think it on her own. Bishop had a hand in that as well."

"Prompts?"

Melika nodded. "Bishop has been sending her pamphlets and brochures from the Red Cross for the last few months. Like I said, I don't know the full extent of her plan, just that she had one and she planted seeds wherever they would grow."

I nodded. "I can't imagine New Orleans without her."

"The New Orleans that used to exist does not exist any longer, my dear. Our once grand city will never return to the way it was. Perhaps that is why this is a fitting time for her to go." Melika closed her eyes and lay her head back on the pillow.

"I should let you rest."

Opening her eyes, she shook her head. "No. Enough about Bishop. I want to talk about you and how proud I am of you. Tip told me how brave you were out there. She said you stepped into a leader role with great ease."

"I don't know about that."

"Yes, you do. She said you are a natural-born leader. That's high praise coming from a woman who takes orders from no one but me."

"I don't really want to give orders, Mel. That's Tip's job."

She shook her head and smiled. "Power without patience is a road to disaster. It sparks misunderstandings. It creates situations that needn't be created. As strong and as wonderful a woman as Tip is, she does not possess the necessary patience to lead."

I knew what was coming, and felt a little like a fly caught in a web.

"You have learned a great many lessons in such a short amount of time, but there is one thing you've learned above all else, isn't there?"

I nodded. "The short version is square peg, round hole."

She chuckled. "Oh, my dear, don't be so down on yourself. Every single one of you who leaves the bayou truly believes you are striking out on your own; that you're through with your lessons, and that somewhere out there, a normal life is waiting for you. The question isn't if you'll realize that it isn't there. The question is *when* will you realize it. You simply have done what the rest have already experienced."

"Everyone?"

"Well, Zack struggles, but that's because he believes he has complete control of his powers." Melika pulled me closer. "Don't worry, my dear, I am not asking you to abandon your life in San Francisco. It is not your time yet. You have much to learn. You have merely stepped one toe on the path of your next journey. You have learned all the rudimentary skills you needed to exist in the world; now, it is time for your real studies."

"Why didn't you tell me?"

She smiled. "You were eighteen. You had spent the last four years of your life in the only place you'd ever called home. You were ready to face life in the world as a young adult. Do you really think you would have listened?" She stopped me before I could answer. "Why do you think I allowed you to tell Danica when you were barely fourteen years old?"

"Because you knew she'd always be in my life?"

"Because I knew you needed someone in the real world to know who you really were. I knew you needed someone to experience the real world with, and when you were ready to accept the totality of who you are, you would accept her help to get you through it all."

I looked down at her hand on mine. "If it isn't my time, what time is it?"

"It is time for you to learn about your secondary powers and to discover all of the hidden abilities nestled in your primary ones. It is time for you to acknowledge that, while you may move about in the natural world, you shall never truly be a part of it. It is also time, my dear child, for you to find out where you came from so you can see the true extent of your powers. Both your future and your past await you, Echo. It is time for you to embrace them both," Melika let go of my hand and lightly brushed hair away from my forehead. "Take the time to rediscover yourself, my dear. You are a gift waiting to be unwrapped."

I felt her energy ebbing, so I rose. "You need to rest, and apparently I need a bath."

She grinned. "Yes. Get some rest and then tomorrow, you can take me home." She closed her eyes and leaned her head back on the pillow. "Home. The bayou seems a strange place to raise children, doesn't it?"

"I had no complaints."

The grin faded from her face as her energy dropped. "Like a hand in a glove, my dear, and when you're ready…the bayou will be your home again."

I kissed her forehead and was almost out the door when she said, "One final word."

"Yes?"

"Cinder."

I bit my lip.

"She has killed for those she holds dear to her, not out of anger or any innate violence. She's killed because she loves you, and her greatest fear is that you, too, will be taken away from her. She will remain safest here with me, as we learn how to control her powers better. But when she is done, when it comes her time to leave, she will need a new home with someone who knows who and what she is."

I nodded.

"You will always be her heroine. You released her from the hospital, you cared for her, you've given her a great deal of love. There will be a time when she leaves here. When she does, she will make a beeline for you and Danica. Consider this a heads-up."

"Will do."

"You have such a big heart, my dear, and so much to give. Remember that always."

She fell asleep almost the moment after she said it, leaving me there to ponder the idea that I could be raising Cinder some day. I could barely keep up with the care and feeding of my three-legged cat. By the time Cinder finished her training she'd be what? Fourteen? Fifteen? My God, I couldn't even keep a plant alive longer than a week. But a teenager?

So...is this what she meant about leading? About family? Was that path I stepped on going to be filled with experiences I knew nothing about? How was I ever going to manage my life back in San Francisco when all my questions went largely unanswered?

"I love you, Mel," I said softly over my shoulder as I gently tossed the flap back. As I took two steps and turned toward Danica, I ran smack into Finn.

"Echo," she said softly, hugging me to her tightly. She was sweaty and smelled of that musk people get when they have worked too hard. "Dani told me you were in there with Melika. How is she?" She pulled away to look at me.

"Sleeping now. She's going to be fine, thanks to you."

Finn studied my eyes and face as if she hadn't seen me in years. "How about you? You all right?"

When I saw myself through her eyes, I realized I probably looked like one big mudpie. The shirt I had "borrowed" from a house on a bayou clothesline was far too big for me, my hair looked like it belonged in Jamaica, and I was pretty sure there were enough bags under my eyes to carry everyone's luggage home. Still, her eyes searched mine with so much tenderness, I had to look away. I was not worthy.

"You want the short list?" I said, trying to sound light and airy.

"I'm probably looking at the short list, huh?"

I smiled, feeling the final pieces of my psionic energy fade away. I had nothing more left in me, and I needed some in order to construct a wall between me and her. This was going to be a whole lot harder if I could read her feelings for me.

"Later," she said softly. "That is…if you want. I'm just so glad to see you're okay." She threw her arms around me and crushed me this time. "I have missed you so much."

Before I could respond, Tip took three long strides and extended her right hand. "You must be Finn. Thank you for taking such good care of Melika. We can't thank you enough."

Finn released me and shook Tip's hand. I had not told Finn anything about my past here on the bayou or about Tip; instead, I had told her the many horror stories of growing up in nearly a dozen foster homes. I never anticipated she would meet anyone from New Orleans until after I had prepared the way. I hadn't done so yet and this moment felt awkward.

"Uh, Tip, Finn. Finn, Tip." I couldn't look at Tip, afraid Finn might see something pass between us. Finn was not a stupid woman, and there was a *lot* of water under that particular bridge. Thank God Dani had flawless people-reading skills, because she whisked Tip away in the bat of an eye.

"Big gal," Finn said, watching them as they walked away.

"Yes, she is." I had nothing left, nothing witty or creative or scintillating. Stick a fork in me…I was done.

"Hey, I need to get back to the guys over at the Dome. Things are fu…are totally messed up over there. They're shipping families to different parts of the country, and there's no order anywhere. It's pretty frightening, really."

I nodded. "Of course."

"And then I'm helping some of the guys on the Ninth for a couple of days. Think we can hook up for dinner or something?"

"I would love that." I kissed her cheek, lingering longer than I should have. Somehow, having someone from the outside world here with us seemed to ground me. "You have the vidbook number, right?"

She nodded.

"Thank you. So much. You saved her life. I would love to catch you for dinner. Call me."

She grinned. "Will do. Oh, and don't worry about any police reports on this little incident. My buddies made it go away, but I'd love to hear what the hell was going on if you want to share."

"You're the best. Maybe when we get back, okay?"

"And you're not half bad yourself, though..." She looked over at Tip with her left arm in a sling and Zack with his head bandaged. "It would appear you've had quite a time of it."

"If only you knew."

Leaning down, she kissed me softly. "If you'd trust me, Echo, I *would* know."

Looking up, tears filled my eyes. "I'm trying."

Wiping a tear away with her thumb, she kissed my forehead and whispered. "That's all I ask. I'll call you, okay?"

I watched her saunter out of the triage unit, a woman unafraid of who she was or where she was going; a woman willing to put her life on hold to help others. She was a kind woman, a decent person, but was our relationship at a point where she was a woman I could trust with the biggest truth in my life? Was there any such person?

I had no idea.

"Danica, would you walk with me to get some fresh air?"

She was at my side in an instant.

We walked about two blocks until we found a park bench. The weather had cooled off, but not substantially.

"Well, Clark, I would say they all lived happily ever after, but that's not the case, is it?"

I shook my head. "Not really. I miss Jacob Marley so much."

Danica heaved a sigh. "Let's face it: you miss this place. I know you can't see it, but your physical appearance changes a lot when you're down here. Your shoulders relax, your eyes sparkle, hell, even in the midst of all this mess, you seem happier."

"I'm not staying."

Danica nodded. "Not time yet."

"No."

"And Finn?"

"I've decided I can't really deal with her down here and so out of context. It's time I learned about my true potential, not as a reporter or someone's girlfriend, but as a being with extraordinary powers. I've run from myself long enough."

"Good. It's about time. Besides, it sounds like you're going to have a lot more responsibilities on your plate soon enough."

"You were listening."

"It's a tent, for Christ's sake. Hell yeah, I was listening. And now, it's time for you to listen." Danica rose. "Stay or go, love or don't, you need to figure out how to cut the big Indian loose. She's still in love with you. If you aren't going to return her affections, you need to find some way of letting her go." As she walked away, I saw Tip coming toward me. "You deserve to be loved, Clark," she said over her shoulder. "You just need to figure out how to make that happen."

Tip sat down on the bench in place of Danica. "Seems like a nice enough woman."

"She is."

"Saving Melika goes a long way in my book."

I grinned. "Thanks for being so nice to her."

She leaned over, bearing a wolfish grin. "I'm anything but nice, kiddo, and you know it, but anyone who has your back like she did is okay."

We sat in silence for a long time, feeling the heat of the sun bearing down upon us. When she finally spoke, her voice was softer than I'd ever heard it. "I miss you, Echo. And even though we lost Jacob Marley and this whole thing turned into one helluva battle, there's no place I'd rather be than fighting the good fight at your side."

"Is that what this was? The good fight?"

"We won, didn't we?"

I shrugged. "Sure doesn't feel like we won."

Tip laid her hand on mine. "Some days, that's just how it is."

"Some days? Do you do this often?"

She smiled. "More than you could imagine."

"Is that what Melika was talking about?"

She rose, favoring her shoulder. "You know how she likes to speak in riddles. When the time is right, you'll know what she meant. The next twelve months or so might be very trying. Just know I am always here for you. Always."

When she left, I felt like curling up on the bench and sleeping for a week. I had come down here, I thought, to help locate those who were lost after Katrina hit and instead, managed to find myself…or at least, the beginnings of myself. And, as usual, the bayou had supplied me with a rough sketch of where to begin my new journey.

Stretching out on the bench, all of my energy gone at last, I was so tired of thinking, of feeling, of trying to keep my shields up, that I just let it all go.

Behind me, someone was crying from having lost a loved one in the big move out of the Superdome. To my right, some guy was having sexual fantasies about a movie star on a torn poster. In front of me, a woman held on tightly to her rage over the government's impotence at helping Katrina victims.

As the feelings around me sputtered out, and my eyelids were too heavy to keep open, someone crept into my brain and whispered, *Before you know where you're going, you must find out where you've been.*

Where I've been.

In the dim haze that seeps into our minds before sleep mercifully whisks us away, I knew exactly where I needed to start looking.